SALVAGED

FROM THE

RUINS

A NOVEL OF 1945

AL MCGREGOR.

Salvaged from the Ruins, A Novel of 1945

Copyright 2022 by Al McGregor.

This is a work of fiction. Apart from well known actual figures, events and locales that figure in the narrative, all characters, places, and incidents are the product of the author's imagination or are used fictitiously. Any resemblance to persons living or dead is entirely coincidental.

Paperback Edition 978-0-9950900-4-0
Kindle edition 978-0-9950900-5-7
Kobo edition 978-0-9950900-6-4

Cover design Quantum Communications.

Al McGregor Communications
www.almcgregor.com

History with its flickering lamp stumbles along the trail of the past, trying to reconstruct its scenes, to revive its echoes, and kindle with pale gleams the passion of former days.

— Winston Churchill

PROLOGUE

Quebec City, September 17, 1944

A SMATTERING OF APPLAUSE washed over the small crowd as the open convertible slowed. A secret service agent hefted a revolver but decided the spectators posed no serious risk. From the rear seat Winston Churchill flashed an exuberant 'V' for victory but beside him, Franklin Roosevelt, managed only a feeble wave. A moment later the car picked up speed throwing a small shower of stones.

Vincent Russel scowled, brushed at the dust and stepped away from the onlookers before speaking to a Canadian army officer. "A big change from the first Quebec City Conference a year ago when they planned for D-Day." His eyes followed the car. "FDR is definitely aging but he'll make history in November as the first four-term American President."

The limousine slowed and stopped. Churchill could be seen pointing across the field of the Plains of Abraham. "Winston, the historian, must be waxing eloquent on the deeds of Wolfe and

Montcalm," Russel guessed. "War time heroes of another age." He lifted a straw hat to feel the late summer sun. His much younger companion glanced about to ensure no one else was watching before loosening his tie.

"Two years and you're not comfortable in uniform." Russel sighed. "The army likes your type, athletic build, pushing six feet, but a million other Canadian men and women are in uniform. That's a lot of competition if someone intends to leave a mark and most of your marks are demerits. You're twenty-five. Time to make something of yourself."

Duff Stewart never enjoyed a lecture but Russel controlled the payout from his father's estate and army compensation didn't allow for the lifestyle he preferred. "What do you suggest?" He too raised his hat. An army barber had trimmed the brown hair close to his head. "I may look like a soldier. I don't feel like one."

"I can see that. But, in the next year or so the army may de-mobilize and those with a sterling record will have the pick of civilian jobs. Unfortunately, your record is far from sterling."

Stewart's face twisted to a smirk. "A lieutenant who passes paper from one desk to another doesn't meet your standards?"

"Service on the home front is no longer enough." Russel's tone showed his frustration. "At this point I wouldn't want you to join the firm. Your father and I positioned the company to profit from major business projects or confidential jobs for government. I won't see our work damaged by a slacker."

"Again, what do you suggest?"

"Volunteer for duty overseas and do it before there's a draft. Conn Smythe, the owner of the Toronto hockey club, is home from Europe. He claims wounded men are sent back into action before fully recovered. Howls will erupt demanding conscription. Too many men are playing it safe, volunteering for service but only at home. Zombies, we call them and you are one."

"But most people think the war will soon be over," Stewart said.

"If General Montgomery seizes the bridge at Arnhem he'll drive through to Berlin."

"And, when the fighting ends, the Allies will begin the occupation. Roosevelt's friend, Henry Morgenthau, the American Treasury Secretary, wants to turn Germany, the most industrialized state in Europe into small farms and pastures. Occupation armies could make it happen."

"Find a farm boy from Alberta." Stewart turned to watch the limousine fade in the distance. "I know nothing about agriculture."

"Don't be so dense. Young officers will de-nazify Germany and set up a new administration. Serve with distinction and return home covered with peacetime glory. Future leaders won't be Zombies."

"Why would the government policy change now? Mackenzie King is opposed to conscription."

"He is but men in his cabinet will make the Prime Minister see the error of his ways." Russel thought of what he'd learned in a series of private meetings. "King was hoping the Allies wouldn't ask for more men. The last thing he wanted was a bigger army but he may not have a choice. And, while the photographers captured him at dinner with Churchill and Roosevelt, he was little more than a glorified waiter. The other two make the decisions. He hasn't been invited to join them at the Roosevelt home in New York state. I think that private tête-à-tête has something to do with a major new weapon."

"No doubt your sources will whisper the details." Stewart slipped the hat back on his head and turned to leave. "I feel no need for hasty decisions."

"No!" Russel shook his head in frustration. "No…the sooner you volunteer for overseas the better. And, here's a bonus, one that should overcome your hesitation. My connections can keep you from any real danger." He paused before he offered a last piece of advice. "And that little tart in Montreal. She's not going to fit into postwar society. Say goodbye. Find someone more appropriate."

Ottawa, November 16, 1944

"The answer is no. I am not sending you overseas."

As managing editor, Bert Thompson would make the decisions on staffing for the Ottawa newspaper and sending reporter Todd Aiken to North Western Europe was not part of the plan. "I have war stories coming out my ears. I don't need any more. The *Sentinel-Guardian* needs help at home. We've the makings of a conscription crisis that will make 1917 look like a Sunday school picnic. The casualty numbers have climbed in the last few months. The army needs more men and now this…" Thompson waved the latest wire copy. "A report from British Columbia suggests a mutiny. Canadians fighting Canadians."

"I don't believe it, a story blown out of proportion." Aiken scoffed. "If the Zombies shout loud enough, politicians will back down."

"Not this time." Thompson shook his head and fingered another dispatch. "The army needs sixteen thousand men for duty overseas. General McNaughton was tasked to find them. He failed and as a result the country is split. Quebec asks why anyone should fight to save foreign empires while English Canada is ready to shed more blood."

"Forget politics. We should be covering the boys in action. We should have a reporter in Northwest Europe."

"Not going to happen. The Parliament Hill bureau needs help. Their hands are full, writing about conscriptionists, anti-conscriptionists, leftists and the odd fascist. The Prime Minister fears a cabinet revolt and if he doesn't change his mind on conscription, those 'boys' overseas won't see reinforcements. Cover that story. I'll think about a European assignment next spring."

CHAPTER 1

January 2, 1945

THE PLANE LANDED hard and bounced back into the air. A second lurch came as the wheels again touched the runway and a third before the pilot slowed the transport for a safe arrival at a French airfield.

Duff Stewart woke at the first jolt and by the time the aircraft stopped felt the return of nausea. "Sick on takeoff and sick on landing." The Air Force officer beside him laughed. "Good thing you're army. The Air Force would wash you out."

"It's not the flying," Stewart replied. "I had an extended New Year celebration. A friend got me to the airfield just in time." He pictured her in his mind. Bright red hair, flashing green eyes. But what was her name. Veronica? Vicky? It wouldn't matter. He shook his head to clear the cobwebs but instead felt bile rising in his throat. "Concentrate," he told himself and managed to hold the contents of his stomach until the feeling passed.

"Hangover, huh?" The seat mate guessed. "Should have been here yesterday. Everyone had one. The Luftwaffe surprised us with a New Year's Day raid."

The door to the plane swung open and as the men began to disembark—the smell of burning oil and rubber wafted into the cabin. On the tarmac, planes were burned to skeletal shells and firefighters continued to spray foam on smouldering wrecks. "A real mess," the airman told him. "Hundreds of planes were destroyed but the Germans took the worst of it. Everyone hopes this was the last act for the Luftwaffe. The Allies can build more planes but the Nazis can't have many left."

"I thought the Germans were finished. But now this Hangover Raid and the breakthrough in the Ardennes, the Bulge?"

"We're flattening the Bulge. Montgomery came galloping to buck up the Americans. Without him, Hitler might have reached the coast and that would have been a true disaster."

"Stewart, Lieutenant, D.," a sergeant called and waved toward a waiting car. Stewart slipped a duffel bag over his shoulder and followed across the pavement. In minutes, they were on the main road but moving slowly behind an armoured column.

"About two hours to Headquarters," the sergeant announced and slipped an unlit cigarette in his mouth. "Permission to smoke, Sir?"

"Oh…of course."

"Some officers object. Like to lord it over lower ranks."

Stewart shrugged. "Doesn't matter to me. By the way, what should I call you?"

"Murphy, Sir. Sergeant Tim." The driver was medium height, stocky, every pound packed tight to his frame. He lit the cigarette and took a long drag. "Spend much time in England?"

"I had a few weeks in London and hoped for more but suddenly the orders changed. I don't even have a weapon. Supply officers are to fix me up."

Murphy went silent, intent on the road for a few moments before abruptly asking, "Are you a Zombie?"

Stewart thought quickly and tried to sound convincing. "God no. I volunteered. I'm no slacker."

"Good to know. Zombies, or to be polite, the National Service Mobilization Volunteers, aren't popular. The whole bunch tried to sit out the war in Canada while in Europe the army combed the ranks for anyone who could carry a gun; supply guys, cooks, you name it. Most hadn't seen combat and made a lot of mistakes. That's one reason our casualty counts are so high. Then high command gave us the dirty job of clearing Nazis from the channel ports. We lost good men fighting from Le Havre to Antwerp and clearing the Scheldt became a bloodbath. And don't forget we're another army in Italy that's starved for men. And so finally, the Prime Minister agrees to send the Zombies to war. Like they say—a Snafu. Situation normal all fucked up."

"How long did it take to reach that conclusion?" Stewart asked.

"Right from the start. I came in ten days after D-Day." Murphy tossed the spent cigarette out the window. "I was in action for a few weeks and busted something in my foot. The Doc knew I wasn't fit but with the shortage of men they won't ship me home. Brits are in the same position, stripped clean, no reinforcements. The Yanks have men but the wrong type. Lots of administrators but they need riflemen. Did you get special training?"

"No. I was scheduled for a rifle range but never got there. For the record, sergeant, I am a damn fine typist, can organize a file drawer in seconds and speak a smattering of German. Those apparently are ideal qualities for the Canadian Forces."

"Hope it works out. Wouldn't want you disabled by a paper cut."

"Yah. That's cute but I'll take care of myself. But first things first. Would an enterprising sergeant know where to find the hair of the dog?"

"There's a place just ahead. The drink is fine and I haven't heard of food poisoning but don't expect a warm welcome. Air attacks in the last few months killed thousands of French civilians. Homes, businesses and factories were destroyed by our bombs. We took out anything the Nazis might use."

"Do the French not appreciate Allied priorities?"

"How would you feel if it was your house?" Murphy didn't wait for an answer and wheeled onto a rubble strewn lot. Stewart suspected the burned-out structure had once been a café. The business had been moved to a nearby house where a young woman led them to a table. Murphy smiled as she took their order. His hand ran across her rump and she gently pushed it aside.

"A close friend?" Stewart asked.

Murphy watched her move toward the kitchen before answering. "We know each other. Notice that scarf tied tight to the head? Paulette got too close to the Germans when they were here. Locals gave her a hard time, shaved her head and were ready to douse her in tar when I put a stop to it. Since then, I've been getting my reward. I understand why the 'Jerries' liked her."

"Well, aren't you a gentleman."

"No, Sir. I'm a mercenary. I take what I can get. This war is almost over. I'm going to stay safe and on the odd night with Paulette will stay warm…unless…the bloody doctors send me back into action."

Eastern Germany, January 10

A trickle became a flood. First a few cars, army wives she suspected, sent to shelter in the west. As Greta Heinzel watched, a horse-drawn wagon appeared and then a two-wheeled cart, both piled high with family valuables. More people followed on foot. Most carried a suitcase or a bag of possessions. German women, old men and children on a trek to an uncertain future.

The door slammed as the farm manager entered the kitchen. An accident left Heinrich Steinbergen unfit for army service. Instead, he ran the estate with the help of foreign labour. "Anymore to pack,

Frau Heinzel?" He limped to a pair of suitcases and carried them to the door.

"No. I'll travel light," she answered. "My sister and I are the same size. I'll borrow what I need. She's so pregnant her clothes won't fit. And I'll be back in a few weeks."

"Are you sure there's room on the train?"

"Oh yes. I'm guaranteed a seat. But Heinrich, we need to talk about what happens while I'm gone. If the army demands shelter send men to the barns. I don't want dirty soldiers in the main house."

"The baker in the village heard guns yesterday." He nervously rubbed calloused hands together. "Big guns, the noise louder than a summer thunderstorm. And, the old woman who lives above his shop says owls are hooting every night. That's a sign of doom."

"Don't repeat such silly ideas. The Fuhrer promises new weapons to repel the enemy. He's never failed us." She waited until Henrich grudgingly nodded agreement. "Now where is the maid? That Russian sow disappears when work needs to be done."

"Larissa is frightened," he replied. "No Russian was to be taken alive and she surrendered. She fears what will happen if the Reds break through."

"They won't. Don't be so alarmist. While I'm gone, she must clean the entire house. Before the war we had good German servants..." Her voice trailed off as she glanced again toward the road, where refugee traffic was growing. She took a deep breath before continuing. "Polish women were better than the Bolshevik. Make her work and don't let her steal food. The pig would eat us out of house and home."

"I'll see to it. I also have a paper your grandfather gave me before he died. A family member should look at it..."

"...Not now!" She sounded angry. "Set it aside until my husband returns."

"Yes, ma'am," Heinrich answered sadly. He suspected her husband was a prisoner or in an unmarked grave in Russia.

The sound of a car horn caught her attention as an army staff car crunched through fresh snow. "A young officer will take me to the train. You are in charge, Heinrich. We'll discuss spring planting when I return."

The journey to the local station took twice the normal time. Despite the markings of an official car people were slow to give way. Along the road lay bundles of household goods cast aside by earlier travellers, an attempt to lighten the load on man or beast.

At the depot a train with a single passenger coach and a line of cattle cars waited. Passengers crowded the platform but gave way as her army escort pushed toward the carriage.

"Full!" A conductor barred their way. "Squeeze into a cattle car. She has warm clothes. She won't freeze."

The escort snapped to attention with the Nazi salute. "Heil Hitler!"

"Still full." The conductor shook his head.

"Make room!" The officer pushed into the carriage. "Them." He pointed to a woman and two children. "Out."

"You can't do that." The conductor objected.

The officer presented a sheet of paper. "On the orders of the Gauleiter, Frau Heinzel has a reserved seat." The conductor glanced at the form before speaking to the young family. "We'll fit you in somewhere. It will be less comfortable but no one on this train will have heat or light."

"Raus!" The officer pulled the mother to her feet and pushed her to the platform. The conductor more gently followed with the children. Greta's two suitcases were placed where the youngsters had been.

The train made a series of unscheduled stops. Twice, lines of prisoners shuffled by the windows to repair damaged track ahead. After a particularly long delay she heard gunfire and when the train moved forward saw a body sprawled beside the rails. Guards had no time for prisoners who were slow in their work.

Hours later, the conductor stopped beside her seat. "Almost to Berlin. We go in the black of night." He had decided if the woman had important connections, she should be kept informed. "The British are bombing and their fighter escorts strafe anything that moves."

A whistle sounded and the train ground to another halt. Flashes lit the night sky and passengers tensed as something struck the carriage roof. "Just flack, shrapnel, coming back down," the conductor assured her. "Our men, in the antiaircraft batteries, give them a fight. We don't quit." As if to underline his words, a whistle sounded, the train jerked and moved forward. "Be dawn soon. Berlin gets a break for a few hours. The British go home but by midday Americans planes will come. Don't delay. Streets aren't safe during a raid."

Another officer met her at the station. He forced a path through the crowd on the platform, through what was left of a waiting room and to a car idling in the street. Foreign workers and prisoners from across Europe, worked to clear debris from the latest bombing but she felt no desire to survey their work or the damage. She pulled the curtain on the car window and sank back in the leather upholstery. The heater made her drowsy and in minutes she was asleep.

"We're here." She woke to peer at a narrow track through rubble and her escort led the way to what had been a four-story apartment building. The upper floors were badly damaged. Only the lower levels appeared intact.

"Leave the luggage," she suggested. "My cousin will be home soon. We'll move the bags later."

"It's a risk. The police try to prevent thefts but can't be everywhere. My orders are to ensure you and your property are safe."

"Very well, then. Apartment two. This building was damaged over a year ago. I'm surprised it hasn't been repaired. Although, I suppose the war effort must take priority."

Darkness was falling when she heard footsteps and the door opened to the silhouette of a young women. A plain wool cap covered her head while the collar of a light coat was fastened by a scarf.

Greta extended her arms. "You've lost weight."

"Lots of exercise," Karin Werner smiled and returned the hug. "I walk to work. I got your letter but wasn't sure when you would arrive. And this morning the radio reported a strategic withdrawal in the east."

"A trap for the Russians," Greta told her. "We'll pull back and surprise them with a counterattack. They never learn."

Karin removed the scarf and hat, shaking her head to let blonde hair fall to her shoulders. "Keep your coat close. We seldom have heat. The gas has been out for several days." She rummaged in a drawer, produced a candle and lit the wick to throw a faint glow across the room. In a corner was a single, unmade bed and a dresser. Across the room, a couch was pushed tight against a wall. She placed the candle on a table and sat on a wooden chair. "You can have the bed or the couch. I sleep in my clothes. Through the night we hear the British bombers but don't always need to shelter."

"The couch is fine. I'll only here for one night. Lotte's baby is due next month and my sister is such a scatterbrain she won't be prepared. And, I'm sorry, I didn't realize how difficult city life had become. At home we don't have the help we once did but the house is warm and there's plenty of food. I brought a few extra supplies."

"Take them to Lotte," Karin suggested. "Dresden has escaped serious attacks but the food ration will be tight. She'll need to keep her energy up."

"And you don't?"

"I get by."

"I'm sure the party takes care of the faithful. And, when the Fuhrer's new wonder weapons are introduced, we will triumph."

"I hope so. We've been lucky on this street. But I've seen horrible things—the dead and the dying, mangled bodies and…"

"Don't do that! Don't dwell on what you can't control. Have faith in the Fuhrer."

"Yes, he's never failed us." Karin tried to sound strong. "And what of you? Is there any word of Gunther?"

"No, nothing since last fall but an SS officer has more to do than write letters. I believe my husband is alive and refuse to approve a death notice. I hate those black bordered announcements—'*Fallen for the Fatherland and the Fuhrer.*' But enough sad talk. I've been looking forward to seeing Dresden and exploring the old city."

Karin reached to touch the candlewax that dripped toward the table. "People say Churchill has a distant relative in Dresden. That's why it hasn't been bombed as much."

"Churchill! The man is a war criminal. Look at the terror he creates. But his day is coming. Churchill, Roosevelt, and Stalin. We'll settle with them."

"Yes…yes. I'm sure we will. It just that sometimes I feel…uneasy."

"Better if a man took care of you."

Karin shook her head. "No, I'm better alone."

"Those officers that Gunther brought home would have been good providers."

"And are they still alive?"

"Probably not." Greta shrugged. "The Russian campaign. But there are others."

"I was never interested in producing babies. And, in these conditions…"

"…The party would have provided."

"I wouldn't want the Mother's Cross. A woman needs five children to qualify. And, have you seen the children of Berlin? Orphans run in gangs."

"That will be corrected when we destroy our enemies."

"Oh Greta, I do hope that happens. Remember how we carried flowers when the Fuhrer returned after the French surrender. That was a marvellous event or what about the military parades and entertaining the young officers? And, we had the summers on the estate. The car accident had taken my mother and father but Grandfather was there…"

"…Enough! Grandfather resisted National Socialist policies. Gunther and I used our connections to protect him. The heart attack may have been a blessing. Eventually he would have run afoul of the authorities. We tried to warn him as I warn you now. The war can be won. Those who stand fast will have their reward."

Eastern Germany, January 18

The thunder of guns was constant as the German army reeled from Red Army artillery. A Russian Colonel watched dense smoke rise from the enemy lines. He loosened the cord on a fur hat and lifted the ear flaps before addressing a punishment unit, men who had broken army regulations.

"Comrades!" He shouted, his eyes ranging across their faces. He saw no emotion. No anger. No fear. Instead, simple resignation. "I am Colonel Peter Petrenkov. The hour of redemption has arrived. Your crimes will be pardoned. Tonight, as heroes you will sit by the fire, eat meat and fresh bread and have your choice of plump German women. You will again be proud members of the Red Army."

The expressions did not change, except perhaps for the young man in the front row. He motioned the soldier forward. "What was your crime?"

"I'm accused of desertion but it's not true."

"I remember you. A brave soldier as we fought across Poland." The Colonel offered a cold smile. "Prove your innocence. A guilty man shrinks from danger. A small enemy detachment is beyond those trees. At my command, the unit will advance." He pointed to a pair of guards who carried short machine guns. "These comrades will follow. If extra help is needed, they'll finish the Nazi scrum. Advance! All of you!"

The men cast anxious glances at each other and at the guards before entering an open field and moving cautiously forward. Twenty yards, thirty, fifty before an explosion and two men fell bleeding in the snow.

"Run! Advance!" The Colonel shouted from the rear. "Don't stop in a mine field. Forward!"

A prisoner took only a step before disappearing in a fiery blast. The others froze.

"Force them," he ordered and the guards carefully followed the path of foot prints in the snow, firing into the ground near the heels of anyone who hesitated. Another explosion and yet another showed their progress. The deserter led the way forward and was close to the tree line when a blast shredded his body.

The Colonel fastened the flaps back over his ears and called to an orderly. "Bring the tanks forward. This minefield is cleared."

Belgium, January 24

Loud voices carried from a meeting room in the headquarters of General Bernard Montgomery's 21st Army Group. Two field armies, one British and one Canadian, were combined with Americans, Poles and a smattering of other nationalities. The men fought across France, Belgium, part of the Netherlands and now stood on the doorstep of Germany.

"A bit of row going on," Duff Stewart said and tugged at the woollen gloves to expose the finger tips before he began to type. "One of Monty's liaison officers, the eyes and ears for the General, is back from the front. He must have seen something important. It's causing quite a stir."

"Doesn't concern us," a captain snapped and dumped a set of handwritten notes on the desk. "We need transcripts of prisoner interrogations."

A half dozen typewriters were ready for action but only Stewart was on duty. He strained to decipher a scrawl before pecking at the keys. "I wonder if anyone reads this stuff. It's the same every day. A few Nazis relieved to be out the war but most still eager to die for the Fatherland."

"You are new, aren't you?" the captain asked.

"Yes, Sir."

"You'll learn German determination is actually fuelled by our radio broadcasts. Repeated demands for unconditional surrender are considered proof we aim to destroy everything. They'll have no families or homes to return to and so fight on, martyrs for the Third Reich. And, they're determined to take more of our men with them."

"What about the kids, the boy soldiers?" Stewart waved another prisoner statement. "We've underage men in our army but this prisoner admits he's only fourteen. He probably had pimples on his face and foamed like a rabid dog."

"They've been indoctrinated, fed propaganda for years. At home, at school, in training for Hitler Youth. They don't know anything else."

"I wouldn't mess with the little bastards. A kid might hide a grenade in his pants."

The voices in the next room grew louder but the words were indistinct. "I can see why Monty prefers to sleep elsewhere." Stewart motioned toward the door. "He wouldn't get much rest with the noise from that crowd."

"Yes, the Field Marshall is wise to retire to his caravan, his private trailer," the captain said. "I prefer whiskey but Monty likes a glass of milk and privacy at bed time."

"Hopefully he doesn't have to offer more apologies. Claiming he saved the Americans in the Ardennes wasn't tactful. He may have been right but to say so and in front of the Yankee press corps was certain to cause a ruckus, especially after the losses they suffered."

"I'm sure he'd appreciate your advice."

"Don't get me wrong, Sir. He's here with the men. I hear of officers living in luxury while the rest of us freeze our butts off."

"That lip will get you in trouble. Button it."

The voices in the next room rose, this time with a crash as something was hurled against a wall. Seconds later, the door opened to the bark of an angry officer. "I can't process these damn reports if you keep stealing my staff." His eyes came to rest on Stewart. "Collect your gear, Lieutenant. We need more men at the front."

CHAPTER 2

"**A**CHTUNG! ACHTUNG!"

Karin Werner roused as someone pounded on her door, the warning almost lost in the wail of an air raid siren. She rose quickly, fastened her coat and felt for the emergency kit that everyone in Berlin carried; identification, ration cards and a few small personal items. Thankfully, Greta was gone, safely on her way to Dresden. Karin glanced around the room before opening her door. "Go to the Zoo bunker." She urged those running along the hallway. "We'll have heat and with the antiaircraft guns the enemy can't get close."

"I don't go there anymore." An older woman rejected the advice. "The smell is awful and young people are…well…copulating in the stair well. Once it was orderly. The mothers kept baby carriages lined in neat rows but now everything is confused. I'll take my chances here."

Another siren joined the chorus and with it first thump from an explosion. Another neighbour brushed past. "Go to the cellar. I looked outside. The sky is full of red, green, and yellow flares. My husband calls them Christmas trees. They show where the bombers will aim. Hurry. There's no time to waste."

A mother led a youngster toward the stairway while another child clung to the woman's skirt. "Take my hand," Karin clasped the toddler's fingers and began the descent. In the crush, she was pushed from behind but somehow kept her balance.

In the flickering candlelight of the basement, she found other tenants, a few nervously braced against the wall, others standing silently, as if in shock. The room shook and a rush of air forced the door on an abandoned furnace to swing wildly, first open and then violently shut. The same air current snuffed out the candles. Only a kerosene lantern spluttered in the gloom.

"Here." The mother gathered the children. "Sit here." The children dutifully sat on the latest addition to the shelter, a wooden bench anchored to the wall.

More explosions prompted cries and groans. "It will hold," a man called. "This is the worst attack in months but these apartment blocks are built to last."

The minutes seemed like hours. The basement walls shuddered and dust hung like a dense fog. But a few blocks away, new fires attracted the attention of British bombers and as the aircraft swarmed toward a new target an uneasy calm settled on the shelter.

"I'm going to leave," a young woman spoke. "My father has a house in the country. I won't spend another day in Berlin."

"I doubt you'll be allowed to go," a man warned. "The party fears a panic. Streams of people leaving the city would damage morale. It would be a sign we're giving up."

"I'll stay!" A boy shouted and squared his shoulders. "I'll fight for the Fatherland."

"Shush!" His mother caught Karin's eye. "He's big for his age. Carl is only twelve, too young for active service."

Daylight allowed a full assessment of the damage. The upper stories had collapsed onto the apartments below. The hallway and

Karin's apartment were open to the sky. She moved cautiously to what was left of the dresser. Ripped clothing, the tattered remnants of her wardrobe lay on the floor.

A child laughed and she turned to see the boy tugging at a bra strap tangled on a piece of wood. "Carl, stop!" The mother was a step behind. "Let go of that. Help the lady move the mattress to the cellar. She won't have to sleep on a cold floor."

An elderly man had taken charge by the time Karin returned to the shelter. "Don't worry. I spent months underground on the western front in the First War. As soldiers, we didn't have bricks and concrete above us, only a few feet of dirt."

"I'm sure we'll survive," she answered. "We'll make do until the party arranges new accommodation."

"Privacy will be an issue," he told her. "But take the old coal storage room. There's only room for one person anyway."

Carl arrived and dropped the mattress. He stood as if waiting for more instructions. "Could you find a blanket?" Karin asked. "Even a cloth door would make me feel better."

Ottawa, February 8

Vincent Russel was a regular hotel guest and used his influence to claim a room in a capital packed with wartime travellers. A quick word with the manager produced a bottle of the best Scotch plus a plate of sandwiches and pastries. "Help yourself." Russel motioned to the food while leafing through the afternoon newspapers. "Canada is going to need a new Defence Minister. Andy McNaughton lost the by-election that was supposed to secure his place in cabinet."

"Never met the man and I won't have to bother about him now." Ben Willey wore the uniform of a US army officer but had never seen action. He did however offer access to the upper echelon in Washington. "McNaughton is a mere domestic trifle and hardly matters in the grand scheme of things."

"Matters to the Canadian government." Russel snapped and

tossed the newspaper aside. "The General stepped into the political crisis over conscription when the Prime Minister feared a military coup. Amazing how a silly idea can take root in a politician's mind. But I guess that doesn't matter anymore either. McNaughton will be out."

"And Canada joins the world in conscripting soldiers. What's the big deal? In the States, we had a draft before the shooting started."

"To those beyond Canadian borders this must appear a tempest in a teapot but we've been through years of debate over conscription. An all-volunteer army overseas made us stand out among the Allies."

"Oh, come now. Other countries didn't notice or care. Especially when many of your volunteers chose not to leave the country."

"Oh, I suppose, it's a uniquely Canadian issue. But the defeat of a cabinet minister will upset the Prime Minister. He hadn't counted on the old religious animosity. A whisper campaign claimed the General's wife was Catholic and that doesn't fly in parts of Ontario."

Wiley reached for a pastry. "Maybe time to grow up and set aside the prejudice."

Russell smirked. "I seem to recall Americans rejecting Al Smith, a Catholic candidate for president. None of us are enlightened as we like to think. I wonder what other old hatreds will emerge as the war draws to a close. The big three might add that to their agenda."

The American relaxed. The conversation was back on safer, secular ground. "Yes, the secret is out of the latest conference. Churchill, Roosevelt, and Stalin are planning for a new Europe or to be blunt, how to punish Germany. They've gathered in the Russian Crimea, at Yalta, in palaces originally built for the late and unlamented Tsar. Winston can regale them with tales of Balaclava and the charge of the Light Brigade."

"One would hope they don't make a hash of things as in 1919."

"The school masters will revisit the lessons of the Peace of Versailles but with a new curriculum. Here's a hint. Roosevelt never liked Germans. And, unlike after World War One, America will play a major role. We'll have to." Willey slipped into his coat and prepared to leave. "England is bankrupt. The British Dominions are too small to play a major role. France, Belgium, and the Netherlands need to rebuild. Only America has the military and manufacturing might that will be needed."

"What about the Soviets?"

"Oh, don't worry about Uncle Joe Stalin. He'll fall in line."

"Is that an official Washington view?"

"About as official as can be. We'll worry about the Reds after we've kicked more German butt. And, we have no reservations about kicking them when they're down."

"I've another matter," Russel said and produced a sheet of paper. "A young Canadian acquaintance has found himself—well—a little too close to the front line. I wonder if the American forces might find him useful?"

Wiley took a moment to study the resume. "This Stewart fellow needs a safe transfer, eh? I'll see what I can do."

"And, I may have more news from Europe soon. Two of my associates have returned to France. Evers Chance has great connections across Europe. He joined our firm in '42. He and his wife usually find interesting material."

Le Havre, France, February 13

Blackened bricks and the remains of a chimney were all that remained of a once prosperous farmstead. An attractive middle-aged woman choked back tears as she surveyed the wreckage. "It's all I had and there's nothing left. The house and barn were either destroyed by the Nazis or by Allied bombs. It would take years to rebuild."

Evers Chance slipped an arm around her and she leaned against him for support. "Maria, we knew it would bad. Le Havre was bombed repeatedly and there were months of hard fighting on the ground." Gently he took her hand. "Buildings can be replaced but I've more bad news. Maurice is dead, killed in an ambush last summer."

"Oh no." Maria's voice quavered as she thought of the friend who worked with the French resistance. "I liked Maurice and I feel guilty. We were safe in North America. And, in these last few days, working with UNRRA in Normandy, I'm still safely behind the lines." She brushed at tears and turned from the wreckage.

Chance handed her a handkerchief. "I have trouble remembering the full name. The United Nations Relief and Rehabilitation Agency? Did I get it right?"

"You did, and what an odd mix of people. Retired British army supply specialists; Washington bureaucrats who worked on FDR's New Deal and a few plain old activists anxious to save humanity. Collectively, an earnest bunch. I tried to introduce a bit of realism but doubt I succeeded. We won't know until they come face-to-face with the refugees...or...that new designation...Displaced Persons, D.P. for short."

"I've seen some," Chance said. "The numbers will only grow."

"And, so complicated. No one expected to find Russians fighting in the German army. I'm glad I don't have to sort it out."

"Not just Russians. Men from across Eastern Europe fought alongside the Nazis, sometimes by choice and sometimes there was no choice. And, it's not just Europe. Men from India fought with the Japanese. They saw it as a way to win independence from British rule. Nothing has been simple these last few years. Thank God, we got you out of France." His mind flashed to a desperate escape in late 1941. "I'm not sure I could have gone on without you."

"Come on, Chance. Don't get sappy. You're the strong one."

He chuckled. "Only when you support me."

The pair were an odd wartime pairing. Chance was twenty years older than his wife. The first meeting came during the Russian revolution but romance only blossomed in the early 1940s and since then they had grown inseparable. In his eyes, she had very special gifts: intelligence, courage, and the slim body of a woman who refused to age. The long black hair showed only the odd strand of grey.

"What now?" Maria asked.

"On to Paris. Hitler ordered the city burned but his men never struck the match. I have briefings with SHAEF, another great name, the Supreme Headquarters Allied Expeditionary Force. The staff have appropriated the Palace Hotel at Versailles."

"And then?" She knew Chance usually thought several steps ahead.

"Berlin."

"You feel up to this?" She worried about his age. How long could a man in his late sixties withstand wartime conditions and the constant tension? In recent years, he'd gained weight, the hair had thinned and the wire framed glasses became an absolute necessity.

"Long as you are close, we can do anything," he told her. "You keep me young."

"There you go…sappy again." She managed a weak smile. "Did you want to see Dieppe?"

"No. I know what happened. The raid in '42 should never have been mounted. Hundreds of young Canadians dead on the beach. It was stupid and accomplished next to nothing. Military leaders would like to forget but the rank-and-file definitely remember." He began to fill a pipe with tobacco. "The army mounted a special ceremony when Dieppe was liberated last fall. And then, another mistake. General Montgomery's nose was out of joint because the Canadian Commander went to the memorial service instead of a meeting with the top brass. Monty is a superb soldier but can be a pompous, unfeeling ass."

"Yes. You've told me before. Men like Montgomery or the American George Patton are not really nice."

"Of course, as I've also explained, nice men do not win wars."

Maria nudged her boot into a pile of ashes. "I never understood why you were obsessed with Dieppe. You weren't part of the planning and we were in Canada."

"I was meeting with auto industry executives in Windsor when the word came and the Essex Scottish, a local regiment, was involved. I've never seen so many telegraph delivery boys on the streets at the same time and each one carrying bad news; of the dead, the wounded, or the missing. The day haunts me. It never should have happened but even Franklin Roosevelt was prepared for a 'sacrifice raid', ready to spill American blood and build interest in the war against Germany. After the attack on Pearl Harbour the US developed a hate for Japan. FDR had to keep reminding them of the Nazi threat."

"We're told the lessons from Dieppe were used on D-Day."

"Oh, but so many missteps." Chance sucked on the pipe until the tobacco began to glow. "Think of the tanks bogged down at Dieppe because no one considered the type of gravel on the beach. And think of how the Normandy invasion nearly stalled because no one thought hedgerows would slow the advance. Mind you, D-Day was a colossal feat. Brave men fighting for a foothold in France, the prefabricated Mulberry harbours, a pipeline to carry gasoline from England. I only wish people were told the full story, mistakes and all."

"Berlin must see the war is lost." Maria starred again at the wreckage. "My little farm is a tiny example of what's been destroyed. Magnify that a million times for how the world has suffered."

"It's been obvious since '43 that Hitler will not get what he wants. He's held out in hopes of a negotiated settlement but there's nothing left to negotiate. Oh, the odd general may offer to surrender his force or try to save himself. But it's too late."

Chance bent to tap the pipe against a stone and ground the embers into the ground before he slipped an arm around Maria's waist and guided her to a waiting car. "And, I'm sorry. I don't mean to harp over the mistakes of the past."

"I know you too well. You'll find new mistakes to harp on. You must watch that temper. Too much excitement is bad for an older gentleman."

He laughed and gave her a squeeze. "We'll watch from Paris. Great Britain and America will compete on the race through Germany. But neither will take Berlin. The Red Army will be there first."

CHAPTER 3

"**H**ERE." A CAPTAIN'S dirty finger stabbed at the map. "A Lancaster went down and parachutes were sighted. The enemy is close but you should be able to locate any survivors and bring them back."

Duff Stewart's face turned pale. "Wouldn't it better to send men with more experience? My guys are green. The only one who has seen action is Sergeant Murphy and he's recovering from an injury."

"No. Time for the baptism of fire. Get a move on."

Stewart saw Tim Murphy's eyes roll. Finding him among the other replacements had been a stroke of luck. The sergeant guided the rookie lieutenant through hurried training exercises and away from anything that suggested danger.

"But, Sir." Stewart tried again. "We've no idea what to expect and well, I'm not sure my men are up to speed on their weapons."

"Too bad." The decision was obviously final. "Check the map. Round up those flyers and bring them back. That's an order and the safest job I'll assign today."

"Safe my ass," Murphy said when the senior officer was gone. "That area could be crawling with Krauts."

"Another suggestion?" Stewart asked.

"Not unless we want to spend the rest of the war in the cells."

Murphy used his contacts and arranged for the use of what he called a Kangaroo. Engineers had cut away the turret on an obsolete tank and the squad crammed into what became an improvised armoured personal carrier. In two hours, they reached the site designated on the map.

"Rough ride but better than walking," Stewart said as he sprang down from beside the driver. Murphy watched as the unit began the search. "This may not be so bad," he whispered. "The Riley's and the Scottish are supposed to be close."

"The what?"

"Our guys. The Royal Hamilton Light Infantry and the Essex Scottish are somewhere nearby."

"I thought those outfits were decimated at Dieppe."

"They were; but with new men, they are back in action. Of course, Dieppe is not the only mistake the brass made. Lots of men have been lost through bad planning, stupid accidents or friendly fire — when we open up on our own people, or how about officers who are replaced when they refuse to accept high casualties…"

"What are you talking about?"

"Just trying to make you see the brass aren't as smart as they claim. We have to look out for ourselves. It's a question of whether we leave the army with an honorable discharge or they chisel our names on a cenotaph…"

"…That's enough, damn it. Find the fly boys and get out of here."

Stewart took a moment to study the landscape. He rejected a search of a burned-out farmhouse and instead ordered the men toward the trees on a nearby ridge.

A shout from behind took them by surprise. "Hey! Back here!" The men spun, weapons at the ready, to see first one airman and then several others emerge from the shell of the farmhouse. "Glad to see you mate!" a voice called. "Give us a lift?"

Stewart was embarrassed. "Where were you?"

"The cellar. We were all cozy and warm and waiting for a cab. I've got two men missing. I don't think they got out of the plane but the rest are hail and hearty."

"We should go," Murphy hissed. "Get them away quickly."

Stewart waved everyone toward their transport. "We were ready for anything." He faked bravado. "I was ready to shoot my way through, ready for a real firefight."

"We came from one of those," an airman replied. "Big raid on Dresden. God, you should have seen the firestorm. The whole city was burning. I could feel the heat inside the bird. The Air Force thinks mass destruction will shorten the war."

Murphy offered a broad smile. "Anything to shorten the war is welcome."

"Yah...I guess so." The airman spoke slowly, the image of the burning city etched on his mind. "I'm glad I'm wasn't on the receiving end. I pity the people on the ground." He was silent for a moment. "But best not to dwell on it. And ...hey...we're glad to see you. A captured flyer is more likely to face a noose than a prison camp. Bomber Command is not popular in Germany. But, let's move. I want to be home for last call."

Berlin, February 17

The shop was in the only intact building left on the street. A sign propped in a row of sandbags announced the location at the National Socialist Welfare Organization. Inside was a low counter policed by an older woman and behind her were rows of boxes, crates and half empty racks of clothing. From the rear, came the sound of classical music, a regular broadcast from Radio Berlin.

"I've a letter from my local party leader." Karin Werner slid the note across the counter. "I'm desperate for clothing. My rooms were destroyed. I've tried the few stores that are open but there's nothing left."

"What do you need?"

"Everything. Underthings, a dress, a skirt. I have nothing but what I'm wearing." She opened the coat. "I salvaged my uniform from the League of German Maidens. I was a bit pudgy when I was younger so the skirt fits at the waist but is much too short. I work in a records office and must appear respectable."

"Hmm…maybe you dazzle the men. Too many young women take advantage of what nature provided."

"No…no. There is no time for mindless flirting…"

"*Achtung! Achtung!*" The radio station interrupted the music program and a few seconds later, an announcer began to read a statement. "*British and American criminals have conducted a terror raid on the city of Dresden.*"

Karin gasped and leaned on the counter for support.

"*Thousands are dead after the treacherous firebombing of a peaceful city. Dresden is a scene of mass destruction. Dr. Goebbels will have a full statement later this afternoon.*"

After a few seconds of silence, the music resumed.

"I have two cousins, the last of my family is in Dresden." Karin's voice broke. "One is pregnant. They thought it was safe."

"Sit." The clerk produced a chair. "Take some time." She turned and retreated into the rabbit warren of crates and boxes.

In her mind, Karin saw Lotte and Greta and happy smiling faces as the three cousins played on their grandfather's estate. She remembered how Greta convinced them to volunteer for the women's organization and of how smart they looked in their uniforms; the crisp white shirt, the blue skirt and black beret, always pushed to a jaunty angle. The future had seemed full of promise.

The clerk returned, carrying a bag. "I found skirts worn by older girls. And socks. Pull them high. Up to the knee. That would appear proper."

"Thank you." Karin wiped at her eyes. "I'm sorry. The news from Dresden is so horrible."

"Wait." The woman again disappeared among the boxes. A minute later she returned with a fur coat. "This came in a shipment from Auschwitz, a labour camp in Poland. There's a mend at the collar but it's been deloused and the fur should keep you warm."

"I can't thank you enough. There's a small stove in our shelter but it's terribly cold."

"You must stay well to continue the war effort. The Fuhrer demands complete dedication."

"Yes. Yes…I suppose…he does." Karin removed her old coat. "Perhaps some one could use this?"

The clerk shook her head. "No. Foreign workers wear better rags than that."

Karin slipped into the fur and lifted the small bag of clothing.

"Don't give up," the clerk warned. "We've all lost family and friends but we can't lose hope."

The Rhineland, February 20

"I don't like the looks of this." Tim Murphy pointed to a line of jeeps, loaded with wounded men on stretchers. "We're taking too many casualties. More men will be needed in the front line."

Duff Stewart shivered under the partial shelter of a camouflage net. The netting might offer protection from German aircraft but not from the steady soaking rain. He sat with his back against a tree, hoping the pine boughs would deflect the deluge. "Nowhere is safe." he told the sergeant. "London and Antwerp are being hit by the new buzz bombs. And, here, the bloody Krauts fire shells into the top of the trees. The falling limbs and branches injure men as badly as bullets."

"We'll be flat on our bellies if we move forward." Murphy warned. "Turn the Air Force loose and bomb the hell out of them."

"They are. Even German broadcasts admit major damage in

Dresden. Nothing left but acres of smouldering rubble. Thousands of Nazis were literally fried."

"The hell with their cities. Blast their Siegfried line to hell. Drop more ordinance on the pill boxes and bunkers. It's their last fortified barrier."

"Pilots can't fly in rain and fog." Stewart shifted position in another vain attempt to avoid the cold downpour. "When the weather clears the bombers will be back."

"What's with you? Why are you so complacent?" Murphy looked for a dry spot and he too wedged against the tree. "Don't you understand? They'll need more men at the front."

Stewart was silent. He had decided not to share the latest news from home where his mentor was working to arrange a quiet transfer.

"Stewart! Murphy! On your feet." A captain slogged through mud as he came toward them. "We've a bunch of prisoners on the way to the cage. Go up the road to collect them. Another unit is bringing them part way."

"All disarmed?" Murphy asked. "I don't want to frisk them, never know what they might be hiding."

"For Christ's sake, yes. All disarmed, captured two days ago. If pistols or knifes haven't surfaced by now, there aren't any."

Passing traffic churned the roadway to mud and the two men were forced off the track and into the edge of the forest. The first hour was quiet but then a burst of small arms fire sent them scurrying for cover. "That's close," Murphy whispered from behind a tree.

Stewart held his breath for a full minute before shouting. "Hey, we're Canadians, sent to pick up prisoners." He waited. If the gunfire was from the enemy they were finished. A shouted reply came in English. "Ok, move where we can see you."

"Go ahead," he told Murphy. "I'll cover you."

"Frigging hero," the sergeant snorted and slowly rose. Stewart followed as Murphy cautiously inched forward. Seconds later they met a soldier in British battledress before spotting four other soldiers, and a group of downcast prisoners.

"Had a spot of trouble." Another Lieutenant spoke with a thick English accent. His troops were covered in mud and had a haunted look, the effect of weeks of constant combat. He pointed to three German bodies; the back of each uniform riddled by bullets. "Bastards tried to overpower us and escape." A soldier bent and rolled a body to expose a face. "This one was a tough old bugger. Had to watch him like a hawk. The others won't give you trouble."

"How do we account for this?" Stewart asked. "We were expecting thirteen."

"Forget it. Nobody gives a damn. Fewer Krauts to feed."

"Yah, well, just in case who are you? Sorry for the questions but I'm new to this game."

"Hmm......ok...uh...I'm Wilton...uh...Fourteenth New Brunswick. Any questions, the brass can find me through regimental headquarters. Don't worry about the bodies. A pioneer brigade can put them under." He kicked a living prisoner and after a motion with the rifle the others stumbled to their feet.

Murphy led the way to the stockade while Stewart took the rear, rifle at the ready. He was only steps behind the prisoners and caught whispered words in German. "The leaflets from the British promised an honourable surrender. Not murder."

"Do nothing," a companion answered softly. "But remember everything." Stewart broke the conversation with the prod of a gun and the only sounds became boots sloshing in thick mud. A half hour later the prisoners appeared relieved when herded into a barbed wire pen but immediately turned to glare at their captors.

"I'm Lieutenant Stewart," Duff explained to a sentry. "Officially, I guess, I'm assigned to Monty's H.Q."

"Sign." A weary corporal offered a pen. "Name and unit."

"I wasn't given paperwork." Stewart scratched his name.

"Don't worry. Someone else can sort it out."

"Yah, don't worry about it," Murphy said as they left the prison cage. "Shit happens. Those Krauts were shot in the back. A few more minutes and we wouldn't have had anyone to escort."

"No wait. They were trying to escape..."

"...If you believe that, you believe in Santa Claus. The rest of the prisoners were scarred shitless and expected to meet their maker. But don't sweat it. We lost men in Normandy. Germans killed them after they surrendered. Everyone talked about it and everyone planned for payback."

"But that's not right. That's murder."

"Duff. You delivered ten prisoners. That's all there were. Forget what you heard and forget what you saw."

Eastern Germany, February 25

In only hours, drifting snow covered the inert shapes along the road. The wind lifted the odd piece of cloth, a stripped pyjama, or a torn uniform, mute testimony of a death march. The SS units drove prisoners west only hours before the arrival of the Russian Army. Those unable to keep up lay by the road, dispatched with a single bullet.

"Germany must be desperate for workers." A Red Army officer spoke as he surveyed the scene. "Why else take prisoners on a retreat."

Colonel Petrenkov turned his back to the wind before he answered. "Perhaps there is something they don't want us to know."

"But we've seen the camps. Men starved to death. Only a few were alive."

"Russians survive. A few may be contaminated by insidious foreign influence but after re-education can return to the fight."

"As you order, Comrade, and we have a British soldier. He's asked for someone who speaks English."

"Bring him to the house," Petrenkov said and pointed to the ruins of a building.

Minutes later a scarecrow like figure emerged from the storm and offered a weak salute. "Sergeant Ewen Armstrong. I wanted to thank you. I've only a few men left."

"We will help an ally. Your men will be fed."

"Most welcome." Armstrong appeared to stagger from the simple effort of speaking but after a moment regained his balance. "Most men who are strong enough to walk are under German guard, somewhere ahead." He pointed up the road. "The sick and the frail were left behind. We'd be dead if not for your arrival."

Armstrong was gaunt, a grey face covered with a scraggly beard. His uniform was ragged, matted with dirt. "My men had a rough go. The Nazis were low on supplies. If we didn't have food from Red Cross packages, more would be dead. Russian prisoners didn't get packages but we slipped them what we could."

"*Red?*" Petrenkov was confused. "Russia sent food?"

"No, no." Armstrong explained, "Red Cross or Red Crescent. Relief packages were sent from our homes and Germans passed them out or at least they did sometimes. Guards often kept the best for themselves. We were glad to get anything."

"The more I see the less I understand. Food was hidden in these houses." Petrenkov pointed to the wreckage. "In once fine German homes. Why attack Russia? They had everything. We had much less."

"Afraid, I wouldn't know except that Hitler wanted to rule the world. I was captured in France back in 1940. Prison life wasn't bad at the start but grew progressively worse."

"Tell me, sergeant, why did you surrender?"

"My commander issued an order."

"What an odd command." The Russian cocked his head. "And, when you go home, you'll be punished for giving up?"

"Not bloody likely."

"The Soviet army finds no honour in surrender. Any Russian will be interrogated by political officers. Cowards might face hard labour or in extreme cases…execution."

"Poor buggers."

"No Sergeant. No pity. Our policies make Russia stronger."

Berlin, March 1

The air raids never seemed to stop. The 'Amis', the Americans, concentrated their daylight attacks on the city centre and only a few errant blasts fell near the Karin's underground office. 'Tommis', the British Air Force, would likely return tonight but for the moment she felt safe.

"Frau Werner. A new assignment," her supervisor called. "I need the delicate hand of a woman." Herman Hauptmann leaned from a doorway and ruefully waved an artificial hand. "We must complete the insignia for the latest Volkssturm unit. An official crest will give units of the Peoples' Storm greater pride. Our new militia will fight harder."

Karin followed him to a work bench to find a swastika stencilled on a page.

"Draw crossed swords at the top and the bottom," he ordered, "No time for impressive artwork. The men will be in action soon." She followed his instructions and the insignia was soon completed. "Good," he nodded approval. "Each man will be given a copy, something to boost the spirits. Old men and young boys need encouragement. They've not seen battle."

"You saw action in Russia?" Karin asked. Hauptmann had only recently been transferred from a hospital to the record centre. "I don't mean to pry," she spoke gently. "But the radio warns against the Bolsheviks. Our troops will no doubt drive them back but why do the Russians hate us so? The Americans and the British deliver terror attacks by air but Russians are portrayed as much worse."

"Why do Communists hate us?" He considered the question. "Think of animals which lack intelligence. Severe measures were taken to bring them under control."

"But what measures? What makes them so dangerous?"

"A young woman should not think of such things. Those broadcasts are to encourage our men. If homes and loved ones are in danger men fight harder."

She looked puzzled. "I wondered if something happened in Russia that people don't know?"

"War is harsh." He struggled for the right words. "When we captured a village, we had to destroy it."

"And what of the villagers, the peasants?"

"We couldn't leave them to rampage in the rear."

"Women and children?"

"What of them?" Hauptmann showed a rare display of anger. "Did they care about this?" He waved the metal hand. "Men were angry; feelings ran high. Peasants were liquidated. I am not proud but it happened."

"Women were…abused…were raped?"

"Frau Werner! Soldiers are rarely celibate. But what was done, is done. It is beyond our control."

"But the Russians remember? And want revenge?"

"Pray they are kept at bay. I shudder to think of what could happen if they reach Berlin."

The Rhineland, Feb 24

Tim Murphy returned with a bag slung across his shoulder, a rifle carelessly cradled under his arm. "Did a bit of foraging, found food and a bottle of cognac."

"Standing orders warn against looting." Duff Stewart smiled. "But nothing was said about foraging."

"The cupboard in the house was picked over." Murphy pulled a bottle and a roll of meat from the bag. "A sapper got there before me and showed me where an explosive charge had been planted under silver ware. Warn our guys. Any souvenirs, helmets, lugers, or anything that looks valuable may be booby trapped. The Nazis prepared ugly surprises."

"At least they didn't tamper with the food," Stewart said, using a bayonet to slice the meat.

"Actually, they may have but other men were wolfing it down and nothing happened to them."

"Monty must be ready to attack." Stewart washed the cognac around in his mouth and passed the bottle to other members of the squad. "Thousands of men, tanks, artillery, extra ammo, food and fuel. Something big is coming."

"Yah, the attempt to cross the Rhine is only days away." Murphy watched anxiously as the bottle made the rounds. "Montgomery has a reputation for thorough planning, with maximum artillery and air support. And better yet, he aims for as few casualties as possible."

"Let's hope so." Stewart wiped his sleeve across his mouth. "We're moving up at dawn."

"Ah shit." Murphy shook the near empty bottle. "I hoped we'd be sitting tight for a few more days."

"It may not be that bad. We're to support an armoured unit. Let them play hero."

Morning brought another day of miserable late winter weather.

The retreating German forces destroyed dams, flooded thousands of acres of land and with the hint of spring a seasonal thaw added to the sea of mud. Truckloads of rocks and debris were dumped onto paths in an attempt to create passable roadways. But four-wheel drive jeeps, powerful trucks, half tracks and tanks fought for traction.

"Let's hitch a ride on a tank," Stewart suggested. "Why slog through mud?"

"We should stay on foot and a few yards back, quite a few yards," Murphy warned. "German artillery, their big 88 cannons, can tear apart an armoured column. Everyone thinks the tank crews are safe and dry but extra fuel cans are strapped outside. If they're hit, they're like a teapot on a stove. They 'brew up' but go ahead, if you want, climb aboard."

Stewart instead waved the men to the side of the road. "We'll wait and hitch a ride on something else."

"Choose carefully," Murphy warned. "A bunch of our universal carriers have been modified as flame throwers, what are called Wasps. They're loaded with napalm, a jellied gasoline, or other fiery concoctions. Men call them Ronsons, like the cigarette lighter, cause if they're hit, they burn and burn. We're safer on foot."

"Stewart!" Neither man had seen the captain approach. "That bush on the right has been cleared. A reconnaissance unit is dug in a mile ahead. Take your platoon and back them up."

"Cleared my ass," Murphy muttered two hours later, "This place is like a jungle."

"Oh, it's cleared." A British soldier surprised them and stepped from behind a tree. "If it wasn't your whole outfit would have been wiped out. Make less noise and follow me."

The reconnaissance team lay in shallow foxholes behind an improvised cover of tree limbs and branches. A captain waved them to the ground. "We heard enemy movement last night but nothing today." He handed over a set of binoculars. Below, in a shallow valley was a village with a handful of houses and barns, a peaceful scene that might have graced a prewar post card.

Stewart passed the binoculars to Murphy before he spoke. "My men are tired. We should wait for the armour. No sense taking unnecessary risks."

"No! We're going in. We'll split up and hit them from both sides of the village."

"Something's funny." Murphy interrupted as he studied the scene. "There's a strong breeze. The trees are swaying but the curtain hanging from that window hasn't moved."

"I'm not worrying about any curtain." The captain prepared for a fight. "Take five men and move to the right."

The squad had barely left shelter when a burst of machine gun fire erupted from the village followed a second later by the blast of a shell. The men scurried back and dropped to return fire.

"A frigging pill box!" Murphy yelled. "I saw the blast. A tank is hidden in that building. The curtain was painted on the wall to fool us. An attack would be suicide. Wait for armour and burn them out."

The captain scowled but slid to where a radio operator had raised headquarters. Stewart and Murphy were too far away to hear the conversation.

"We wait," the officer said as he returned. "The armoured column will be up in an hour. But Lieutenant Stewart won't be here. New orders. You are to return to H.Q. for re-assignment."

Murphy smiled in relief.

"Oh no, not you sergeant. You stay with us. Only the Lieutenant is going back."

"But…"

Stewart served up a wide smile. "Sorry Murph. You know the army. New assignments come right out of the blue. Maybe we'll cross paths later."

CHAPTER 4

MOST OF THE windows were broken or missing completely but the street car on freshly repaired track offered proof Berlin still functioned. Karin Werner sat behind the conductor and raised the collar of the fur coat to protect against the wind whistling through the car. A briefcase filled with documents was at her feet. The demand for orders, requisitions and paperwork showed the armed forces too still functioned.

A pair of Wehrmacht soldiers sat behind her. Their uniforms were clean, fresh from army stores and each carried a field pack.

"Why go back?" She heard one say. "It would be different if we had seasoned reinforcements but old men and boys will run at the first sign of trouble."

"Desertion means a firing squad," his companion whispered. "Besides where would you go?"

"Away from the Russians. I'll take my chances and surrender to the British or Americans."

The car swayed and threatened to derail before the wheels caught and rolled on. "What's left to defend?" The first soldier waved toward the ruins around them. "Berlin is a wasteland and the bombs keep falling." And, at that moment an air raid siren sounded and the car ground to a halt.

"There's a shelter in the basement across the street. Hurry," the conductor called. Karin snatched the briefcase but almost lost her balance as she jumped to the pavement. A tall officer in a long leather coat reached to steady her. "Fraulein. Let me help."

"No, I'm fine. But the two soldiers behind me are planning to desert. I overheard their conversation."

Instantly, he drew a gun and waved to where police were supervising a band of foreign workers. "Leave them," he ordered. "I am Kempler, Gestapo. Arrest those soldiers, suspicion of desertion."

"No. That's not true." One soldier shouted as he realized the danger. "We're on our way to rejoin our unit."

"Arrest them," Kempler repeated and waited only long enough to be sure the order was followed. An explosion sounded a few blocks away but he stopped Karin before she could reach the public shelter. Instead, he guided her to the next block and down a set of stairs. An entrance showed recent damage but deep underground a large room was unscathed. Tables were arranged as in prewar nightclub.

"This is better." He commandeered two empty chairs. "We'll have a drink, something to eat and won't need ration coupons. The party operates this shelter."

"But I've documents that must reach the Reich Chancellery."

"Unfortunately, there will be a short delay." He ignored the explosions and signalled for a waiter.

"What will happen to those deserters?" Karin asked.

"The Fuhrer has issued orders for flying court martials. Justice will be delivered on the street."

"I'll be called as a witness?"

"No. No need for a long process. We know what they are."

Someone began to play a piano and several women and a group

of uniformed men with decorations and gold braid surrounded the entertainer. "For a few minutes we can forget the war," Kempler said and leaned closer.

"But those deserters," she persisted. "A prison sentence..."

"...No. Desertion brings the death penalty. Forget them."

The encounter became surreal. The group around the piano broke into song while the Gestapo officer began to stroke her hand. "Relax, Gretchen. We can spend the night together."

"I'm not Gretchen. And no!"

"Russians call every German woman Gretchen. Better a night with a German officer than ridden by a wild Russian beast. I can protect you or send you west."

"I have to go."

"A foolish woman! Go then. Another will take your place."

The next day Karin described the encounter. "The men in the shelter weren't fighters. People call them 'Golden Pheasants', party officials who are abusing their position."

Herman Hauptmann sorted through files before he responded. "Frau Werner, you must be mistaken. Party officials need time to relax, a short break from other duties. And, the Gestapo officer would be concerned for your safety. I doubt any indiscretion was intended."

"I'm not so sure." She brushed flakes of snow from the coat and hung it on a peg. "I was treated with respect when I delivered the papers at the Reich Chancellery. The building and the beautiful garden have been ruined by bombs but the Fuhrer is safe. The men say his bunker is four stories under ground."

"The men should not be sharing secrets." Hauptmann frowned. "In the future I will make those deliveries. A young woman may attract undue attention." He studied her for a moment. "Men see a girl who needs protection, the skirt, the woollen stockings and braids. You could pass for a teenager."

"I have nothing else to wear and I braided my hair because there is no water to wash."

"Don't misunderstand. Under the circumstances, your appearance is appropriate but people misinterpret. No one would guess the fur came through the party welfare agency. But set this aside, we have a new assignment. The records of the earliest party members are to be moved."

"It's been so difficult to arrange any kind of transportation… why…"

"Frau Werner, please. Start with the records from the early days of National Socialism."

She had little time to think in the next few hours. SS Officers arrived to supervise and appeared to know what files to take. Prisoners handled the heavy lifting but packing took longer than expected.

"Where do you take them?" she asked as the last crate was pushed into a truck.

"I'm not allowed to say," the driver answered. "But the papers must be important. Only a few vehicles are available." As he locked the tail gate, he dropped his voice. "Berlin is no longer safe. We hear the Fuhrer will soon leave for a last stand in the mountains."

On the Rhine, March 15

"Holy shit! Check out Johnny Canuck!"

An American major rubbed at the Canada insignia on Duff Stewart's shoulder. "Looks like the real thing." He rapped his fist on Stewart's head. "Plus, an authentic Canadian helmet, a wash basin, like the Brits wear. You fellows really should try to look different. But I thought the British and Canadians were further north. Or, should I say, resting on their butts while Americans win the war."

US Forces had taken control of a key crossing on the Rhine. The bridge at Remagen was badly damaged but a steady stream of men crossed into central Germany. General Montgomery was making final preparation for his attack.

"Oh, Monty is coming," Stewart promised. "I came through the rear areas on my way here. Guns, tanks, one of the biggest armies in Canadian history."

"Wow! Canadians will save the day? What a relief." The sarcasm was obvious.

Stewart wanted to avoid an argument. "Look, I was just transferred to the US Army. I have civil administration training which I know won't be needed until the shooting stops, but I can wrangle papers and…"

"You speak German." Major Ben Cooper interrupted. "That's what the record shows."

"I took a course at university a long time ago and can muddle through…"

"Bauer!" The Major yelled, "Check this one out. Bauer knows the language. Talk Nazi. Tell him what you ate this morning."

Taken by surprise, Stewart cleared his throat, tried to remember a hurried breakfast and the German words to describe it. Slowly, he began to speak but after only seconds Bauer shook his head. "The right words. But he's too slow and the accent is awful. He wouldn't pass as a native. He sounds like an old textbook."

"Shit!" The Major fumed. "But he'll have to do. Buddy up with him over the next few days. All conversation in German. Keep him talking maybe he'll improve. Tell him our mission."

Bauer spoke rapidly in German.

"I didn't get it." Stewart confessed. "Something about the Kaiser and moving fast and I don't see what this has to be with administrative duties."

"It doesn't, bud. But there's no time to find a substitute. You're it."

Washington, March 17

"Great day for a visit to Washington." Ben Wiley laughed. "Spring and the warmest St. Patrick's Day in years. I'll wager Ottawa is frigid and buried in snow."

Vincent Russel carried a coat over his arm and silently congratulated himself for the timing of the trip. The civilian and the American officer casually strolled on Pennsylvania Avenue but were careful to keep a distance from other pedestrians.

"I have no news of that Stewart fellow," Wiley spoke softly. "The War Department thinks his file was misplaced. I wouldn't worry. He's shuffling papers somewhere."

Russel nodded. "I wouldn't be surprised. The young man has a knack for avoiding danger or for that matter hard work." He glanced around to be sure no one was close. "But what else do you hear? Prime Minister King spent time with the President last week."

"Anything to do with secret projects," Wiley continued to speak softly, "is on a need-to-know basis. Although, I expect King was given a briefing. He stayed at the White House for a couple of days and he and FDR must have talked about more than old times."

"King and Roosevelt have known each other for years. The Prime Minister would want to hear the details from Yalta."

"In other words, you wonder how much he was told." Wiley laughed. "When FDR addressed Congress, he talked of beating Germany and his hope for the new United Nations. After World War One, President Wilson failed to win Congressional approval to join the League of Nations. Roosevelt wants to avoid a similar fiasco."

"Canadians won't learn much from King. He's going to the founding meeting of the United Nations. Beyond, that…"

"…Washington is more worried about the President's health." Wiley steered the conversation in another direction. "Roosevelt didn't stand when he spoke to Congress and allowed people to see him in his wheel chair. That's a first. Those close to him, say there are times, he's…he's just not there."

"It's only weeks into the new term. Can he last four years?"

"Now that is a question only his opponents are prepared to raise. One hears rumours that he might step aside but not yet. Finish the war, get the UN established and we'll see. He may disappear, rest for a few weeks at that polio retreat in Warm Springs, Georgia. The military can run the show. Churchill continues to insert himself in the minutia of war but FDR has finally agreed to leaves things to the professionals."

CHAPTER 5

SERGEANT TIM MURPHY was determined to remain safe and inconspicuous. He curled into a ball against a shallow ditch bank as an artillery barrage struck German positions on the Rhine's eastern bank. The first units of infantry were crossing the river in boats, in special landing craft, and with a few men perched on tanks, engineered to navigate the frigid water.

Throughout the night, search lights were aimed at the low cloud and the reflection created a bright, artificial moonlight. The barrage ended as abruptly as it had begun, a sign Murphy suspected, of an imminent advance but instead the roar of engines came from above with a vast armada of Allied bombers. Minutes later, another wave of aircraft dropped parachute regiments and were followed by a fleet of gliders and more men for the landing sites east of the Rhine.

"Soldier!" He felt a sharp kick and rolled to see an officer towering above him. "Get out of there. Stand up!"

Murphy pulled himself erect and began to brush at the dirt.

"Clean this one up." The officer turned to an orderly. "At least make him look like a soldier." He leaned close to Murphy's ear. "For your own sake, shape up."

A half hour later, a car fishtailed through the mud and came to a stop where Murphy and a line of soldiers stood at attention. A British staff officer emerged, shook his head in disgust and opened the rear door. "Not much of an honour guard, Prime Minister…"

"Couldn't care less," Winston Churchill muttered. "Which way to the river?"

"Straight ahead and you did promise not to expose yourself to danger."

"I'll decide on any danger. I want to see Monty across so he can beat the Russians to Berlin. Now, out of my way. I've waited for years to piss in the Rhine."

As Churchill moved off, Murphy felt a hand on his shoulder. "If you won't fight, we'll send you packing." The officer had returned and with a jackknife removed the sergeant's stripes. "Be damn glad, I've decided on only a field demotion. We don't have time to waste with cowards."

Eastern Germany, March 27

"That man but not the next one. He's too thin, wouldn't survive the trip, a waste of space." The Russian Colonel Petrenkov made a selection from a group of prisoners. The men in the line represented all facets of German society, the army, a few navy cadets and men in civilian dress.

He stopped in front of a prisoner. "SS?"

"No."

"Papers?"

"Lost."

"I don't believe you. I could have you shot but instead we'll make you work." The prisoner was destined for a cattle car on a waiting train. In days he would be rebuilding Russian cities or working in the Soviet camps that begged for labour.

"Colonel." Another officer smiled. "More wise choices. But what about the man who was too weak?"

"Perhaps he'll recover and be sent on the next train. Perhaps he'll die. It doesn't matter. Others can take his place."

"And next? Will you be with us as we attack Berlin?"

"No. Marshall Zhukov's shock troops are trained for house-to-house fighting. My unit will follow. The second wave will strip the city. Anything of value will be sent home."

"Colonel?" A soldier approached. "We need more prisoners to fill the train."

"Round up civilians. Grab men from the street, healthy ones. Don't accept arguments. Shoot anyone who resists." He turned back to his fellow officer. "As to Berlin. We must be there before the British or Americans. Encourage the men. Let them know the rewards. Each man can ship five kilograms of captured goods to his home each month and officers can send twice as much. As to the women, treat them as our women were treated."

Paris, March 28

American army staff cars lined the street but only pedestrians with a special pass could enter the restricted complex. A sentry scanned her papers. The woman was attractive but definitely middle age. "I doubt there's work for you. You're too old."

"Let the proprietor decide," Maria said as she retrieved her pass and pushed through the doorway. Inside, lights were dim and the staff scurried to serve the officers and the attractive young women who sat alongside them.

"I'm to see Madame Teresa," she told a waiter.

"Second floor. First door on the right."

As she climbed the steep staircase she glanced below. Business was obviously good for a high-class French brothel.

"Enter." A woman's voice answered her knock and she stepped into a room decorated in red velvet. "I don't have many female clients." The woman smiled. "But I'm sure we can arrange something."

Maria laughed. "No, no. I want to thank you for what you did several years ago. Evers Chance brought me here to elude the Gestapo back in 1941. You were very brave and very kind."

Teresa studied her for a moment. "I remember, a memorable moment of the occupation." She paused. "I'm glad you escaped. So many didn't."

"I often think of being spirited out the back door as the Gestapo came in the front. I thought you would be arrested."

"Oh, how could I be in trouble for an accident? The soldier who was searching for you took a nasty fall on the stairs and broke his neck. And, although he might have been pushed, my German clients stopped any investigation. Everything was kept very quiet. And you, obviously recovered. Why are you back in Paris?"

"I'm going to write for North American magazines. I should re-introduce myself. I'm Maria...Maria Chance."

"Chance?" Teresa laughed and clapped her hands in delight. "Hah! You married him. As I recall he was smitten. I'm happy for you! But, call it professional curiosity. He's older. Do things still happen."

"I have no reason to complain and neither does he." Maria laughed. "Ask him? He'll be in touch. I think...I hope...for another kind of business. He would have come today but had meetings with the Americans."

"Ah yes. Most Americans are fine people but a few 'entrepreneurs' run lucrative black-market operations. I try to stay above it. And, I must confess I am wary of my own people. I had ties to the resistance. But today it's hard to keep everyone straight."

"I'm not sure I understand?"

"Many men and women claim to have worked against the Nazis when they didn't. It's difficult to know who was a collaborator and who was a patriot? It will sort itself out, eventually. In the meantime, I've a business to run."

"I'm glad to find you safe," Maria told her. "My story could have ended in another way. Perhaps I can return the favour."

"Nothing is expected. Chance and I worked together and I'll look forward to working with both of you. Let's have a drink to celebrate our reunion."

Western Germany, March 29

"Here's the best one I could find." A mechanic led the way across an abandoned airport hangar. "The truck is a Mercedes Benz L3000 and the Luftwaffe didn't use it much. Even the tarp doesn't show wear."

To Duff Stewart, a truck was a truck; but Major Ben Cooper paid special attention. He ran his hand across the frame before he spoke. "I need something that will run for a few hundred miles, carry six men and a small cargo."

"Can't guarantee anything," the mechanic replied. "It's captured equipment. If it breaks down, you're out of luck. Our truck makers build on the same pattern so parts are interchangeable. But Germans used different designs. Parts from an Opel won't work on a Mercedes. A breakdown is harder to fix. Like we say stateside, buyer beware."

The Major waited until the mechanic was gone before turning to his men. "I want a few modifications. Something that looks too new will attract attention." He lifted heavy wrenches from a tool box. "Put dents in it. Make it look like other German equipment—used and abused." And with a swing of his arm, he bashed a taillight. "Slash the tarp and work on the seats. Cut through the stuffing."

"Ya-vool, mien commandant." Stewart mimicked a German accent. He smashed a side mirror, climbed to the cab and used a knife to slash the seat.

"Leave the glass in front of the driver," Cooper ordered. "Smash the other windows. Throw bolts against the hood. Make it look like shrapnel bounced off. Fire a few bullets into it but don't hit the engine or the tires."

As the men worked, Bauer arrived with captured German uniforms.

"Too clean," he told Cooper. "But we can roll in the mud before we leave. The helmets are fine. Dents and scratches would be expected."

"Major?" Stewart called from the cab window, "Uh sorry…mien Coronel. When do we get the details on what this is about?"

"Stewart! If I hear another word in English. I'll ram a wrench up your ass. But this is as good a time as any. Gather around." The men dropped their tools to form a half circle.

"All of you have at least a smattering of the German language. But when we leave, Bauer and I will do any talking." Cooper waited as the men nodded their understanding. "High Command thinks the Nazis are working on a new type of bomb. We are going to raid their research facility in Berlin and it's vital we get there before the Russians."

"Wait?" Stewart gasped. "Berlin? In German uniforms, we could be shot as spies."

The Major slapped a wrench against his hand. "One more word and I'll beat you to a pulp."

Stewart glanced at the wrench and suspected the threat was real.

"It's not all bad," the Major continued. "The Russians are about to launch their assault but we'll be in and out before they arrive. The Germans are in retreat and can't have much fight left. Think of it. The first Americans into the German capital. And, with luck, we and our Canadian friend, will also be the first to leave."

Berlin, April 1

The teleprinter stopped midway through a transmission. It was to be expected Karin decided, the communication lines had been damaged yet again. Constant bombing was taking an ever-greater toll.

"Frau Werner," Hauptmann called. "No more work today. There is too much confusion. The Fuhrer ordered a scorched earth policy, what's called a Nero order. Are you familiar with Roman history?"

"No…not really."

"It means nothing is left for the enemy. Buildings and supplies are burned, the bridges and transportation destroyed. But, just before the teleprinter failed, a new directive arrived from the Minister of War Production. Albert Speer says to save as much as possible. I think it means secret negotiations have begun. The Western Allies are coming to their senses and will join us to fight the Communists. Anything we save can be used in that battle."

"And our files?" She thought of the days spent trying to maintain a semblance of order. "Are they to be preserved or destroyed?"

"We'll wait another day. New instructions may come when communication is restored."

"But if we are going to fight with the west, why would they continue to bomb us?"

"Don't ask so many questions. Go home. Rest assured the proper decisions will be made."

Public transport like so much else in Berlin had been all but destroyed by the bombing. Stubborn fires burned and the smoke left a dirty, grey pall over the city. Karin stumbled on foot through streets clogged with debris. Buildings were little more than empty shells, with windows, doors and roofs missing. Damaged apartments showed gaping holes with living areas exposed, a bed frame, a kitchen table or part of a toilet teetering above the street.

As night fell only a few people remained above ground. The queue for rations would begin again at first light, part of a grim struggle for survival. Yet, at the entrance to her shelter, she heard the sound of laughter.

"Hah, Karin. A rare treat. Meat for supper, a fresh cut from a dead horse." The residents of the cellar hovered over a sizzling frying pan. "And, we found a stovepipe. We can vent to the outdoors. No more choking on smoke."

"And more good news," the Great War veteran told her. "The Russian advance has stopped."

Another neighbour, a man badly injured in the African campaign, disagreed. "That's not what I heard. Radio Berlin urges a fight to the very end and the newspaper *Das Reich* calls for more volunteers to repulse the Bolsheviks."

As the men argued, a woman pulled Karin aside, "The police were here," she whispered. "Carl was arrested. I'm almost glad his mother was killed last week. She didn't have to see him led away. He's a big boy but barely a teenager."

"Taken by the police? Why?"

"He hadn't reported for duty in the militia. We told them his age but they took him anyway."

"A boy can handle a Panzer Faust." Schroeder, the Great War veteran, had been listening. "He balances the antitank gun on the bars of a bicycle and peddles into battle. A single shell will destroy a Russian tank. Unfortunately, the Panzer Faust fires once and then is useless." He bent to smell the meat. "And I'm not sure Carl is brave. He might run at the first sign of danger. But, never mind, it's one less mouth and more for everyone else. Come. Eat before the Tommis ruin dinner."

"If we had wine, we could toast Carl," Karin said. "He'll help to reclaim the eastern territories."

An early April morning in Berlin dawned with a brief respite from the bombing. No longer able to clear an entire street, a prisoner work gang broke a narrow path through the rubble. Karin waited as the men manoeuvred large cement blocks from the roadway.

"A faithful Nazi." A skeletal prisoner leaned on a shovel and spoke to Karin, "You are one of the few who continue to report for duty."

"We must do our best for the Fatherland," Karin replied.

"Be careful. The Russian hordes are closing in. A full-bodied woman is a tempting prize. They'll take turns with you."

"Stop it!" Karin looked for the guards but saw no one close.

"The truth is harsh," the prisoner continued. "I know what Germans did in the east. The tables have turned and you are too pretty to pass over."

"Stop! Our men will drive the Russians back. I could have you shot."

"No. Hitler needs men with strong backs. There are more graves to dig."

She twisted to go around him. "Germans are turning on each other," he hissed as she brushed past. "Look down the next street. See what Hitler ordered. The end is near."

"Bastard!" She swore, squared her shoulders, and walked on.

The cross street showed another ruined avenue where only the posts of street lamps remained but today sported gruesome new fixtures. Bodies, men in German uniform, hung in a line, victims of a mass execution. A rough, hand-drawn sign hung from the neck of the first body. "This man was a coward!"

With a mix of shock and horror she recognized the lifeless form of Carl, the boy from the cellar.

CHAPTER 6

A SMALL PLANE WITH American markings circled slowly above a forest. The collapse of the Luftwaffe left the pilot free to meander about the sky.

"That didn't take long," Stewart spoke in fractured German as the plane wings waggled in parting and returned to the west. Major Ben Cooper, wearing the uniform of a German army colonel, stomped from a clearing, carrying a small portable radio. "The pilot says no enemy units are close but more refugees are coming. Remember. Bauer and I do the talking. Stewart, fix that bandage over your throat. Twist it to show the bloodstains." Duff adjusted a dirty field dressing, taken from a body, a ruse in case someone questioned why he didn't speak.

The Major set the radio on the floorboards of the truck. "The contact in Berlin is close to our objective. I don't understand the scientific mumble jumble but he knows what to look for. So, if he says something is valuable for 'Tube Alloys', we grab it. After that, we get the hell out."

"We've company," a sentry called. "Looks like mostly women and children."

"Keep quiet. Let them pass," Cooper ordered.

"Too late! A woman is coming this way. She's seen the truck."

"Food?" the refugee called. "And a ride?"

"No. Going the other way." Cooper stepped in front of her. "We need the rations. My men will defend Berlin."

"Food." She repeated and opened her coat to show a baby pressed against her chest.

"Food is for those who fight, not those who run."

"For the baby?" She lifted the child.

"No!" But a second later Cooper reached inside his uniform. "Chocolate. Go before I change my mind."

The woman scowled but hid the bounty in her clothing. "Nothing," she called to the other refugees. "Our men refuse to share."

"Let's go." Cooper started the truck. "We rendezvous with another plane tomorrow morning." Stewart slipped into the cab while the other men climbed into the rear. "I wonder if anyone, anywhere cares about the innocent?"

"Don't go soft on me, buster. Germans are getting a taste of their own medicine."

Berlin, April 4

"I have made a decision." Herr Hauptmann announced. "The Fuhrer directs the war effort from his bunker. The fate of the records would be only a minor concern so I will ease his burden and take it upon myself."

Karin waited. The near ceaseless attacks suggested the Battle of Berlin was nearing a climax.

"I have dynamite to destroy the entrance," Hauptmann told her. "The floors underground will survive the blast. The documents can be recovered later."

"Our work is finished?" she asked.

"I will detonate the explosives myself." Hauptmann rose. "I thank you for courageous service. In another time, I would recommend a medal but I've done the next best thing." He lifted a folder. "Your record from the League of German Maidens. I added a note praising your diligence in difficult times."

"Herr Hauptmann, that is very kind."

"It will be of value when the archive is unsealed in our ultimate victory. Now go. I must set the charges."

She tried to find words but nothing would come.

"Heil Hitler!" Hauptmann clicked his heels and snapped to attention.

By instinct she raised her arm and returned the Nazi salute.

Western Germany, April 8

The mass of refugees ran for cover at the sound of an aircraft, hoping the shallow ditch or a bit of shrub would protect them from strafing. But this time the pilot surprised them and merely circled above the road.

"Kee-rist. Why not bring more attention to us," Stewart said as he squirmed under the truck. "Let's hope the pilot isn't nosing around for a target."

"Relax." Bauer told him. "If he was going to shoot, he'd have done it by now. He was talking with the Major." Stewart raised his head in time to see Ben Cooper leave the shelter of a barn, the portable radio draped over his shoulder. Allied technicians had devised a relay from the headquarters to the plane and then to the ground, a low power transmission that escaped enemy interception.

Cooper scowled when he saw the men under the truck. "What a stupid place to take cover." He grasped a collar and hauled a man from the shelter. "The Air Force may be squeamish about shooting refugees but they wouldn't think twice about taking out enemy transport. Get on your feet. Open that other crate and change clothes. Orders have changed. The fellow in Berlin says the Kaiser Wilhelm Institute, our objective, has been abandoned. I don't know why we'd trust a German but the brass does."

The men quickly exchanged uniforms for civilian attire. Four wore the rough clothing of labourers while Copper and Stewart slipped on suits to pass as fleeing office workers.

"Split up," Cooper ordered. "Stewart comes with me. The rest fan out and join the refugee columns. Everyone goes west. The American army has stopped at the River Elbe. The Russians can fight the fanatics in Berlin. The Red Army has no qualms about bloodletting or casualties."

Stewart shook his head in amazement. "We sneak into Nazi territory and all for nothing."

"Cut the bullshit," Cooper said and buttoned a vest. "Keep your eyes open. Nazi big wigs are mixing with refugees. Watch for anyone throwing his weight around. Watch how common folk react. If they kow-tow to someone, there's a reason. Now, divvy up the rations. Everyone takes a share."

Stewart watched as the four men began to blend into the stream of refugees.

"Burn the truck." Cooper ordered. "No sense leaving anything for the scavengers."

Washington, April 10

Vincent Russel stepped from the train and into the bustle of early morning commuters. As in other wartime capitals, Washington's work force had exploded. Each day thousands of people pushed toward desks where their war was fought. Russel hailed a cab and in minutes was at the entrance to the new Pentagon complex. A young soldier checked his identify before leading him to where Ben Wiley waited.

"Too early for the hard stuff." Wiley smiled and waved Russel to a chair, "But the coffee is hot. I've only got a few minutes so we'd better get to it." He pushed a tattered tourist guidebook across the desk. "I can't allow access to military maps but Germany hasn't changed…yet. Your young friend is somewhere between the River Elbe and Berlin and yes, that's enemy territory."

"What in hell happened?" Russel demanded as he studied the guide to prewar Europe. "The transfer to US forces was to put him in a safe job."

"A big mix up, I'm afraid. What the men call Fubar, Fucked Up Beyond All Repair. But we're in contact with the unit. They're returning to our lines."

"I don't understand." Russel shook his head. "Duff is not endowed with what I would consider great intelligence—or courage. Why would anyone pick him?"

"Because he speaks German. The mission was secret and since he may have accessed sensitive material, we'll keep him for a few weeks. He probably doesn't know much but we're being careful. Security. Hush hush and so on."

"I'll feel better when he's back behind our lines."

"Shouldn't be long." Willey slipped the guidebook back in the drawer. "What's happening in Ottawa? Everyone must be pleased with the performance of the Canadian army. Boots on the ground in Germany and the Netherlands and an excellent show from all I hear."

"Except for the casualties. The last few months have produced the greatest losses of the war but the Prime Minister has turned back to pure politics. He's planning for an election and is worried about the strength of the CCF, the Cooperative Commonwealth Federation. The party under Tommy Douglas has taken power in Saskatchewan and…."

"…I don't care about petty Canadian politics." Wiley threw his arms in the air. "America has bigger issues, including the wellbeing of the President. The trip to Yalta almost did him in. His daughter, Anna, appears to be playing a bigger role in the administration. It wouldn't be the first time that a family has quietly taken control at the White House. Old timers remember when Woodrow Wilson's wife pulled the strings. Congress may look the other way on the daughter but won't let Eleanor anywhere near decision making. The wife is far too progressive. Even FDR kept her on a short leash."

"Hah. Are women going to run America?"

"No! Of course not. Although…" He dropped his voice to a whisper, "Gossip says FDR has been meeting with a lady from his past. Apparently, they were close—very close—about twenty years ago. Her presence seems to lift his spirits. He and Eleanor had an unconventional marriage so this mystery lady may be part of a larger secret."

"Any more thought of Roosevelt stepping aside?"

"Oh God no. That would open a real can of worms. FDR keeps his cards close to the chest. Vice President Truman has probably been kept in the dark. No. Let Roosevelt rest and see what happens. With the war in Europe ending, we'll concentrate on the Japanese."

"When does Washington get serious about the postwar and peace."

"Don't get too far ahead of yourself—we'll be fighting for another year and probably longer."

Berlin, April 12

Karin returned to the cellar to find men breaking through the brick wall to a neighbouring basement. "The party block leader gave the order," Schroeder, the Great War veteran, explained. "An escape route. Once the hole is open, we can move underground to the next street."

"But there's nothing on the next street but more wrecked buildings. The local shops are out of food and the only water close by comes from the old hand pump."

"Are you suggesting the party has let the people down?" Another man paused in the demolition and studied Karin. "Strange words from an ardent little Nazi. You sound defeatist."

"Nnn…no," she stammered."

"Our soldiers have but two choices." The man returned to chipping at the wall. "Advance toward the enemy and be shot or retreat and be shot by their German compatriots."

A woman lifted a finger to her lips and pulled Karin aside. "Don't argue. The men can't protect us. They're invalids with barely enough strength to move a few bricks and they're all that's left."

Karin scowled. "I won't listen to this."

"Don't be a fool. I'm trying to help. Those men can't. I was at the emergency hospital yesterday. Women refugees from the east are asking for abortions after multiple rapes. The Bolsheviks line up, take turns and aren't choosy. Young girls, the middle-aged, and even old women are raped again and again. Protect yourself. The little perks won't last much longer. You are the only one with a private room."

Karin seethed with anger. "That private room is a coal bin, a tiny space that no one else wanted. It didn't come through the party."

"I'm trying to help. Change your appearance. Cut that long hair. Don't wash. Become a woman no man would want."

"Are you serious?"

"Deadly serious. It will be every woman for herself."

CHAPTER 7

FROM THE BANKS of the Elbe only a few isolated gun shots could be heard in the distance and scouting parties had found no evidence of any large enemy force. An American Intelligence unit had commandeered an undamaged house near the river.

Major Ben Cooper, back in US Army uniform, raised his feet to a kitchen table and angled his body to hear the conversation from the next room where Duff Stewart stood in front of another officer.

"At ease, Lieutenant. I'm Baker from Intelligence. Just a few questions."

"I've been through this." Stewart shuffled his feet. "There's nothing more to tell. It's almost midnight. I'd like some sleep."

"Sleep later. Start with the refugees. Tell me what you saw."

"The younger men are in the German army so the refugees were mostly women, children, and old men."

"Suspicious civilians?"

"Cooper spotted a guy that didn't look right. I'd have never looked at the pants but Cooper noticed the difference in colour, where the red stripe had been removed. He figured the fellow was senior staff and pointed him out to military police when we got to our lines."

"What about the incident with the plane?"

"Finally, the army is asking the right question. Someone should be called on the carpet."

"The plane was American?"

"Yup. Big American stars on the wings. Mustang, I think. He strafed what was obviously a refugee column. We ran for shelter but a few Krauts were killed. A German medical unit was nearby or more would have died."

"It's hard to trace a single plane."

"Ah, come on. I gave you the location and the time. There weren't that many US planes in that sector. Ask around? Look for a cowboy."

"We probably won't waste much time on that. We're more concerned with Nazi crimes." Baker hadn't bothered to take notes but now picked up his pen. "What about the first part of the mission, going to Berlin?"

"We didn't get there, did we? The scheme was hare-brained. We could have been shot as spies."

"What about the objective?"

"Cooper didn't tell us much."

"What were you looking for?"

"Damned if I know. Something about a Nazi weapon, Tube Alloys? Nothing made sense."

"Ok." Baker set the pen down. "That's it. Get some sleep. And, by the way, we're keeping you. The accent may be bad but we need everyone with a feel for the German language. We'll send you back to the Canadian army later. For now, you are dismissed."

Stewart saluted, wheeled but as quickly turned back. "Uh, I'm curious. Our mission? Any citations or medals for that sort of work? A decoration would be very useful postwar."

"God no! Everything is classified. As far as the world is concerned you weren't there."

When Stewart was gone Cooper joined the Intelligence officer. "Like I said, he doesn't know much."

"Maybe but we'll watch anyway and keep him busy for a few weeks."

"Sir?" A young private burst into the room. "Radio…just now." His voice broke and he sagged against the doorway, "President Roosevelt is dead."

Cooper's face registered the sudden shock. "Are you sure?"

"On Armed Forces Radio. That's official isn't it."

The men fell silent. For many in the armed forces, Roosevelt was the only President they had known. The young soldier began to sob. "My father and I listened to his fireside chats and I saw him in a motorcade in New York. Pouring rain but he was waving to the crowd from an open car. But now…what will happen now, Sir?"

"Get a grip," Cooper warned. "What happens when we lose a man in combat? We take a deep breath and move on. Sad but it doesn't change anything." Yet Cooper turned aside, rubbed at his eyes and thought of FDR bringing hope in the depths of the depression and guiding a reluctant nation into a global war. It was several minutes before he could speak. "Henry Wallace was Vice President. He'll become President?"

"Cooper, don't you keep up on anything but Germans?" The Intelligence officer was disgusted. "The Democrats replaced Wallace before the last election. Truman was Vice President."

"Yes." The private agreed. "Harry or if he's now President, we should call him Harold Truman."

"Who the hell is he?" Cooper demanded.

"A former senator," the intelligence officer answered. "Hails from Missouri."

"Isn't that great." Cooper rolled his eyes. "A yokel from the middle of no where. Roosevelt knew his way around. He was rich and well connected. This new fellow will have a lot to learn."

Berlin, April 14

"We're saved," Schroeder shouted to make himself heard over the din from explosions. Out of breath, he stumbled into the cellar. "The miracle has happened. Roosevelt is dead. With that Jew-lover gone, the Western Allies will join us and drive the Russians back to Moscow."

"Are you sure?" Karin found false rumours as devastating as bombs.

"My friend has a secret radio receiver. He heard it on the BBC."

"Then your friend could be shot." Another cellar dweller joined the conversation. "Listening to foreign broadcasts is still a crime. But Roosevelt? Was he assassinated? The Americans have a history of shooting Presidents. And why would they change sides now?"

"No…I don't know. What does it matter? Everything will change for the better."

"What if someone takes over who has similar policies?" Karin asked. "What if nothing changes?"

"Stay strong. Our future is assured. The Fuhrer will lead us to ultimate victory."

Washington, April 15

By late Sunday, the funeral services were complete.

A ceremony at the White House had been followed by an overnight passage of a special train carrying the body of the late President to Hyde Park, New York. Franklin Roosevelt planned to retire to the family home and write his memoirs but time ran out. A short graveside tribute was held in early spring sunshine before the mourners scattered and the official party returned to the capital.

The telephone connection from Ottawa that night was poor and Vincent Russel could barely hear the voice of his American associate.

"A little late to extend condolences," Ben Wiley shouted into the receiver. "FDR is in the ground. Your Prime Minister was there. Mackenzie King was one of the few foreign dignitaries. Churchill didn't come, sent Anthony Eden in his place." Wiley pulled the receiver from his ear and banged it against the wall. The connection improved immediately.

"America should be impressed," Russel told him. "King doesn't like to spend money but chartered a special Pullman car to get him to Hyde Park."

"Things are already changing." Wiley's voice crackled through static. "The Presidential train returned to Washington at normal speed. The engineers kept their speed down when FDR was on board. No one wanted him bouncing out of the wheel chair. He had that special armoured carriage, the Ferdinand Magellan. Truman will keep it. We don't know yet what will happen to Roosevelt's plane. The Sacred Cow may be retired. Apparently, Truman doesn't enjoy flying." Wiley snickered. "Don't we sound like a pair of gossipy undertakers. By the way, King will appear in the newsreels. The photographers have a shot of him standing by the grave. And the former Canadian ambassador Leighton McCarthy was one of the few invited guests."

"Ah yes. McCarthy's son had polio." Russel remembered. "Which explains why he became a close friend of the President. He was with Roosevelt at the Warm Springs resort earlier in the week."

"The mystery woman was there too." Wiley's voice dropped to a conspiratorial whisper. "She was with Roosevelt at the end. But no one in official circles wants to admit it. Give Eleanor a break, at least, for a while."

"King did meet that woman, Lucy Rutherfurd, at the White House last month." Russel added to the gossip. "He found her charming and thought she was part of the extended family. Someday perhaps the relationship will be seen as a great wartime romance. I presume the shock of the death is wearing off?"

"Oh, I think so. The cabinet is jockeying for new positions. Truman speaks to Congress tomorrow. A new President must appear decisive."

"Do you expect any change in foreign policy?"

"Not sure. We'll have to see what the Russians think of our new leader."

"Here in Ottawa, we don't know much about Truman? It's sad. The Prime Minister got on so well with FDR."

"The new man is an old-style politician, served in the First War before drifting into politics. As a senator he ran a committee looking at army contracts and found too many hands in the cookie jar. The costs were often inflated."

"That's no big surprise." Russel thought of the Canadian experience. "We needed the industrialists and they expected to be paid."

"Truman rooted out the blatant abuses," Wiley continued, "But like many politicians takes care of his own. His wife and another relative were on his Senate payroll. Other legislators won't make a big deal of that for fear someone would take a close look at their own staffing."

"The new President will be well versed on domestic affairs," Russel suggested. "But I'm more concerned with the international picture."

"We'll see how he acts in the next few weeks. His committee on the conduct of the war included a review of secret projects. He may know more about what's in the weapons pipeline than we first thought."

"Meanwhile, Mr. King has lost a great friend. I hadn't appreciated that Roosevelt had such respect for him. Maybe we underestimate the Prime Minister."

Berlin, April 20

Despite the rumours, nothing changed for the people of Berlin. A frantic search for food continued.

"That's it. That's the army warehouse." The scavengers moved slowly, fearing their approach would be met with a burst of gunfire. A door to the building dangled from a single hinge. Large holes, blasted through the walls, offered easier access. "Did they abandon everything?" Karin asked and stepped inside.

"Looks that way." A civilian answered and balanced a typewriter on his shoulder. "Nothing of value was left in the back but a couple of boxes of ammunition and this typewriter."

"What good will that do?" Karin shook her head in amazement but her eyes roamed around the warehouse. She saw an open crate and a stack of clothing, jumpsuits, the coveralls used by airmen. She lifted one and tossed it aside. Too big. At the bottom of the pile was one that fit. She pulled it over her clothes before looking through other boxes.

"Karin. Help me." She turned to see Schroeder, the veteran from the shelter. "Grab the other side," he motioned to a wooden chest. "Take the rope handle." She hesitated until he whispered, "Field rations. Enough for days."

But before they reached the street a policeman blocked their path. "Looting is a crime punishable by death…" but the rest of his words were drowned by a screaming howl and explosion. "Get to a shelter!" a soldier screamed. "Those are rockets. Stalin's organ—the Katyusha. I heard them on the Eastern Front. The Reds must have reached the suburbs."

Karin and the veteran exchanged a quick glance, saw the policeman was distracted, reclaimed the crate and trotted away, each step taking them further from the detonations.

"Rest." The old man panted. "Let me catch my breath." His breathing while ragged slowly returned to normal. "We don't have to run. The rockets are aimed at the bunker in the Reich Chancellery where the Fuhrer is celebrating his birthday. In other years, the day was a time of national rejoicing. Military bands, flags and celebration but not today. Today, his 'volk' wonder if they will live to see tomorrow."

CHAPTER 8

NEWLY DEMOTED *CORPORAL* Tim Murphy sat behind the wheel of a three-tonne truck with an anxious private beside him. Murphy had been transferred to a transportation unit and today led a small convoy threading the top of a dyke in the Netherlands. He geared down as water lapped over their path.

"I'd feel better in a boat." His assistant, Private Bowen spoke and glanced warily at the waves. "Maybe I should walk ahead. The dyke may be undermined."

"Walk if you want but the engineers think it's safe." Murphy flipped on the wipers as a gust of wind lifted spray onto the windshield. "Push the door open so you can jump. As for me, I'm going down with the ship." He touched the gas and the truck lurched into the water. The tires spun but took hold. He stuck his arm out the window and waved the other trucks forward.

"I can't pronounce the name of the village ahead." Murphy shifted to a higher gear. "But the mayor says his people are starving. Food and even animal fodder was sent back to Nazi land. Nothing left for the locals but tulip bulbs and whatever they could scrounge. And, when the Krauts flooded the land the salt water likely damaged the soil. The Dutch may have to be fed for years."

"You come from a farm background?" Bowen saw the track ahead was safe and slammed the truck door.

"Hell no. Cut my teeth in Montreal and Toronto."

"I miss the Canadian cities. I miss walking out and not fearing a gunshot."

"Bull! You miss the ladies." Murphy began to laugh. "But never fear, my lad. We'll get lots of nooky. Just stay in one piece for few more weeks."

The streets were deserted when the convoy reached the village but people quickly began to wave from windows and doors and spill onto the roadway. "Wish I knew what they saying," Murphy said then smiled with relief as a man with an aura of command and a bright orange sash pushed his way through the crowd.

"I am the mayor," he spoke in English. "Mayor Vanderkirk. We're been waiting a long time." He jumped on the running board. "I see the Canada badge. We like Canadians. You sheltered our Princess in Ottawa."

"Afraid I don't know her. Don't run in royal circles," Murphy answered. "More important, where do we unload? Three trucks, lots of crates and bags. I need to move fast. Germans may come back."

"Go to the town hall. We can distribute from there."

"Bowen. Help the men unload." Murphy ordered when they reached the building. "Do it fast. We're sitting ducks for an ambush. The frigging Wehrmacht is only a few miles away."

"Come with me," the mayor said and led Murphy to an office. "I have a bottle of liquor saved for this occasion. The Nazis were thugs and conditions have grown worse in the last few months. The railway strikes last fall made them especially angry."

"Railway strike?"

"When General Montgomery attacked at Arnhem the Dutch

trainmen were enticed to strike. When the attack failed, the Nazis took revenge. Collaborators told them who to grab. And to make matters worse, food supplies were cut. We suffered through a winter of great hunger."

Murphy lifted the bottle and took a deep swallow. His eyes ranged around the room. On the top of a fireplace was a large silver candelabra. "Oh, isn't that something. Pure silver?"

"Yes," the mayor lifted it from the mantle. "A gift, for you and the men."

Murphy thought quickly. The candelabra was valuable but he felt no need to share. "We've a small chapel at the base. This would look great on the altar. All the men could see it. But…" His mind was racing… "Do you have a bag or some cloth? I'll keep it as a surprise. A big unveiling for the rest of the unit."

"Yes, of course." The mayor said before moving to another room and returning with a sack. "The villagers will be pleased that the men see it during their devotionals."

"Yah, the boys will appreciate this." Murphy was already thinking of where to sell the treasure and fished a pack of cigarettes from his pocket. "Try Sweet Caporals, Canadian cigarettes."

The mayor beamed. "Oh Yes. We've had nothing but foul tobacco for years. Cigarettes are valuable, as good as cash."

"Plenty more where that came from," Murphy smiled. "We get a regular ration and friends often send more from home. But…uh… like a currency? Would people trade for them?"

"Oh certainly. With a few packs of cigarettes, a man is rich."

"Keep those," Murphy said, "I'll be back. We'll do business together."

Berlin, April 25

Karin dumped an armful of wood scraps at the bottom of the stairs. "It's all I could reach. There's more, lots more, but the rockets come at random." The wood was destined for a primitive kitchen. A bent element, salvaged from a ruined stove, rested above a rough firepit of bricks.

Another woman began to pile the scraps. "Those SS officers down the street threw up a barricade. Why? There's nothing nearby of military value and they're drunk. Better they put down their guns. The diehards must see the war is over." She glanced at Karin expecting a lecture on the need to fight on but today there was no response. The girl was changing and no longer appeared to care about her appearance. She hadn't washed in several days. The blonde hair was dirty and ragged from a hurried cut. Her coverall was caked with mud.

Karin turned to Schroeder. "What happened at the end of the First War?"

"We came home and nearly starved but we had shelter. Our houses were cold but intact. There was talk of an uprising and fighting in the street but we stopped a communist revolution. Of course, in 1918 and '19, thousands were sick…a nasty strain of influenza."

"And what of the enemy?"

"Parts of the country were occupied but in Berlin we barely noticed. It won't be that way this time, not with the Russians."

"Maybe we should signal, raise a white sheet, a sign that we're no longer fighting."

"Not as long as our soldiers are about. Anyone, military or civilian who tries to surrender is shot. Our men have their orders."

Karin sighed and took a seat beside him. "When I was out, I could see signs of spring. It was amazing. I saw a lilac. Blocks and blocks of ruin and yet a single plant was in bloom. Perhaps, it was the result of heat from the fires but I hope it's a sign of renewal, a new beginning."

San Francisco, April 25

"Taxi!" The reporter shouted as he ran from the train station and almost bumped into a railway porter. "Sorry, I'm running late." He wrenched a cab door open and jumped into the rear seat. "The Opera House, the United Nations conference."

The cabbie glanced at his passenger before methodically adjusting his metre. "The session has started. I doubt you'll find a seat."

"Let's just see," Todd Aiken snapped. His superiors had finally freed him from the parliamentary duty but the reporter's elation at a new assignment turned to anger when the *Sentinel-Guardian* booked a coach seat for the cross-continent journey. He could only look with envy at passengers with sleeping accommodation or a private compartment. Only in the last few hours had he managed to commandeer a washroom to shave.

"Quite a gathering," the cabbie spoke and steered into San Francisco traffic. "Folks from around the world. Men in pinstripe suits, army uniforms, Arabs in robes…a real menagerie. Where do you hail from?"

"Canada."

"That's not exotic." The cabbie took his foot off the gas as if deciding the fare was unimportant but sped up again as the traffic cleared. "I can give you a special rate to see the city. The Golden Gate bridge, the prison of Alcatraz, or the Kaiser plant where the Liberty ships are built. I'll wait if you want to ride a Trolley car."

"Maybe later."

Aiken sorted through the papers in his case. The assignment desk had sent details on the Canadian delegation. He would be expected to file on the luminaries, the Prime Minister and his Quebec lieutenant Louis St. Laurent, Lester Pearson, the Ambassador to Washington and the opposition Tory, John Diefenbaker.

"The Reds are here," the cabbie touched his horn and swung past a truck. "Fellow called Molotov sent by Stalin himself. Apparently, a gesture to the legacy of Franklin Roosevelt. But the conference is on shaky ground. The Russian and President Truman had a set-to when they met in Washington."

"How does a cabbie know all this?"

"Drove a couple of reporters to their hotel and eavesdropped. Amazing what a dumb cabbie can learn."

"What else?"

"A lot of talk of the four freedoms, another Roosevelt legacy. Free trade, free elections, freedom from want, freedom of religion and so on. Doesn't it sound grand?"

"You sound unimpressed?"

"Not sure what I think but those reporters believe it's overblown."

"I guess reporters would know," Aiken slipped the papers back in the case.

"Yah and they were assessing the latest war news. You probably missed it on the train. Our boys have linked up with the Reds on a German river...the Elbow or something like that. Germany is finished and in the next few months we'll knock out the Japanese."

"So, the UN is founded as peace breaks out. Maybe, that's a positive sign."

Paris, April 26

Other dinner guests moved to the dance floor but Evers and Maria Chance lingered over desert while listening to an army band. Weeks of waiting were almost over. Maria would continue to file magazine articles from Paris while Chance moved closer to the front. "Don't do anything stupid," she warned him repeatedly. "Don't get too close to the action. You are not as young as you think."

"I am quite content to watch the action through a pair of binoculars, good ones like Germany used to make."

"It's a shame Versailles and Paris aren't enough to excite you." She glanced around a former ballroom converted to an elegant banquet hall. Pressed white table cloths were set off with flowers and liveried waiters dashed about with champagne, wine and liqueurs.

"I'll need time to recuperate from the dinners and long, boring meetings." As Chance spoke his eyes too ranged over the room. "The Americans have learned from the British. Give a man a rank and the meetings go on for hours."

"There can't be much left to settle. Montgomery is moving north and east to cut off Denmark. General Patton is pushing through southern Germany and threatening Austria. With Russians coming west the war is almost over."

"Yes, and the outline for occupation zones was decided in Yalta. The Russians get the east. The British and Americans will share western Germany. Although the French are annoyed and demand a slice of the pie. They've a few scores to settle with the Nazis."

"Monsieur would prefer more desert." A waiter interrupted and without prompting set another plate on the table.

The band struck up a slow waltz and a round of applause ran through the room as the Supreme Allied Commander led an attractive woman to the dance floor.

"Hmm…there's General Eisenhower. He's performed well?" Maria asked.

"As well as can be expected. He has the diplomatic skills to keep a fractious coalition together and by that, I mean the generals under his command. Equally important he's satisfied the leaders of the countries in the Allied Force."

"Who is the woman?"

"His driver, Kay Summersby. Beyond the good looks, she's intelligent. She and Ike spend a lot of time with each other."

"And dance well together," Maria whispered. "A sign of familiarity, a deep friendship or maybe more?"

"Another secret, I'm sure. Ike has a wife in the states. No one asks too many questions. Americans claim to be very modern but prefer high moral ground."

"As with race," Maria spoke softly. "The only coloured man in the room is the piano player."

"Yes. Their army is segregated even though the coloured did splendid duty. A few fought in the front lines and their flyers proved a surprise. No one expected such superb fighter pilots. But when they go home, the barriers go back up. Only recently the American Congress was debating an anti-lynching law. A black veteran could still a face a mob and a rope."

Chance toyed with the desert, slowly licking the sugar from his fork. "And a good thing the ordinary people of Europe don't see the feasting. So many are starving but, as is often the case, those at the top," he flashed a smile, "and their associates eat very well."

Western Germany, April 27

The jeep hit a pothole and bounced. The driver recovered only to swerve hard to avoid a shell crater. Duff Stewart clung to the steel frame and wished for more than a hard metal seat. Beside the driver, Major Ben Cooper shifted on a thick pillow. "Slow down," he ordered. "Don't want to break something. I don't want to walk."

Along the roadway were the shattered reminders of war; A burned-out tank with a charred corpse in the turret, a decomposing body in a roadside ditch, dead animals in the fields and the constant smell of decay. But nature was at work. The brown winter grass was dappled with the green shoots of spring.

Stewart casually looked about, no longer shocked by what he saw. "Where are we going? I'm tired of surprises."

"Driver, stop at the top of the hill," Cooper ordered. "We'll take a break before we go in."

As the jeep slowed, Stewart saw a cluster of buildings. American trucks blocked the entrance to a compound and a bull dozer scrapped out a pit. The machine reversed, spun and began to push what appeared to be a pile of sticks. In the next second, he found he could still feel a profound sense of revulsion. What he first thought were sticks were emaciated bodies.

"Not a pretty sight." Cooper reached into his pocket for a small vial. "Coat the nose with this mentholated concoction. The place stinks like hell. They moved the last of the prisoners yesterday, the ones still breathing. There are more bodies to collect while others are in that pit."

The men were silent as they approached the gate. "What caused this?" Stewart was appalled. "An outbreak of disease?"

"No, this was a slave labour camp." Cooper spoke quietly as though in deference to the dead. "Dozens or maybe hundreds of similar camps are spread across the country. Prisoners were worked to death, starved, or were guinea pigs for medical experiments."

Inside the compound Cooper, led the way. "Near as we can tell the prisoners were fed just enough to keep them going. It's hard to believe but other sites are worse. We found death camps, box cars filled with bodies and giant ovens for mass cremations. This began as a way to remedy a German labour shortage. Jews, Gypsies, Poles, Russians. Anyone considered inferior could be worked to death."

"How long has this be going on?" Stewart asked. He glanced inside a filthy barracks, had a glimpse of bodies laying in stacked bunks and quickly turned aside.

Cooper too avoided a closer examination. "Hitler and his gang opened the first re-education or prison camps in the '30s. With the war came facilities for prisoners of war, for forced labour and finally death camps. We do wonder however if there might be more pleasant surprises, more secrets or ideas we could use."

Stewart stopped in his tracks. "What's to learn?"

Cooper adjusted his helmet and for the first time Stewart noticed a new symbol, a large red 'T'.

"For starters T Force." Cooper tapped the helmet. "T Force is ordered to look for the V1 and V2 rocket launchers or new chemicals or equipment. We have men seeking art works, stolen antiquities, and even rare books. But that's too tame for me. I'm looking for bigger prizes."

"Wouldn't it better to destroy everything?"

"Wow. You're thinking like a Nazi. That's what they've been trying to do in the last few months."

"Can't we just be happy we stopped the scum before they did further damage."

"Don't be naïve. The world goes on. Bigger weapons, more killing power. You ain't seen nothing yet."

Holland, April 29

"Down! Those planes are too low." Tim Murphy threw himself to the ground as two Lancaster Bombers barely cleared the village rooftops. He had a glimpse of Royal Airforce markings before the aircraft lumbered out of site. "Those planes must be loaded with food. If the asshole that commands the German forces would negotiate a ceasefire, we could move a lot more and faster."

"The first shipments have helped." The Dutch Mayor struggled to his feet. "But people are still starving. We're desperate."

"Help is coming," Murphy assured him. "The army and air force don't mount a major operation without a code name so this one is 'Operation Manna.' In the next few hours, hundreds of planes will drop food instead of bombs. But warn everyone to eat slow and not too much at once. Too much after months of starvation and a stomach can explode."

"We tell them." Vanderkirk bent to lift a box. "But people are so hungry and more have emerged from hiding. I've been surprised at the number of Jews who have appeared, hidden for months in cellars or attics. The people who helped them could have been shot."

Murphy balanced a sack on each shoulder. "Where do we put these?"

"In the townhall." The mayor fished for a key. "I keep it locked so we can dole supplies out fairly." The door opened to a room filled with the most recent shipment. "This will be gone by tonight. Can you bring more today?"

"We'll try. If the airdrop works, the ground will be covered with supplies. Guns were taken out of the planes to allow room for more food."

The mayor set the crate against the wall. "Tell them to hurry."

"I will," Murphy said, "and I brought a carton of Sweet Caps. I'll let you run a tab."

"A tub?" The mayor was confused.

"Na…a tab…a North American term…means pay me later. Don't worry. I'll keep track. And, in addition to infantry rations I have access to booze and luxuries. They're expensive but I can deliver."

France, April 30

"Hitler is dead!"

The signals officer produced a broad smile and offered a headset. "Want to listen?"

"No. I trust you." Evers Chance rocked in a chair. The background hiss of static filled the radio room, overwhelming the faint murmur of voices. The radio specialist began to read from his notes. "Radio Hamburg made the announcement. It said the Fuhrer died leading his troops."

"Almost certainly sanitized," Chance decided. "He was in the bunker in Berlin. Maybe it was suicide? If he's dead, fine, but everyone will want confirmation. It truly appears to be *Gotterdamerung,* the twilight of the Gods. Hitler dead, Mussolini killed by his own Italians and FDR gone to his reward. All within the last few days."

"German radio is talking about new units, called Werewolves. We picked up transmissions ordering them to a bastion in the Alps. What we don't know is how many men are involved?"

"And we need to know who is in command," Chance said. "Hitler's henchmen started secret negotiations but were only trying to save themselves. Anymore interesting broadcasts from North America?"

"Lots of talk about the new United Nations. I heard part of a speech by the Canadian Prime Minister. This UN sounds a lot like the old League of Nations, which didn't accomplish much."

The radio operator adjusted a dial bringing the clear sound of Russian voices into the room. "I don't have a translator available."

"You won't need one. The Soviets are breaking through. Berlin is falling."

San Francisco, May 1

Todd Aiken pushed to the door of the hotel reception room only to be blocked by a heavy-set man in a dark suit. "Where do you think you're going?"

"To join the other reporters." Aiken tried to push by. "There's a whole bunch of them in there. I'm from Canada, the Ottawa *Sentinel-Guardian*. This is big news day. Hitler dead. The Russians in Berlin. I need reaction."

"Sorry, Sonny. This area is restricted to Americans. See that fellow at the front of the room. That's John Kennedy. He's writing for a big New York magazine and he's an American war hero. Only important people like him and important publications are welcome at this briefing."

"Look, Fella. We're all part of the United Nations or hadn't you noticed?"

But, before he could say more, the man shoved him to the hallway and closed the door to the suite. "This is invitation only."

Aiken knew when he was beaten. His copy from the final day at the United Nations founding convention would lack the hoped-for punch. The conference, everyone agreed, would be considered a success. The major nations, the United States, Great Britain, Russia and perhaps China would have seats on the top-level Security Council. Smaller countries, like Canada, would take a place in the General Assembly and would have less influence. Ottawa insiders hinted at Mackenzie King's disappointment and his determination that Canadian Forces would not play a major role in any future UN military actions. His fear of casualties remained firm. Beyond that, the Prime Minister put the best face forward and praised the formation of the organization.

Aiken made his way to the hotel lobby and heard his name called. "Are you coming with us?" He recognized a Vancouver reporter. "A special train is going north. King's election campaign will start from British Columbia. We'll finally see how popular or unpopular the Prime Minister really is."

"No. I'm heading back to Ottawa but won't be there long. The managing editor found a little extra cash. I'm off to Europe soon. A little late for the war but in time for the occupation."

CHAPTER 9

WATCHING FROM THE entrance to the Berlin cellar Karin saw first one and then another soldier slink away. "The men on the barricades are leaving," she called to the others in the basement.

And then from the street someone shouted. "The Fuhrer is dead!"

The old veteran was the first to react. "So much for his Thousand Year Reich. Get that white sheet up." Karin helped Schroeder carry a faded white sheet to the entrance. "With our men gone, it's better the Reds know the rest of us won't fight," he said and tied the cloth to a broken pipe.

The mortar and rocket attacks had eased, except for continued explosions in the direction of the Reich Chancellery. Back in her room, she buried her head in a few remnants of clothing and for the first time in weeks was able to block out the noise.

She woke a few hours later to a shouted warning and the sound of heavy boots on the basement stairway. A half dozen Russians descended cautiously armed with guns and knives. "They shot

Schroeder," someone whispered. "He was holding his hands above his head and calling 'Comrade' but they shot him."

"Uri." A Russian yanked a watch from the wrist of a shocked German. "Uri," he repeated, waving his gun and the rest of the cellar dwellers surrendered watches. "Hmm," he grunted and tore a necklace from an elderly woman. Then he and the other soldiers were gone, moving through the broken wall to the adjoining cellar. "Uri," he called again and again until at last the voice faded.

"That wasn't so bad." The robbery victim managed a smile. "I can live without a watch and a cheap necklace."

Karin retreated to her room and began to implement her plan. She coated her stomach and the top of her legs with coal dust, spitting and rubbing the saliva to produce the impression of black, festering sores; pulled on a tattered dress, and piled the coverall and the fur coat in the darkest corner before working more coal dust onto her face.

"Schroeder is dead," a German called. "I got close enough to the entrance to see the body. More Russians are in the street. Stay quiet."

The next wave came an hour later. Their arrival announced by a quick round of gunfire, the demands for 'Uri' and—more ominous, another guttural command—"Fraulein Komm!" Karin covered her ears at the sound of screams, hoped in the confusion her room would be overlooked but in minutes found herself in the glare of a flashlight. "Fraulein Komm!" Two men seized her as a third laughed from behind the light. The dress was ripped away.

"Nyet!" She screamed in Russian. "Stop. I have a disease. Don't take this home to your women."

The light sprayed across her body, stopping at the black mass. "Disease. I am contagious." But her words had no effect. Two men forced her to the mattress while another fumbled at his belt. "No! This is not what Comrade Stalin would want!" She tried to kick free but rough hands forced her legs apart.

"Stop!" A second light blinded her from the doorway. "Not this one," a deep voice ordered and she felt the hands freeze. "This one is mine. Have sport with others." The hands dropped away. The first men shuffled from the room and the voice barked another order. "Zev. Watch the entrance. I need to learn how this one speaks Russian."

Blinded by the light, she could see only the outline of a uniform.

"Stand up!" He ordered and when she was slow to respond delivered a vicious kick. "Up!"

Karin staggered to her feet, trying to cover herself with what was the left of the dress before it too was ripped away. The light shifted over her breasts and stomach, lingered before drifting down her legs and slowly returning higher. His hand touched the dark mass before he held his fingers to his nose and began to chuckle. "A cleaver Gretchen. But coal dust would not have worked." Inch by inch the light again explored her body. "Usually, my men prefer a woman with more meat, the stocky peasant type. But it wouldn't matter. They'd have had their way. Now, where did you learn to speak Russian?"

She answered quickly, hoping conversation would distract him. "I took it in school and later I worked as a translator, transcribing war bulletins broadcast from Radio Moscow."

"For the army?"

"No, the Foreign Ministry. But I wasn't there long. I was moved to a job in the archives."

"The Foreign Office must have been an important position." The light continued to play across her body. "Turn around." Reluctantly, she faced the wall. Tears formed as the hand slowly travelled over her naked back and thighs.

"Tell me about this work," he ordered.

"I wasn't fast enough. I missed important words."

"To have such work." The hand was rising again. "You must have been a dedicated Nazi."

"I was, until the last few weeks."

"Hmm…preceptive too. Cover yourself. No more talk tonight. I have more important things to do."

"Zev!" She had forgotten the guard in the doorway. "Protect this one. Keep the men away. Tell them Colonel Petrenkov has chosen an occupation wife."

In the next few hours an uneasy calm descended. But mixed with sporadic bursts of gunfire Karin heard screams. Bands of Russians were claiming their prize—the women of Berlin.

The Colonel returned at dawn. "Prepare the truck," he told Zev and studied Karin.

"What do you want?" she asked, fearing she already knew.

"A guide." The answer surprised her. "Take me where I want to go. If all goes well, you'll be fed and sleep soundly. If not, the men will give you no time to rest." He lifted the coverall from the pile in the corner. "Put this on and come outside."

She emerged into a strange Red Army contingent, the men and women who supported the front-line troops. Only a few were in full uniform. Most wore odd pieces of clothing collected over years of desperate fighting. On foot, on horses, the odd car or truck, a few on rough, teetering carts and at the rear, a small herd of cattle. "We brought our own supplies," he told her. "But that part of the war is over. We'll live off Berlin."

She sensed no reply was necessary or expected.

"Get in," Petrenkov ordered, pushing her to where the guard Zev sat behind the steering wheel of a battered truck. Studebaker, a name plate in English, caught her eye as she was forced into the cab. "Show us Berlin. Take us to the Reich Chancellery. It will be decorated with a Red Flag."

The Russian settled back like a tourist delighting in each new attraction. Most streets were blocked by rubble but eventually she found a way and felt a surge of relief on arriving at the Brandenburg Gate. "I know this," Petrenkov said. "We'll walk from here."

Parts of the monument remained but little was left of the famous streetscape of Unter den Linden. Smoke streamed from the wreckage of the once prestigious Adlon Hotel. Burned-out vehicles and rubbish from battle littered the street. And, in the air, the smell of death from bodies lying exposed or decaying under rubble.

The Russian kicked at an abandoned helmet. "So much for the German army. The Soviet Union held Leningrad and Stalingrad for months. The Battle of Berlin lasted only days." Karin followed him through the debris. The memories of ceremonies and processions flashed in her mind, the nights she walked under lime trees that now were little more than splinters.

"Hitler headquarters?" he demanded. She pointed ahead, amazed by how little was left.

Russian soldiers snapped to attention as the Colonel approached the wreckage of the Chancellery and the Fuhrer bunker. "Wait here," he ordered when another officer emerged. The second man studied Karin before both disappeared underground.

Karin found herself alone with the guard and wasn't sure if he was preventing her escape, protecting her or both. She found herself drawn to what was left of an office. A desk was covered with a thick layer of dust and several drawers were open as if someone had mounted a hurried search. A small box caught her eye and inside she found a medal, the German Iron Cross awarded for bravery. She fingered it gently, wondering if the man who was to receive the honour was alive or dead.

"Come!" The Russian had returned. As Zev moved to follow, she slipped the medal in her pocket.

A shout echoed through the ruins. "Hitler Kaput!"

"Da!" The Colonel laughed as a wooden box was dragged to a waiting truck. "Dead." He made a motion of a revolver pointed to his head. "They tried to burn the body but we found it. Death from a bullet or maybe poison."

"The Fuhrer?" She whispered and watched as the box was unceremoniously shoved into the cargo box.

"Hitler Kaput!" The Colonel repeated and slapped his gloves

as if clearing dirt. "A shame. Comrade Stalin wanted him alive and delivered to Moscow in a cage."

Russian soldiers began to collect other material from discarded weapons to file cabinets. "Nothing else to see." Petrenkov glanced about. "We did find a field hospital in the tunnels of the subway. Germans flooded it and killed their own wounded men. What kind of people are you?"

She had no answer.

"Come!" He began to retrace his steps. "Gretchen will direct us to the Kaiser Wilhelm Institute." He raised a hand and motioned two men in civilian dress into the back of the Studebaker.

Several hours passed with Karin and the guard waiting outside the research complex while a search was underway inside. "What are they looking for?" she finally asked.

"SMERSH does not share secrets," Zev answered. He had decided the woman was no risk. And to pass the time would answer her questions.

"What is SMERSH?"

"In the west it would be considered an intelligence service."

"The Colonel is part of the organization?" She stepped closer to the truck to avoid a cold breeze.

Zev shrugged. "Or, he might be NKVD, the secret police. Sometimes it's best not to know. The same way, it's best not to know what he wanted from this building."

"Berliners were told of secret experiments at this complex and were warned to stay away because of dangerous chemicals." Karin felt an urgent need for talk, a few words to break the odd silence that had suddenly fallen across the city. "Why did he choose me?"

"That should be obvious. An attractive woman, despite the dirt. And, one who speaks our language. I too was selected for my language skills?"

"You speak more than Russian?"

"I get by in English and speak Yiddish."

She froze. "You're a Jew."

"Jews are everywhere." He laughed at her shock. "But we do not run Russia as Hitler claimed. Anti-Semitism exists in the Soviet Union but we survive. You should not be surprised."

And yet she was. "I believed what our leaders were saying. And now…well…."

"Bring the truck!" Petrenkov's command echoed down the street. The two civilians had assembled boxes of files and the collection was stacked by the door. Zev backed the truck to the doorway and began to load.

"The documents may be useful," she heard the Colonel say. "The Germans slowed their work on the new bomb but the British and Americans are pushing ahead."

One of the civilians nodded. "The Western Allies were sending a team to plunder this complex for their 'Tube Alloys' project. I convinced them it would do no good. I claimed to be part of the underground, the opposition to Hitler, a 'Good' German."

"Da." The Russian laughed until he noticed Karin listening.

"Good Germans keep their mouths shut, Gretchen. Bad Germans are shot."

Holland, May 4

"Murphy! Where in hell are you?" The shout interrupted a pleasant dream and as he rolled in the bed discovered it was no dream. His hand came to rest on female breasts.

"Murphy! There's a fire." He recognized the plaintive voice of Private Bowen. "I'm coming." He answered while patting his bedmate. "Stay here, Peggy. Leave when I'm gone." But the bedroom door burst open. The private looked on in shock. "Jesus! What are you thinking? That's the girl the captain was banging."

"Stuff it." Murphy growled and began to dress. "Take the chocolate and cigarettes, Peg. I'll be in touch." As he fumbled with the buttons on his uniform, he turned to Bowen. "What's the fuss? A man needs a few hours relaxation."

"A fire in the building with all of our records."

Murphy bent to retrieve his boots. "I was there a few hours ago but I know I stuffed out my cigar."

"The fire brigade worked hard," the private reported. "But there's not much left."

Murphy shook his head in apparent disgust. "And, after all the time I spent completing the latest reports."

"We've had our share of problems." Bowen had begun to calm. "Yesterday a full truck ditched in a canal and now this."

"Yah. All those supplies will be written off as war time losses. We'll never have an accurate assessment." In the distance, he heard the sound of approaching planes. "But the Air Force is dropping food. What we've lost will hardly be noticed."

It was several hours before Murphy caught up with the relief effort. He lit a cigarette and watched the latest food shipments unloaded before he swung from a jeep and approached the mayor. "Get everything I promised?"

"A bit of a struggle with the truck in the canal." Vanderkirk smiled. "But we salvaged all of it. Your men will find the truck easier to remove with the cargo gone. Food rations are welcome but we haven't seen such luxuries in years. Tobacco, liquor, chocolate, bags of sugar."

"And for me?" Murphy asked.

The mayor pointed to a pair of wooden boxes. "Silver, a complete dinner service and pieces of jewellery. I hope it is adequate compensation."

"I suspect it will be." Murphy strained to test the weight of the boxes. "I'll be back in a few days."

"In a few days, we should be at peace. The Germans are going to surrender."

"Yah, be that as it may. People will want 'special' goods."

Southern Germany, May 6

"This is the way to travel." Ben Cooper settled deeper into the leather upholstery. "A German general's staff car, all arranged by the helpful Mr. Kissinger. Turns out the Sergeant was a German Jew, escaped to America in the 30s and came back with the occupation army? Good man. I didn't fancy bouncing in a truck."

Duff Stewart pretended to sleep. Rest had been difficult in the last few hours. A short flight on an army transport plane followed by a long wait before the major secured the car and driver.

"Look at this." Cooper poked him as they met a procession of men on foot, "The remnants of the German army." A long line of disarmed troops marched toward the west. A few straggled and their commanders struggled to keep them in formation. "Ike warned them to accept unconditional surrender or escape routes to the west would be blocked. No Kraut wants to be collared by the Reds."

"Sorry about the delay, Sir," their driver called. "Only a few miles to go." He slowed to navigate a section of damaged highway. "A week ago, we thought those 'Werewolves' would make a last stand but most of them were kids. If you ask me, the Hitler Youth deserve a good spanking."

"No one is asking for your opinion. Some of the Werewolves may be dangerous." Cooper leaned forward and tapped his shoulder. "Get us to Berchtesgaden, the quickest way possible."

"What's the rush?" Stewart asked. "If the war is almost over, we can take our time."

"No, not yet. I got wind of a Luftwaffe archive and Berchtesgaden is the site of the Eagle's Nest, Hitler's private lair. Infantry secured the town but I don't want someone wiping his ass with captured documents. A simple G.I. wouldn't know how important a scrap of paper can be."

"Is this more material for use by America?"

"Damn right. The British might be allowed a peek but the Russians aren't going to see what we find. It's not like they rushed to show us what they discovered. Our men are digging for German secrets. Take the rocket scientists, the characters who built buzz bombs, long-range missiles. We nab them and we can learn how they did it."

"Does General Eisenhower share your zeal?"

"Ike? He knows what's going on but I doubt he bothers with the fine details. Lots of time for that later."

"We're here." The driver slowed for an army roadblock. "Please show yourself and quickly. Those sentries get trigger happy when they see a German staff car."

"At ease," Cooper called and sprang to the road. "I'm Major Cooper with T Force. The commanding officers are expecting me."

As Cooper began his meetings, Stewart began to explore. The town and Hitler's Mountain retreat had been bombed before the troops arrived and the resulting debris was the largest obstacle in any inspection. For most American infantry, the tension of the long campaign from the beaches of Normandy was giving way to a search for souvenirs and liquor. Their war would end with the pop of champagne corks.

"Stewart," Cooper returned sooner than expected. "The archives are secure. We don't have much to do. Unless, you like fine art. Priceless masterpieces, Herr Goring's collection, well, artworks looted by Herman, have surfaced. I had a glance but I prefer nudes and most of the stuff looks pretty tame. I thought of having my way with one of the local women, maybe reward her with a can of rations or a pack of gum but most of them look pretty bedraggled."

Stewart nodded. "Yah. I noticed that too."

Cooper smiled. "There's lots of time now. Word just came through. Monty has accepted the German surrender. From here on, we're officially mopping up."

CHAPTER 10

"THIS IS MOST unusual Mr. Russel. Here in Halifax, we normally report through chain of command. But I am ordered to speak with you."

Vincent Russel gave the Navy Captain a look of sheer disdain. "My company often works with the government and can work faster outside of normal channels. After the events of recent days, we should agree this situation is far from normal."

"Yes, Sir. I guess you're right."

The street was littered with glass and rubbish, the aftermath of two days of rioting. "I read the morning paper," Vincent said. "Over 500 businesses, damaged and looted, three men dead and a couple of dozen in custody. A black mark on Halifax. In other cities, people danced in the street, a boisterous celebration of Victory in Europe. But not here. Here we had a riot. The question is why?"

"Booze." The captain shrugged. "Too much to drink. One of the deaths was from acute alcohol poisoning."

"But the liquor stores were closed?"

"That was the problem. The boys had steam up and wanted to celebrate. The town fathers decided that shouldn't happen and stopped the sale of booze so the men broke down the doors."

Vincent stepped into a men's clothing store. Mannequins had been overturned. Suits, shirts and pants littered the floor. "Did anyone really think after six long years of war that sailors and soldiers would gather quietly? Did they expect a hymn sing?"

"It wasn't only V.E. day," the captain said and placed a hat back on the shelf. "There's been bad blood between the forces and the city. Sailors complained of exorbitant prices in stores and restaurants and if a man was allowed to live ashore, he faced unconscionable rent. Landlords stuck it to us. Ask any seaman. Newfoundland treated us well. Halifax had a hand in our pocket."

"So, it's the fault of greedy merchants." Russel stepped back and glanced along the street where other shops were in the same condition. "The navy takes no blame?"

The captain was silent.

"Come on, man." Russel exploded. "I'm not holding you responsible. What happened on the navy side?"

"On the first day, the Admiral felt the men deserved shore leave. He ordered an 'open gangway' so men who were off duty left the ships. But the liquor stores and taverns were closed. One thing led to another and the stores were…forced open. The crowd couldn't be controlled. Fights, fires, looting. You name it."

"And the navy allowed more men to join this—party?"

"The Admiral didn't know about the trouble until the second group was on shore. When he did find out, it was a little late."

"A little late?" Russel shook his head in exasperation. "Someone's ass will be a sling over this. Bad feeling between the city and the armed forces don't justify a riot."

"But the men spent millions of dollars here in the last few years. Surely that counts for something."

"Oh, I doubt it. Ordinary seamen and private soldiers don't have the ear of the politician. Men returning from overseas will now be watched carefully as they disembark. Halifax will offer those returning heroes a cup of tea and a sandwich, force them onto the trains and send them on their way."

"Hardly seems fair." The captain reached into the debris and lifted a woman's shoe. "The men laid their lives on the line, time and time again. And now they'll be shunted aside."

"Oh no. This won't be a repeat of the Great War. Ottawa has plans to bring the men back into civilian life, they'll have new opportunities."

"But wartime plants are already closing. Jobs will be scarce."

"New plants will open," Russel assured him. "It won't happen overnight but people will buy cars and houses and furniture and start families."

"But where does the money come from?"

"Remember those war bond drives, a form of forced savings? Those bonds can be redeemed. That's cash in the pocket for a working man. And, the government will do its share. The trick is to get everyone home without a repeat of scenes like this."

"Did you want to see any more?" the captain asked.

"No. I've seen quite enough."

Paris, May 10

Maria heard footsteps and the sound of a key in the door. She glanced in the mirror, ran fingers through her hair and adjusted an errant strand before the door opened.

Evers Chance laughed and took her in his arms. "Oh, how I've missed you!"

"It's mutual," she said, returning the embrace. "But stop with the wandering hands. A good wife pays attention to more than sexual urges. Supper is warming. And, I've a bottle of chilled wine."

"No reason to hurry." Again, he pulled her close.

"Enough." She laughed, escaped his grasp and began to prepare the food. "I want to know what you've seen."

"An historic occasion but the war's end was anticlimactic and almost immediately we saw the shape of things to come." Chance spoke from the kitchen door. "The Russians weren't satisfied and demanded a second surrender ceremony in Berlin. Historians will decide which was most important."

"I saw a picture from the signing in Reims," she told him. "I filed a short item with Ike's victory message. It was so short. *The mission of this Allied Force was fulfilled at 2:41 local time.* With all the hangers-on at headquarters, couldn't someone create a moving message for an end to war?"

"Maybe after all this time they no longer care."

"SHEAF did release a picture, showing Eisenhower's staff at the moment of victory," Maria told him. "Although, someone was missing from one photo that was sent to America. Kay Summersby was air-brushed out. I guess she wasn't considered appropriate for domestic consumption."

"Hmm…I'm not surprised." Chance lifted a lid on a pot and sniffed. "Eisenhower may have political aspirations. A war time general would make an excellent candidate."

"What will happen to her. Back to the driver's pool?"

"For a few weeks and then she'll be a civilian again. She could write a book."

"Sad." Maria began to serve the food. "But she knew what she was getting into. Women do. I made sure we were married in case you had wild ideas."

"Ah Maria, I am happy and content as long as you are close."

"No urge to visit the ladies of Madam Teressa? She says she saw you frequently over the years."

"Mostly business." He chuckled.

"I've come to enjoy her company," Maria said and poured a glass of wine. "Many people believe the brothels were dens of collaboration but that wasn't true with her. And, by the way, she thinks anyone connected to Marshall Petain and the Vichy regime is in deep trouble."

Chance rubbed his fingers over lip of the glass. "Many Frenchmen found it safer to keep their heads down. The search for those who collaborated with the Nazis will be underway in France and other occupied countries for months or maybe years."

"She doesn't care for Charles de Gaulle."

"Hah!" Chance began to laugh. "Nobody likes de Gaulle. He sees himself as a future French king."

"And what of Germany?" Maria asked.

"The country is devastated. The Allies are pushing ahead with this notion of a hard peace and believe all Germans should share the punishment. The world demands a full measure of revenge."

Western Germany, May 11

"Behold the famous army of the Third Reich!" Major Ben Cooper laughed. "The Wehrmacht is finally caged."

Duff Stewart stood beside the American. In front of them, a high barbed wire fence and behind the barrier, surrendered men from the German army. A few were in full uniform but most wore only the remains of army dress.

Cooper smiled. "We've more cages like this one. Give them a dose of their own medicine."

Stewart scanned the yard. The beaten men milled about, aimless, nowhere to go, nothing to do and faced an uncertain future. Prisoners numbered in the thousands but only a few small tents were scattered around the enclosure.

"What about shelter?"

"Shelter? Hitler made them fight in ice and snow. The rain will wash them off."

"Latrines?" Stewart asked.

"Let them dig their own. Germans claim to be hygienic."

"Food? Water?"

"Have you become a bleeding heart? A few more days on short rations won't hurt them."

Inside the cage, a few men moved toward the wire. Cooper flapped his arms as if scattering a flock of birds. "Likely carrying disease. Guards from the concentration camps could be infected with anything."

"Poor food, poor sanitation is a recipe for disease and death."

"We'll give them shovels and let them dig graves. Eventually we'll have to use trucks to cart bodies away. A couple of loads have gone to a Potter's field. Civilians dig graves in exchange for cup of soup and a slice of bread."

"It's not right." Stewart turned to confront Cooper. "Prisoners of war should be protected. The last time I checked the western world had moral standards."

"Moral standards!" Cooper twisted Stewart to face the wire and the men inside. "After what that bunch did?"

"If we set aside moral and legal rights, we're no better than they are?"

"That's nonsense! A few weeks and we'll sort out the good from the bad, the hard core from the poor sap who followed orders. But we'll take our time. These men are not considered P.O.Ws. Instead, they are 'disarmed enemy personal'. This way we don't worry about the legalistic Geneva conventions, like how much food a prisoner gets. All thanks to a minor change in a legal definition."

"More men will grow sick and die." Stewart waved toward the enclosure. "I can see men who need food or medical care."

"People across Europe have the same complaint and they didn't start the war. Eventually, most of these men will be turned loose and go to what's left of their homes. I'll probably be stateside by then and you'll be back with the Canadian army. The civil administrators, men like you, can deal with them. And, good luck with that."

Berlin, May 14

Karin lost all track of time. The days of the week became meaningless as she guided the Soviet Colonel through what was left of Berlin.

The day might begin with the search of a damaged factory. A quick inspection before machinery, tools or goods were loaded in trucks destined for a railyard where the booty was crammed into box cars and trains, powered by confiscated locomotives, creaked off to the east. All kinds of material in any state of repair. Toilets, bicycles, electrical equipment or the tracks from the city tramways—all destined for Russia.

Karin knew Petrenkov was watching but he made no demands. Instead, he kept his distance while his assistant kept her safe. Zev had intervened to stop a squad of Russians intent on rape and on another day turned aside a cluster of foreign workers about to steal her meagre lunch.

The Russians moved with startling speed. Only days after the ceasefire, feeding stations were established. Soup, sometimes with only a morsel of meat was at least a form of sustenance. On the odd day, when the 'reparation' work slowed, she was forced to join the rubble women who worked with bare hands to clear the streets.

"How does it feel to be a Russian whore?" A fellow worker had demanded.

"I'm not. Do you think I prefer this life?"

"Oh Blondie. I feel your pain." The woman kneeled to lift a chunk of stone. "I see them. An officer and his assistant. You service a pair. The rest of us fend off gangs. My friends are left bleeding and torn after multiple rapes. Others endure the horror and kill themselves later."

"I hear the screams…I know…"

"But you live with the pigs." She waved swollen hands in Karin's face. "At least I have dignity. You've surrendered for the head of the soup line and a pair of gloves." Zev produced the gloves after her first day of street clearing when her hands too had been bloodied and bruised.

Karin kept her voice low. "I'm only trying to survive."

"And should those of us without the blonde hair and the full body jump off a bridge?"

"I'm sorry...I don't mean..."

"Sorry? You have no shame. What will you do when your husband returns?"

"I have no husband. I..."

"Did he die at the front?"

"No. I never married. I..."

"...So, you think your behaviour is acceptable? I hope you catch the clap or mother a Russian bastard."

CHAPTER 11

"**T**HAT WAS A wild goose chase." Duff Stewart shifted the jeep into a higher gear. He and an American sergeant had been sent to look for a suspected Nazi scientist but found no trace of the man. "Major Cooper thinks he has a hot lead but is more concerned about packing to go home than to come with us."

"We'll all be glad to go home." The Sergeant smiled. "I put in for service in the Pacific but what I really want is home leave, a few weeks in the States before I ship out to fight the Japs."

"Bugger for punishment, aren't you? Most men have had enough of war."

"Me too. But I want to see the world. And I think…what's this?"

A stout woman had stepped onto the road and waved them to stop. "The Poles!" She fought to catch her breath. "They're robbing us blind." And pointed up a driveway where a small cottage and barn were almost hidden by trees. Many towns and villages lay in ruin but isolated country homes frequently showed less damage. Stewart could see men running between the house and the barn and recognized the rough garb of foreign workers. "Come," she ordered and despite her weight climbed to the hood of the jeep.

At the house, a man had chopped the head from a chicken and dangled the carcass to let the blood drain. Another chewed on the remains of a loaf of bread. Others clustered near the barn.

"They steal. They're vandals." The woman slid awkwardly to the ground and tried to avoid shattered bits of pottery in the driveway. "I let them stay in the barn overnight but today they come to the house, go crazy and smash my dishes. You win the war. Protect us!"

Stewart stepped from the jeep and walked toward the men. "What's going on?" From the blank stares he realized English wouldn't work and tried a few words in German. This time a man answered. "We're taking what we deserve. We're foreign workers. But now the war is over. No food. No shelter. No one cares about us."

"We'll get you food." Stewart tried to sound reassuring. "An army camp is up the road with food and a shower."

"No." The man backed away. "No camps."

The chicken killer smiled broadly and waved the feathered trophy in the air. "We worked. Now paid."

Distracted by the conversation, Stewart hadn't noticed the woman disappear until suddenly she rounded the corner of the house armed with a pitchfork. "Go!" she screamed, launching a frontal attack. The men easily danced aside.

Stewart stretched to catch her apron. "Stop this." He yanked at the fork, setting in motion a brief tug of war until the housewife surrendered. He gestured to the leader. "Get the men together." And to underscore the command, told his sergeant, "Show them the gun." The appearance of the side arm brought a semblance of order. "How many men?" Stewart demanded.

At first, only silence, and then—"Five. We left our village four years ago with a dozen. Most starved while Germans, like that bitch, grew fat."

Stewart felt the woman tug at the fork but shoved her aside and planted the tines deep in the ground. "Did you work for this woman?"

"No. But others like her. They ate eggs and chicken and bread. We were fed slop, pig feed."

"We can't blame her for what happened. Load the men in the jeep. We'll drive you."

The offer set off another round of shouts and gestures. The man with the chicken, clasped the bloody carcass to his chest. The others argued.

The woman began to shake and cry. "Have the gun ready. Poles, Russians. They can't be trusted. They rape and kill."

"Not this time." He told her and with relief watched the workers climb into the jeep. Except for the chicken killer. Like the woman, he took a spot on the hood, swinging the carcass over his head and splattering the windshield with blood. "Go before they change their minds," Stewart spoke to the sergeant. "And give me the gun." He shook his finger at the woman as she worked to free the fork. "No. You're safe now."

As the jeep moved off the sergeant spoke. "Nice work, Sir. It's my first experience with Displaced Persons."

"You'll meet more in the coming weeks. They may not look like much but they are human."

Berlin, May 16

Zev was anxious, a stark contrast to his usual stoic calm but the day had been unusual. The Colonel ordered baths for the entire squad. Karin was forced to wash in water used by other women but was relieved by a rare show of Russian modesty. Males and females used opposite ends of a primitive bathhouse.

When Petrenkov disappeared for a few hours, Zev brought her to the cellar room and stood guard at the entrance. Dusk was falling when she heard the commotion.

"Zev!" The Colonel's voice boomed through the basement. "Stand guard in the street."

Petrenkov staggered into her room, the smell of alcohol overpowering. "The time has come, Gretchen. Prepare for a man." His words were only slightly slurred and for an instant she wondered if drunkenness was an act. He appeared to trip and fell on the mattress but his words became more distinct. "Remove the clothes or I will."

The moment she feared had arrived.

"Now!" The command was harsh, a tone he seldom used. He pulled himself from the mattress and stepped toward her.

"No. Don't do this!" she said frantically. "No. Please!"

His hand reached and tore at the coverall. In seconds she was naked and pinned against the wall.

"Better." He stepped back. "Do you know why my men rape German women?"

She raised her hands across her breasts but he pried her arms away. "For the peasant soldier, it's an animal instinct. But as important, they remember what German men did to our women." She flinched and tears welled in her eyes.

Then suddenly he began to gently caress her stomach. "Lovely, smooth white skin, the perfect Aryan. Others have noticed." The hands dropped away and he took a step back. "A classic Aryan beauty would appeal to the Nazis. Because of that, my fellow officers believe you must have secrets."

Karin pressed tight against the wall, fists clenched, ready to fend off his attack.

"As a translator who did you work for? Was it the Foreign Minister von Ribbentrop? I want the truth." The question shocked her as much as the attack.

"I...I...I didn't really work for him."

His hand lashed her face. Despite the stab of pain, she tried to think. What had she told him on that first night? "I only worked with the Foreign Ministry for a few months but yes, I did see him."

"See him? You must have noticed something. What? He's been captured by the Americans. What could he tell them?"

"I don't know?"

Another slap made her ears ring. His face twisted in anger. "I don't believe you."

"He…he claimed to be an aristocrat." She tried to remember what she had heard. "Behind his back, men laughed at his pretensions. Money from his wife's family bought him access to German society. And, someone said it would have been better if he had stayed in Canada. He worked there selling wine before the First War."

He appeared satisfied, pulled a flask from his jacket and took a deep swallow. The flask was hardly back in his pocket when his hand reached to her breast. "The day at the Chancellery. What did you see?"

"Nothing. Nothing but wreckage, bomb damage."

The grip tightened.

"What else?"

"Russian soldiers, a box…remains. The body of the Fuhrer."

"No. You are mistaken!"

"Men laughed and said, "Hitler Kaput." She gasped from the pressure. "They said it was him."

"Those men were mistaken. Hitler may not be dead. Rumours of his death may be a fascist plot. Anyone who spreads lies suffers severe consequences."

"But…"

"No buts…" He loosened his grip and threw her to the mattress, "Forget what you think you saw."

She shivered with fear.

"Be a good little Gretchen!"

The colonel dropped his pants, shouted for Zev and waited for the private to arrive before slowly pulling the pants back up.

"She'll be tired." The slight slur had returned. "She wasn't worth the wait."

Western Germany, May 20

"Hold this," Major Cooper pointed to the end of a blood red Nazi flag. "One of the mementoes, I'm taking home. I found it in a supply cache but I'll claim I fought off Hitler's body guard. Maybe I can donate... no...sell it...to a museum."

"Maybe develop a lecture series," Duff Stewart said and helped fold the banner. "First came shootin' then the lootin'."

"Don't be a smart ass. Everyone has something. I shipped a box of 'souvenirs' home, a Luger, couple of helmets and a really nice camera."

"Excuse me, Major." A private appeared in the door. "Telephone lines are repaired and you have a call."

Cooper disappeared leaving Stewart alone. The Major was waiting for orders to return to America and Stewart expected to be sent back to the Canadian army.

But only seconds later Cooper stormed back into the room and slammed the door. "Shit! Frigging bureaucrats run the world. My embarkation date has been delayed. I'm here for a few more weeks. And, my bad luck is your bad luck. The brass say Lieutenant Stewart remains under my command."

"I'm not being transferred?" Stewart wasn't sure if his disappointment came from the dashed hope for a fresh assignment or regret at spending more time with Cooper. He had begun to find the American obnoxious.

"Why would you want to go the Canadian army anyway?" Cooper closed the box of souvenirs. "Most of them are policing Holland. That's small stuff. The big fish, the Nazi brass, are under guard at a hotel in Belgium."

"Who do they have?"

Cooper began to count on his fingers. "Von Ribbentrop, Goring, the submarine guru Donitz, Seyss-Inquart the guy that was the overlord in Holland..." He stopped at his thumb. "Hitler is a question mark. He may be alive but more likely dead. Heinrich Himmler would have answered for the crimes of the SS and so chewed on a poison pill.

Goebbels killed himself too but not before the sick bugger killed his entire family. The Minister of Propaganda and Enlightenment, master of the big lie. Our politicians will probably study his technique."

"And what do those other men face? Firing squads?"

"Ah no, that would be death with a thin veneer of honour." Cooper sneered, "A waste of a bullet. I predict a long trial. War crimes, a veritable field day for lawyers. Completed, of course, by an appointment with a hangman."

"It would have been simpler to order a military court martial, shoot them and be done with it."

"Ah but they may still have secrets."

Berlin, May 21

The gears shrieked in protest as the Studebaker lurched forward. "The clutch is going," Zev said. "The Americans gave us these trucks but have grown stingy since the end of the war. This one is almost finished."

"The Americans forget what we've done." Petrenkov answered. "This truck and others came through Lend Lease. They gave us tools but we shed the blood."

Karin was wedged between Zev and the Colonel. No one mentioned the events in the cellar. She had been forced to resort to an old shirt and skirt when the coverall was destroyed.

"Germans are industrious," the Colonel's hand fingered her bare leg, "Beaten and abandoned but they struggle on."

Zev stopped the truck where a female Russian traffic guard supervised the flow of vehicles. Like Karin, she wore a dress shorter than fashion would dictate. Yet, she was in uniform with a sub machine gun hanging from her shoulder. A quick burst could bring any unruly driver to a halt.

An elderly woman glanced at the traffic supervisor before crossing the street. She pulled a child's wagon, filled with dinner plates, a broken shovel and stray bits of clothing.

"Heading to the market." The Colonel guessed. "The black

market. The old lady may trade for a bit of bread. Those who work are fed but she's too old for a full ration." The hand tightened on Karin's leg. "Anything can be bought or sold on the black market. Food, clothing, a girl or a boy. Everything is for sale. Life is hard for those without protection."

Zev fought the unruly clutch as the traffic girl motioned them forward and Petrenkov waved his thanks.

"Go to the radio studio," he ordered. "The Americans and the British don't need broadcast equipment."

Karin felt one last painful squeeze before he lifted his hand.

"And Zev," he ordered. "Tonight, round up pants and a couple of uniforms. Gretchen should be well dressed."

CHAPTER 12

IN LESS THAN a month, a Wehrmacht base in western Germany was transformed. The symbols of the Third Reich were removed and the Union Jack flew above the parade square. A British guard inspected each vehicle at the gate.

"Evers Chance to see the commanding officer." He leaned from the car window. "I'm expected but I'm late. Didn't count on traffic."

"Have been a lot of people about." The guard ran a finger down a list of names. "German soldiers going home, prisoners of war, refugees from the east and hundreds of foreign workers wandering aimlessly. And, everyone has light fingers. Anything that isn't tied down disappears. Ah, here you are, Mr. Chance. The C.O. is expecting you at his residence."

"I'm curious what goes on in this camp."

"No big secret. With the surrender we're training for occupation duty. The C.O.'s house is about a half mile up the road, big stone mansion with sentries to keep the rabble out."

A half hour later, Chance passed another security check, entered the main hall of an ornate country home and was ushered to a large office.

"Far too long." A rotund British officer rose to greet him.

"Good to see you, Tiny." Chance smiled and used an army nickname. "I hope the promotion to major general hasn't gone to your head? The rank is well deserved and shows how important intelligence operations have become." The men had been friends and shared information since the 1930s. Harley Bennet was a towering figure with an extra-large stomach. The nickname Tiny had followed him through a long army career.

"Hah. Still buttering up the senior ranks, are you Chance? I'm living well and glad to be out of tents and flea infested cottages. The German who owns this place was convinced to move into an old coach house. He and a few servants take care of our needs. I growl every now and again to keep them in line."

"I'll only be here for the night."

"Yes. I understand your network is humming again. I'm to pass along whatever you have."

Chance settled into a chair and lifted a dossier from a brief case. "One of the old crew slipped out of Poland. Our Russian allies have not been as forthcoming as hoped. My man has details on the Russian occupation as well as a long list of atrocities committed in the east. It was a blood bath for both the Reds and the Nazis. Unfortunately, most of this is likely considered ancient history but it may be useful in planning for what's ahead. We knew about the 'Show Trials' where Stalin destroyed his opposition and there are persistent rumours of man-made starvation in Ukraine but we looked the other way in the interest of winning the war."

"Umm…Poland will be a problem." Tiny began to light a pipe. "Joe Stalin has his hand around the country's collective neck. Everything points to a communist government, much to the chagrin of the exiled London Poles who worked with us the last few years."

Chance produced another file. "Thousands of Germans are being forced from their homes across Eastern Europe. Settlers that Hitler moved into the occupied territories in the early 40s would naturally be evicted but others come from regions that have been ethnically German for years and years."

"Well, I have no sympathy." Tiny's voice took on a harsher tone. "Their leaders brought on this war. Someone should have thought of the consequences."

"The Russians will be hard to control. Romania, Austria, Hungary, Belorussia, the Baltic states and Ukraine are effectively under the Soviet boot. Any German in those countries can be considered—*verboten*—and the big three signed off on the expulsions."

"Yalta." The officers face twisted to a scowl. "Churchill and Roosevelt wanted the Red Army to wipe out the Nazis and reduce the casualties among our troops. The Russian butcher bill was enormous. And, confidentially..." He waited for Chance to nod agreement. "...Winston is worried about the Reds. He wants to know if we should turn and fight them?"

"Oh no! My God. That's unthinkable."

"Interesting choice of words. 'Unthinkable' is the code name for the army study."

"We've been on the same side for four years." Chance shook his head in disgust. "Would we actually consider fighting?"

"Hmm. That's what the Chiefs of Staff are being asked. We do have our army. And, it's not well known but several German divisions are intact, along with a large cache of weapons. We might bring the recent foe in on our side?"

"The world has been mad for years but this sounds like the ultimate madness."

"If anything does happen, it must be fast. The Americans plan to demobilize. We'd need their manpower and supplies."

"Good Lord! We wouldn't have won the war without the Russian army. Do you agree with this?" Chance asked.

"Personally, no." Tiny touched another match to the tobacco

before he continued. "I expect high command will express extreme reservations. On the other hand, we are faced with a huge, seasoned Red Army. If it began to move west, I doubt we could stop it."

"But Stalin must be tired too." Chance again shook his head. "Russia needs time to recover. The world can't exist in a state of perpetual war. Yet, I suppose the West fears the old Bolshevik threat, the call for worldwide revolution."

"The best hope is negotiations. Bring the big three, Russia, the US and Britain to another conference. A repeat of Yalta with a new face at the table. President Truman might have fresh ideas. FDR gave too much to Stalin."

"So, there may be time." Chance relaxed. "Churchill must consider domestic politics and an election since his alliance with the Labour Party has collapsed." He managed a wry smile. "Touch of irony, there too. Churchill became Prime Minister through Conservative party wheeling and dealing back in 1940. His selection was never put to the people."

"And what's in all this for you?" Tiny asked.

"Whitehall will need economic advice. The German factories in the Ruhr can be restored if the Russians don't take them as reparations. In any case, Europe will need industry. I have the contacts to get factories back in operation."

Ottawa, May 30

The Peace Tower clock struck four as Vincent Russel left the Parliament Buildings. Most members of the Canadian House of Commons were on the election trail and his hope to 'accidentally' meet and gather information had been dashed. He glanced toward the East Block knowing the government staff would soon finish their workday. The man he was expecting would wait until other employees were gone.

Russel strolled across the grounds, idly scratching at the bites on his neck and face. A weekend at a fishing camp in the Gatineau Hills proved spring had arrived. The black flies were biting but not the senior civil servants at the neighbouring cabins. Attempts at conversation failed to produce anything of value. He hoped for better results from the next meeting and took a seat on bench to wait.

"Mosquito's follow the black flies," Bill Riggert arrived and laughed at the ugly welts on Russel's face, "Nothing like spring in the Ottawa Valley. If the city had been smart, the canal would have been filled in and new office space constructed years ago. We'd have fewer bugs and fewer of those ugly temporary buildings."

"Maybe that could go on the agenda for the next government." Russel smiled. "Unless, the Prime Minister tightens the belt."

"Not much change of that." The civil servant took a seat beside him. "Our Prime Minister is a conservative at heart. He hates to spend. But, with demobilization comes the fear of another depression. He'll loosen the purse strings to avoid that."

"Can King be re-elected?" Russel asked.

"He might squeak through. His Tory opponents do stupid things. A few months ago, we weathered a conscription crisis. Common sense would say let the issue die but the Tories won't let go. The party wants to conscript young men to fight the Japanese. That might sell in British Columbia but not in Quebec."

"I know all that." Russel fought the urge to scratch. "And, the Liberals are promising new social spending, special programs to re-integrate the veterans, unemployment insurance and this new 'baby bonus', extra money to help families."

"And where are the biggest families?" Riggert laughed. "In a Liberal stronghold of Catholic Quebec. The ladies will be rewarded as they produce more little Liberals. But, don't forget, the British are planning new programs to help ordinary folk too. It's never hurts to follow their lead. Churchill and King both want an electoral victory."

Russel took an envelope from his pocket. "I haven't heard much I didn't know. Hardly worth the expense." He waved it back and forth."

"Don't do that," Riggert cautioned, "Someone might notice. What else do you want?"

"I hear of an energy play, maybe oil in Alberta?"

"That's idle chatter. Finding enough oil to pay would be a monumental challenge. Why bother? Alberta has other energy. Any boom will come from coal."

"Hmm…That's interesting. And what of other mining projects?" He set the envelope on the bench and gently pushed it forward. "An outfit called Eldorado and a rare mineral, uranium?"

Riggert snatched the envelope and warily glanced around. "That subject is dangerous!" His voice dropped. "National security. It's highly classified and since Washington is involved, I don't ask questions. I wouldn't get answers anyway."

"But you could guess?"

"Army, secret project, maybe a new weapon. Like I said, it's dangerous. I can work my way through the backwaters of the civil service but I'm not about to tangle with army intelligence. Not ours, not British and definitely not the American."

Near Berlin, June 5

The Russian squad left the city and drove several miles into the countryside. The scenery was drearily familiar. Bombed villages, burned homes, the debris of war scattered by the roadside; wrecked guns, an abandoned truck and the ever-present smell of death. The warm spring air might dissipate the odour but any change in the wind direction brought fresh reminders of the struggle.

Petrenkov ordered them off the main road to a small village when a whiff of fresh bread reached his nostrils. The ovens in a bakery were still warm. "Take it," he ordered, "Everything. Ovens, bowls, the fixtures and find the flour. Don't miss anything."

The bakery was small and the men bumped against each other carrying the material to the truck. In the confusion, Karin stepped away. She loosened the buttons on her new Russian army jacket and absently rubbed at an itch from the woollen pants. To the occupants of the village, who sullenly watched the confiscation, she appeared part of the Red Army.

On the edge of the crowd, a thin young woman watched intently. "What became of the bakery owner?"

"He ran when he saw the Russians," a villager answered. "He served on the Eastern Front. He fears the Reds."

"Is his name, Steiner?"

"Oh no. Steiner sold the business a couple of years ago. He was smart and got out at the right time."

The woman's face showed disappointment.

"Did you know this Steiner?" Karin asked. Any bits of information might impress the Colonel.

The woman hesitated before she answered. "A long time ago. He bought the bakery from my father. That was 1937. We lived above the shop. Our family was happy here."

"At least you have pleasant memories."

"No. Steiner was a dedicated Nazi, an influential party member." The woman began to wring her hands. "He had important friends. He bought the business but paid much less than it was worth. In other words, he stole it. My family hoped to emigrate but we didn't have enough money. We were sent to the camps. I'm the only one left."

"Why the camps. What was your crime. What did you do?"

"We did nothing."

Karin thought of everything she had been taught, in school, by friends and family or from radio broadcasts. She couldn't let the claim pass. "The people in the camps were there for a reason. Criminal activity? Sabotage? Perversion?"

"No...none of those."

"What then?"

"We were Jews."

"Gretchen!" The Colonel shouted from the door of the now empty bakery. "Time to go."

Karin saw the woman take a last glance before moving in the opposite direction, toward the west.

"I hope Sarah keeps going," a villager said quietly. "We don't want her type."

"You call her by name. Did you know her?" Karin asked.

"Of course not. All Jewish women were called Sarah just as the men were named Israel. The party added those names to their identification. But most of them are gone so it doesn't matter anymore."

Western Germany, June 3

Duff Stewart pulled a bandana across his nose and mouth, scant protection from the smell and fear of disease but the only defense available on short notice. The barbed wire fence surrounded a few rudimentary barracks in the compound and was as the Nazis left it. Only guards and dogs were missing.

"This was a small camp," an American sergeant told him. "Maybe a thousand prisoners. The place has been deloused but we can't control the smell. Our guys had the former guards remove the bodies and clean but prisoners are still dying. Tuberculosis? Typhus? Who knows what else?"

"How many Germans were here?"

"Only about a dozen guards when we arrived. When we saw the conditions, we locked the gate and let the prisoners sort things out. Call it the release of pent-up emotions." The sergeant glanced off across the compound and his voice dropped. "A few of the guards must have shown compassion over the years and got away with a nasty beating. The rest were buried with the dead we found in the barracks. Eisenhower said the camps were a lesson for those who didn't know what the fight was about. What I saw shows what we were fighting against. I guess the next few months will show what we were fighting for. I hope it's the same thing."

"I'm not here for a philosophical argument. Did you find any political prisoners, religious types or union men?"

"Uh, there could have been a few but they're gone and this place was a veritable United Nations. It's like I told the Canadian reporter who came through... hey, maybe you know him? Rene Levesque, he's serving with the American forces too."

"No, we're a small country." Stewart frowned. "But not small enough that we all know each other."

"Ok, just wondered. Anyway, we can't keep track of the nationalities in these camps."

"We've going to do a head count, see who is here and who should be repatriated to Soviet territory."

"Repatriated? Send them back?" the sergeant asked.

"That's the plan."

"Bunch of them won't want to go. I've talked to a few who can muddle through in English. Joe Stalin ordered them not to surrender or face his wrath. He actually passed on a chance to rescue his own son." The Sergeant shook his head in disbelief. "The last few years our people have been talking nice about the Reds, calling them valiant allies and all that. The men who lived in the east paint a different picture."

"You and I aren't going to sort that out. Our leaders agreed on the plan at Yalta. We follow their orders."

"Yah, but isn't that what the Nazis did...followed orders?"

"I'll forget I heard that. Now, is anyone from the west?"

The sergeant took a moment to think. "Not many. A few French went home and a couple of Dutchmen left the other day. Most of the rest are from Russia or the Baltic's. I don't know what we do with Lithuanians, Latvians, or Ukrainians. To be honest, I'm not entirely sure where those countries are."

"I'll bring an atlas on my next visit. But we start by finding out who is here, list them by nationality."

"What about Jews?"

"What about them?"

"Shouldn't they be a special case? Hitler tried to destroy the entire race."

Stewart shrugged. "I've seen no special directive for their treatment and there is no Jewish state. Maybe let them go?"

"Most are in pretty poor shape, Lieutenant. Let them stay for a few weeks, get decent food and grow a little stronger."

"Ok, but no special treatment."

"And if they want to leave?"

"Let them go. Although, once they sample conditions on the outside, they may want back in."

Berlin, June 6

The streets were no longer empty as more people felt safe leaving shelter. Former German soldiers wandered in search of family or food while rubble women continued to clear the streets. And a small, yet significant change occurred. Germans began to greet each other with a smile and a friendly good day. The Hitler salute was relegated to history.

"Potsdam." Colonel Petrenkov ordered and directed the crew toward the western suburbs. "The British and American's didn't bomb there until the war was almost over. Capitalists no doubt wished to preserve the homes of the upper-class. Working-class neighbourhoods were bombed repeatedly. Germans did the same thing. The poorer neighbourhoods were bombed in England."

Zev revved the engine and to the shriek from the transmission forced the truck from first to third gear.

"Keep the speed up," Petrenkov ordered. "We're in a hurry." Pedestrians stubbornly refused to give way until the frustrated colonel leaned from the window and fired a revolver in the air. Only then, did the people move toward the piles of debris that created narrow canyons on the streets.

"Do you know Potsdam?" He asked Karin. "A house built for the Kaiser?"

She hesitated before delivering an answer she felt would please him. "I know where it is. It was home to those who exploited the working class."

"Ah yes, good." His influence was bringing success. A few weeks ago, she might have spouted Nazi ideology.

"The Kaiser was a criminal from the First War," Karin continued, "He abdicated and the building became the home of the Crown Prince. It's called Cecilienhof. The family expected to be restored to the throne. What a ghastly mistake that would have been. Imagine restoring a Romanov to lead Russia."

"A good answer, Gretchen."

"If I may, Comrade, my name is Karin."

She felt a sharp sting as Zev's elbow hit her ribs. She glanced to see him shake his head.

"Never challenge me." Petrenkov twisted to face her, "Gretchen will do."

"Yes, of course, Comrade."

A silent half hour later, Zev steered into a driveway and stomped hard on the brake. Men carried ornate furniture from a mansion, carelessly dumping sofa's, chairs and other furniture into waiting trucks.

"Stop!" Petrenkov shouted and stormed toward the entrance. "Take nothing from this building. Unload the trucks. Everything back inside."

Another officer appeared in the doorway. "On whose orders?"

"Comrade Stalin! Return the furniture. Damage nothing." The Colonel didn't wait to see if his command was followed and stepped inside the mansion.

In the truck, Zev spoke to Karin. "Do not upset the Colonel. He has new orders and is under great pressure. He is to find a meeting place for the Allied leaders, Comrade Stalin, the Englishman Churchill and Truman, the new American President. Our commander must ensure everything is prepared. And, with great responsibility comes great risk."

Ottawa, June 11

The piano player beamed at the appearance of another glass of beer and began a rendition of "*Happy Days are here again.*" Beside him an attractive young woman chalked election results on a blackboard.

"Beer, Sir?" A waiter asked.

"No." Vernon Russel waved a finger. "Scotch. Best you have."

"It's a shame, the Prime Minister avoids alcohol." A man beside him laughed. "But it means more for the rest of us. I'm Harry Lyle. Came up from Toronto for election night. I feared it might be a long, glum evening but Liberal support has come through. We've won another four years."

"But not a true majority." Russel cautioned. "Mr. King is a few seats short."

"Won't matter." Lyle beamed. "A cluster of independent Liberals were elected in Quebec. They bolted the party over conscription but when push comes to shove will stand with us. The Prime Minister should be happy."

"Will this be his last hurrah? He's getting on in years. Maybe it's time for a younger leader."

"Hell, man." Lyle slapped his back. "We've four years to worry about that. Although, any smart politician looks ahead. Louis St. Laurent has been doing a great job. Other potential leaders may come from the armed forces, a different type of leadership but, by God, they've done their duty. Still, it's Mr. King's party. He'll decide when to go."

"I'll order another," Russel spoke as the waiter returned. "And one for my friend."

"That's very kind." Lyle glanced at the blackboard as a cheer greeted the first results from the prairies.

"What did you make of the Ontario provincial election last week?" Russel asked.

"I'm never happy to see a Tory victory but the results did clear away another irritant. Mitch Hepburn lost and will never lead the Ontario

Liberals again. He'll be back growing onions on his Elgin County farm. King must be relieved. Those two didn't get along."

"And what of the CCF? People had expected them to do well. Although I'd change the name and find a new moniker for the Cooperative Commonwealth Federation. But tell me. Was there any truth to the story the Ontario Provincial Police were watching them?"

Lyle dropped his voice. "Wouldn't surprise me. They claim to be centrist but I think the party is socialist and so only a small step from communist. Liberal policies are shifting, moving a bit to the left to undercut their support. The new social programs will mean men who might have been relegated to the economic sideline will have a chance to accomplish more in life. Good times for everyone."

"Yes. A group of associates are thinking of buying land around Toronto. They're betting the city is poised for growth."

"Warn them about pipedreams. Hog town will never extend beyond places like Scarborough. Much as I'd love a home on the bluffs, buying out there would be pouring good money down the drain. Besides, we're getting ahead of ourselves. The war in the Pacific continues. We'll be playing a part there too."

"I'm not so sure." Russel leaned toward his new friend. "The Americans don't need or want us. The Yankees built up a hate for the Japanese and want to finish that war on their own. Japanese cities are firebombed every night. With wooden houses, there can't be much left."

The conversation was interrupted as a loud groan echoed around the room. Lyle sprang to his feet for a better view of the blackboard and the latest result before he slumped back down. "The Prince Albert riding. The Prime Minister has lost his own seat. What a bloody shame. Well, some other Liberal will be appointed to the courts or the Senate and King will face a by-election. This sort of thing has happened before but puts a damper on the celebration."

Germany, June 14

"Turn right, the house among the trees." Major Ben Cooper glanced at a map and loosened the cover on his side arm. "I've a tip the fellow who lives there is a mucky muck from a concentration camp. He came home a few weeks ago and locked himself away."

Duff Stewart downshifted and eased the jeep up a steep path. *Perfect spot for an ambush*, he thought and slid lower in the seat. The young soldier with them lifted his rifle and glanced nervously to where a small bonfire blazed.

Cooper, revolver in hand, approached the house. Before he could knock the door opened and a man backed into the yard, dragging a box filled with loose papers. "Far enough," Cooper ordered and saw the man flinch in shock before turning to face the uninvited guests.

"Dieter Krause?" Cooper pointed his gun.

"Ja." A black patch covered one eye and a scar ran across his cheek. "What do you want?"

"You!" Cooper motioned for the young soldier to check for hidden weapons.

"I'm a farmer. Done with the army." Krause spread his arms wide. "No guns."

Stewart began to sift through the papers. "Army requisitions, sick leave requests..." he paused... "Order's for chemicals for someplace called...Auschwitz?"

"Never heard of it?" Cooper shrugged. "Where is it, Dieter?"

Krause appeared to relax. "A research facility in Poland. A small operation. Most of it was destroyed and the Reds stole what was left. Why bother to tell the Americans? So small, no one cares."

"Let's go inside." Cooper kept the gun in hand. "We'll have a look around."

The main room was dark and remarkably bare with only a table and chair positioned in front of a stone fireplace. The search was finished quickly and Cooper returned his attention to the German. "Auschwitz?" he asked. "Are you sure you didn't work somewhere else, maybe the death camps at Dachau, or Bergen-Belsen, Buchenwald?"

"No, I was in the east."

"Didn't work at any of those slave labour sites, where they built the rockets? Dora…maybe?"

"I know nothing of rockets."

"Fellow tells us, a German fellow tells us, you were a camp commander."

"That is a lie. I was a deputy for a short time, only a few weeks."

"Why don't you think for a couple of minutes? Maybe you'll remember more."

As Cooper waited Stewart again glanced around the room. A camera caught his eye and as he lifted it a photo album fell to the floor. "Good quality Leica." He passed the camera to Cooper, "Is this as good as the one you sent to the states?"

Cooper put the lens to his eye and worked the viewfinder. "Yah, this is excellent."

"That's an expensive camera," Krause told Cooper. "But I would sell it—cheap."

Stewart bent to retrieve the album and glanced at the pictures. Several men, dressed in pinstripe pyjamas stood against a wall. A German officer stood to one side, a man in a doctor's smock on other. "The prisoners? What happened to them?"

"Ah, I'm not sure. Inmates often volunteered for medical experiments."

"Oh, I doubt they volunteered. What about this other picture? You and a nurse?"

"Ah, that was Lisle, a lovely girl."

"Those smoke stacks in the background?" Cooper began to take an interest.

"What were they for?"

"Umm…power supply."

"Bullshit Dieter! Those are smokestacks from a crematorium, probably where you learned to burn evidence."

"No…I don't think so…"

"But we do." Cooper snarled. "We'll take the album to keep it safe."

"Why?" The German appeared confused. "Why make a fuss over a few Jews. I don't understand the west. You refused them as emigrants and expected us to deal with them. And, so we did."

The next morning Cooper was in high spirits. His long-delayed return to the United States had been approved and a vacant seat was available on a plane. He laughed and stuffed a duffel bag. "We're breaking up a great team. But I don't care enough to do anything about it."

"Mutual." Stewart answered. "Besides I'm designated for Berlin and the Allied Control Commission, the headquarters for the occupation armies."

"I don't envy anyone going there, sounds drab and dreary. Hey. Keep the camera that we grabbed yesterday. The photo album may be important evidence but no one cares if a Leica is missing."

"I guess Dieter won't need it."

Cooper continued to pack. "The Russians don't tell us much. But that Auschwitz camp was a lot bigger than he claimed. And, we nabbed him just in time. We think there's an escape route for senior officers. Dieter was a prime candidate to disappear."

Cooper closed his bag and extended a hand. "We weren't good buddies but we got the job done. I'd tell you to visit me in the states but I don't think you'd make the effort."

Stewart forced a smile while thinking back over the weeks with Cooper. "And you would be correct. We were at best…reluctant allies. Good Luck, Major."

Holland, June 20

"Shut her down!" Tim Murphy shouted to be heard over the roar of the engine and waited until the machine coughed and died. "We stripped the armour from a personnel carrier. The beast has lots of power and a single driver can make it work. With a plough attached you'll turn a bunch of furrows. The important thing is to get a crop in the ground."

The farmer nodded in agreement. "Glad to have it. Heavy horses were requisitioned—stolen—by the Germans during the occupation. People talk of mechanized Nazi armies but horses did most of the work."

"Now you won't have to yoke yourself to a plough," Murphy laughed. "This machine took a lot of punishment but conversion to a farm tractor should extend the life span and the army agreed to sell it." In fact, the army didn't know of the sale. Military records would list the vehicle as demolished in an accident. Murphy smiled, patted the roll of cash in his pocket and set off for a meeting with the mayor.

"We've had a profitable relationship," Vanderkirk grinned as the corporal arrived. "I'll miss you."

"The army giveth and the army taketh away." Murphy lit a cigar and took a deep puff. "I was beginning to like Holland but suddenly orders came to move on. Thousands of us are off to Berlin as an army of occupation. I'm not enthralled but at least I wasn't selected for the Pacific. Fighting may go on there for years."

The mayor began to shuffle documents on his desk. "And here the paperwork grows. Many people need new passports or other forms of identification. My signature offers a degree of authenticity."

Murphy glanced at a form and saw space for a name, nationality, date of birth, residence and a line for an official signature. "And this will allow people to travel freely?"

"Eventually police or other government agencies will demand more but this is a start."

Murphy fingered the documents. "You wouldn't miss a dozen or so?"

"A government always provides extra forms."

"Sign a few." He pulled a wad of cash from his pocket and dropped the bills on the desk. "Just a signature. Leave the rest blank. I'll fill them in. A little joke for the men in my unit. I'll tell them it makes them honorary citizens of Holland, a memento of their role in the Liberation."

CHAPTER 13

"**C**UT AWAY DEAD leaves." Colonel Petrenkov was back on attack. "Any plant that wilts must be replaced and the smallest weed removed from the Red Star."

Karin wiped sweat from her eyes before patting the soil. A floral symbol of Communist Russia would greet the world leaders and the display must be perfect. Inside the Potsdam mansion, the Colonel was equally demanding. Furniture was requisitioned and cleaned while the cottages for the Allied leaders were scoured for any hint of dust.

Karin's hands were dirty and her back was sore but it felt good to work with the soil and for the first time in months, she saw no visible evidence of war. The courtyard had been carefully inspected and any damage repaired. "Can we watch as the leaders arrive?" she asked. "From across the street, I mean. I'd like to witness history."

"No, Gretchen." He expected disappointment but she had trained herself to show little emotion. "No, you will be inside as an extra interpreter." She brightened as he continued. "Your presence will demonstrate the equal roles of men and women in the Soviet system."

"It will be an honour."

"You will translate for me alone. And, only when I ask."

"Thank you, Comrade."

"Finish the work quickly. We'll go to the bathhouse. You smell."

Berlin, July 17

Duff Stewart could hardly believe his eyes. "I wasn't prepared for utter devastation. The condition of Berlin is much worse than what I saw of the bombing in London."

An army driver was behind the wheel of a car, confiscated from a Berlin businessman, and carefully avoided damage on the streets. Extra rubble women worked to fill holes and clear routes the leaders would follow to the Potsdam conference. "Churchill and Truman want a tour," the sergeant said. "But if they see one block of destruction, they've seen them all."

"Churchill must be pleased." Stewart rolled down the window but quickly closed it again. The smell of death and decay wafted from the debris. "What did Bomber Harris call it? Ah…yes…de-housing? The bombs were to drive civilians from their homes, ruin morale, and disrupt weapon production."

"But the plan failed." The sergeant slowed to navigate a narrow path between two crumbling apartment blocks. "I drove another Canadian last week, a fellow named Ken Galbraith. He was working on a survey of the bombing results for the American army. Arms production was moved underground. Germans built deep, strong shelters, much better than we had."

"I heard about those factories." Stewart continued to gawk at the destruction. "The production only slowed when the supplies, the fuel, the food and the slaves gave out. But it makes me wonder. Did we go too far? Some this might have been unnecessary. And, we might have saved the lives of a few more men in Bomber Command. Afterall, London was blitzed and the British didn't quit. Why would it be any different with Germany."

"Don't think there was much choice, Sir. We had to hammer the Krauts. Stopping the bombing would have prolonged the war on the ground."

The car picked up speed as the roadway widened. "A word of advice." The driver spoke again. "Take care moving about. There's unexploded ordinance in the debris. Months will pass before it's all disarmed."

He hit the horn to clear a group of children. They dashed aside but turned to pelt the car with rocks and stones. Glancing back, Stewart saw them scurry into the ruins. "Miserable little buggers," the driver said. "Orphans mostly. No parents to supervise them. The kids run amok." He slowed again as a bull dozer pushed wreckage to the shoulder of a street. A half dozen civilians began to scramble over freshly exposed debris.

"People take anything." He pointed to where a man tugged at a bed spring. "An old spring or part of a mattress is better than a bare floor. And, a lucky scavenger turns up a cupboard with a few jars of food. Food comes first, then clothing or household goods. A chunk of metal or a sheet of tin can be traded on the black market or used to plug a hole in what passes for a home."

"It must have been sheer hell during the bombing but Germans had it coming." Stewart starred across the wreckage for several minutes before he spoke again. "An intact house? Or an apartment? There can't be many but how would you find one?"

"Ah, senior officers claim the best. You'll be under canvass to start but once a man gets his bearings and has permission, he can move. Maybe turf a Nazi."

"This canvas, the tent, that will be my new home. It is far from the conference centre?"

"A decent walk and I'd be careful. Carry proper documents and a weapon. Sentries will demand identification. Use the gun to ward off the scum. And, don't think unrepentant fascists are the only threat. The DPs are every bit as bad."

A few blocks away, Evers Chance was beaming. "The amazing British army. A few days on station and an Officers Mess is functioning."

Major General Harley Bennet waved him to a table. "Best of all, one of the privates was a hotel cook."

"Where does he find food, Tiny? Berlin is close to starvation."

"Trucked the essentials in. Liquor too. Have a drink and we'll order lunch."

"I wondered if you might dine with Churchill and Truman." Chance chuckled. "Afterall, the Potsdam summit has opened."

"My company was not requested. Besides, I'm no expert on Poland."

"Yes, a major headache. The London Poles are up in arms, again. Stalin invited their representatives to Moscow and promptly locked them in the Lubyanka Prison. No way to win friends." Chance lifted a pipe from his pocket. "Poland is a lost cause. The Reds have control. Presumably, Moscow prefers extra space between Russian territory and the west."

"A little bird tells me Churchill will give in. Stalin will get what he wants."

"He'll never be satisfied," Chance warned and touched a match to the tobacco. "Russian reparation teams are tearing the city apart. I suppose it's to be expected. The Russians saw their homes destroyed. And, the Allies wanted to turn Germany into nothing but pasture and small farms. Officially, that policy shifted but unofficially nothing appears to have changed."

"We remember Versailles. Younger men don't appreciate how a plan for peace led to another war. And that's the fear in Europe. People fret over food and housing but down the road is the fear of another fight. The general staff, by the way, did quietly scupper the idea of attacking the Soviets."

Chance took a deep puff before he nodded. "That's a relief but have we destroyed what little trust remains among the Allies? And what of the people of Berlin? They're caught in the middle. Think of what's ahead for them."

"We do live in interesting times." Tiny shrugged. "Are you staying for a few days?"

"Yes. I want to locate an associate who opposed Hitler."

"Hah. Good luck finding the true resistance. Most Germans didn't turn against their Fuhrer until the shooting stopped."

Berlin, July 21

"I'll be honest," Duff Stewart confessed. He stood on a curb waiting for the arrival of a victory parade. "I know nothing about press liaison. Hell, I don't often read the papers." His latest assignment had come suddenly. He was to escort a Canadian journalist.

"Ah cheer up. Nothing to it." Todd Aiken, the Ottawa reporter had just begun his assignment in Europe. "Just carry my camera bag and don't set it down. Someone might steal it. By the way, how long have you been here?"

"Only a few days in the city. I came to Europe in January. I've a smattering of the German language and was transferred to an American unit. Interesting work, I could tell you about it. Folks back home would be impressed if my story made the papers."

"Sorry, no. I'm more interested in the big picture. Like today. This victory parade is a public relations exercise. I'll need a fresh angle."

Stewart glanced at a list of units on parade. A select few had been chosen to represent the Allied armies on a march through Central Berlin. "What about something on a pipe band, The Argyll and Sutherland."

"A quick picture maybe but I'll leave a marching band for the motion picture units. Besides the Canadian Argyll's are based in Hamilton. No local Ottawa reader would care." Aiken stepped into the street with his camera as the first contingent marched by. "There." He stepped back to the curb. "Three shots. One of them should do."

He brought the camera back to his eye and surveyed a small group of locals. "Ah, a fetching Fraulein," he whispered, "Low cut blouse, an excellent chest. Wanna a peek?"

"No." Stewart sounded glum. "Non-fraternization edict especially when senior officers are around. We're to ignore the Krauts. Can't get friendly."

"Doesn't apply to a civilian." Aiken let the camera dangle by the strap and lit a cigarette. He smiled at the woman. She stepped closer and spoke German accented English. "I can offer many pleasures."

A smattering of applause distracted them as Winston Churchill and General Bernard Montgomery waved from the rear of a truck. Aiken dropped the cigarette, lifted his camera and snapped a picture. From the corner of his eye, he saw the woman bend to retrieve the tobacco.

"Danka." She offered a broad smile.

"Good Lord, what could I get for a pack?"

"A visit to the infirmary." Stewart laughed. "Who knows what you might catch."

Aiken ignored him and snapped more pictures. "Monty is stealing the show wearing his Desert Rat fatigues and the beret from those heady days of the African campaign. Churchill won't like being upstaged." Another ragged round of applause came from the watching servicemen. "Not much love for Winston." Aiken began to change film. "One would expect a huge ovation for the man who led Britain through the war."

"And the man to lead them in peace. The result from the British election is just days away." Stewart tried to sound well informed. "Churchill must have a lock on Downing Street."

"I wonder? Yesterday the Labour Leader Clement Atlee was inspecting troops and was given a much warmer reception than Churchill."

"Will your next dispatch predict a Labour victory?"

"No, I leave predictions for the opinion pages. Look, I've seen enough. I'll file a story and we can meet later. I'll need a uniformed escort when we go to Potsdam for the conference proper."

"You don't need me today?" Stewart saw the woman was hovering nearby.

"No." Aiken reached and touched her arm. "I'll have someone else show me around."

Stewart watched as the couple moved off and saw the reporter lift a package of cigarettes from his pocket.

"Take a couple," Aiken told the woman. "Payment for your time."

"For a pack, we have regular sex." The words were delivered as if by rote. "Or, I take you in my mouth. The fee is negotiable."

"Quite a price list. Let me think about it. What's your name?"

"Inga."

The woman was very attractive; a pretty face, dark brown hair, vibrant green eyes and an amazing figure.

"Will you show me where you live?" he asked.

"I could, but for what you want, we can use an alley."

"I'm not sure what I want. Would I find a husband at your home?"

"No. I was engaged to a soldier but I haven't heard from him since 1943. The only thing I could do was post his picture at the train station with instructions on how to reach me. He may have been captured by the Russians. The Reds put our men to work."

"I've heard. How do you support yourself?"

"Isn't it obvious." She smiled. "I'm a tobacconist."

"I don't understand."

"Our old currency is worthless. We aren't supposed to use British or American currency so we deal in cigarettes. Wait…" She bent and retrieved another half-smoked remnant from the street. "Some days I make new friends. Sometimes I trade for cigarettes."

"That bakery ahead," Aiken pointed. "I'll buy bread. Maybe we could find a quiet place to eat. And, I would like to see where you live?"

A saucy grin played across her face. "Don't like doing it on the street? Too proud? Afraid of being seen? Most men would be finished and on their way by now."

In his mind, he pictured a naked body and as important a first-person story on life under occupation. "I'm a writer, for a Canadian newspaper. For a carton of cigarettes would you tell me about yourself?"

"Hah. I would be rich."

"And after we eat, show me where you live?"

"It's not much, a bombed-out apartment. I share with a friend. For a few cigarettes she would leave for an hour."

"I can meet that price."

"Better to be off the streets in the evening when the Red Army begins to prowl. The Russians take their pleasure and don't like to pay."

"Rape?"

"Not as much as there was a few weeks ago. The British and Americans most times offer something in return. Perhaps, they have a guilty conscious?"

Stewart had almost given up when Aiken finally appeared in Potsdam the next morning. "Sorry I'm late." The reporter smiled. "Had a busy night."

The three Allied leaders, Winston Churchill, Harry Truman and Joseph Stalin were posing for the cameras. Aiken had dropped to one knee and framed a shot when another photographer bumped against him. "Damn! Watch it." His sharp warning carried across the room.

A grim-faced Russian Colonel was at his side in an instant and pointed to the exit. "One more shot." Aiken quickly took another picture. "Ok. Generalissimo, I'll go."

The Colonel glanced to the soldier at his side and a women's voice said something in Russian. A closer look showed a female body tightly packed into a Red Army uniform.

"I'd like a picture of her," Aiken said as Stewart pushed him from the room. Outside, he leaned against a wall. "I got the shot of the leaders and now know what the Russians are doing. Stalin is photographed from a lower level to make him look taller."

"A bit of artistic licence?"

"The Americans did it too. The Yankee press had an unwritten agreement not to shoot FDR in his wheel chair. But that's history. Do you have today's background?"

Stewart produced the press handouts. "The meeting is formally called 'Terminal'. The public relations staff provided so much material that I could write the story. And, by the way, you could have arrived on time."

"Oh yah," Aiken smiled. "About that. That cigarette girl is a really interesting little item. I'll file on Potsdam but her story offers a much better perspective on the end of the war."

Aiken was late again the next morning and Stewart played reporter, an easy task since the leaders spent most of the time in private meetings. In a matter of hours, the conference would temporarily adjourn. Key members of the British delegation would return to England to witness the election result.

"I'm here, I'm here," Aiken trotted into the court yard. After a check of credentials, he and Stewart moved inside.

"Wow, have I got a story," Aiken whispered. "Inga is really something. A gentleman won't discuss certain things but she's showing me Berlin. She took me to a railway station. The trains from the east are overflowing. Refugees actually ride on the roof. And, when the carriages are unloaded, they find bodies, the dispossessed, dead from disease or outright starvation. Trains stop in the countryside for no apparent reason and Russians or Poles climb aboard to steal what little the refugees have. Yet, despite that, more people come west each day."

"That shouldn't be a surprise," Stewart said as they waited for the public meeting to begin. "The Yalta conference gave part of Poland to the Russians and parts of eastern Germany to Poland. Millions of Germans were ordered out."

The bang of a gavel stopped the conversation and their attention focused on the big three but only a few words could be heard at the back of the room. "This is useless," Aiken spoke softly. "I'll have to wait until a transcript is prepared. All I can do is read the body language. Harry Truman is supposed to be bland and boring but is acting like a cat that swallowed a canary, as if he has a big secret. Joe Stalin is inscrutable. No one knows what he's thinking."

"And Churchill?"

"Distracted. Confused? He rambles on but the other two don't care. Maybe Britain has become a second-rate power."

Stewart glanced about. A few aides, some in uniform and others in suits, stood ready to pass a note to the leaders or offer whispered clarification on technical details. The Russian Colonel waited in the shadows with the young woman at his side. Her huge Red Army head dress was almost comically too large and appeared held in place by a set of tiny ears.

The bang of the gavel brought his attention to the conference table as the three leaders smiled, shook hands and retreated with their delegations. Stalin, stopped to speak with the Colonel, a conversation that lasted only seconds but produced a look of consternation or perhaps fear on the officer's face. He spoke briefly with the woman before following his leader.

Aiken closed his notepad. "I'll make it worthwhile if you stay and pick up a tidbit or two. I'm meeting Inga."

"As long as it's business. I've nothing else to do." As the reporter moved toward the exit, Stewart made his way to a reception area and a table piled with food. He edged forward and found himself standing beside the Russian woman.

"Canada?" She read the badge on his shoulder. "Could you help me, please?"

Stewart was shocked to hear English. "Of course."

"I need help with a translation. I'm not sure what a phrase means."

"For a Russian, your English and accent are perfect."

"I'm not Russian. I'm German. The Colonel orders me to be of service. Can you help?"

"Sure. What's the phrase?"

"Tube Alloys."

In shock, he pretended to concentrate as memories flooded back of the aborted mission and the search for a new weapon. "Odd term. Can you tell me anything more?"

"My colonel heard it somewhere. Could it be American slang?"

Again, he pretended to think and said the first thing that popped into his head. "Actually, more likely English. London's subway is called the Tube and was damaged in the Blitz. The English may have developed a new metal for the repairs."

"Yes, maybe." She seemed satisfied.

"I'm glad to help...Miss..."

"I must go." And, he watched as she rejoined the Colonel.

Several hours later Stewart found himself telling of the encounter for a second and then third time.

"Maybe it's nothing." An American Intelligence Officer tapped his desk. "But I'll run it up the chain of command. Where can we find you?"

"I told you. Control council, Canadian Army of Occupation. I'm supposed to work on civil affairs but was temporarily assigned to press liaison."

"Well, keep your mouth shut, especially around the press. And, let us know if you see this woman again."

Berlin, July 27

Evers Chance lingered over the latest newspaper. The articles told of how British voters rejected Winston Churchill, sent his Conservative party to a crushing defeat and opted instead for a Labour Government and a new Prime Minister, Clement Atlee.

"The political grim reaper visits Mr. Churchill," Major General 'Tiny' Burnett said and manoeuvred his heavy body into a small chair in the officer's mess. "Everyone is surprised except those, who with superb clairvoyance, claim the result was pre-ordained. Which camp are you in?"

"Mark me surprised." Chance folded the paper. "In retrospect, we could argue the British had enough of war and sacrifice. And, Churchill did let his mouth run away on him during the campaign. Comparing Labour activists to the Gestapo was not a smart move."

Tiny signalled for a round of drinks. "My colleagues are already in mourning. Labour will spend on new social programs and not the army. Damn shame. We'd become accustomed to top priority."

The waiter brought two glasses and Tiny offered a toast. "To old times and old friends."

"What happens to you, Tiny? Is retirement an option?"

"Might be. Potsdam puts the lid on Europe. The Russians have their way on Poland and by extension Eastern Europe while at home, the English people no longer feel the need for an old 'Tommy'. Rudyard Kipling was right when he wrote that poem... *It's Tommy this and Tommy that...*"

"...I hate to interpret a recital but I may have work for an old soldier." Chance reached for his pipe. "A different kind of conflict is coming. One that will require more brains than brawn. The game is likely to play out in Berlin. Germany could be a bullwork against a red menace."

"Can't see that. For all intents and purposes Germany is finished."

"Don't be too fast. The country will rebuild. And, I can use men who can assess the future."

"But we've both reached the old fart category. Churchill may engineer a return to power. I'm not so sure about codgers like us."

"Oh, don't say that. We've a few more years. Think about my offer. There's no rush. Give me an answer by year end. Why, we might recruit a few like-minded Germans."

"Not sure about dealing with them either, a little early to kiss and make up."

"Maybe we'll find the 'Good' Germans." Chance rose to leave. "Oh, I need a small favour."

"What do you need?"

"Access to the mess store room."

Evening found Chance on the doorstep of a small house. The neighbourhood had been bombed but the home showed only minimal damage. He rapped several times before a woman appeared. "I'm looking for Otto Von Ronstadt," he told her.

"Not here." She began to close the door.

"I'm an old acquaintance." He stuck his foot in the doorjamb. "I won't claim to be a friend but we did business together when he was in intelligence, in the Abwehr. I haven't seen him since 1941."

"You won't find him." She kicked at his foot.

"Wait." He raised a small bag. "I've brought food. Are you, his wife?"

"No."

Chance passed her the bag. "A bit of cheese and a bottle of Schnapps. Otto liked Schnapps."

Her resistance weakened and she waved him inside. "I don't know much. My father rarely spoke of his work."

"We were both in the import-export business and since we were on different sides the relationship was—confidential."

"You are English?"

"English by birth. Canadian by choice."

"A long way from home. Why did you come?"

"Otto helped me once." Chance began, "We…uh…spirited a woman to safety. She's my wife now. I owe him. What he did took great courage."

"Not everyone would agree," she frowned. "He was condemned as a traitor in '44."

"Condemned." Chance steadied himself on the arm of a couch. "Good Lord. Is he dead? I thought he would be clever enough to escape them. I knew him as a proud German—not a Nazi. What happened?"

"The bomb plot against the Fuhrer. I'm not sure he was involved but everyone was under suspicion. They shot him. Others were hung or killed by guillotine. The party had so many victims it needed to speed the execution process." Chance struggled to control the chill that swept his body. "His superior, Admiral Canaris, was arrested at same time. He was alive until April and then they hung him."

"Canaris dead too?" Chance found it hard to believe.

"Hitler and those around him took steps to eliminate any opposition even at the end."

"And were they successful?"

"Who knows? More people claimed to be anti-fascist when the shooting stopped and a few German Communists sat out the war in Moscow. A couple of them came to see me."

"Why? Otto was no communist."

"From their questions, I believe they were looking for what the Fuhrer called 'wonder weapons', the rockets and powerful new bombs."

"New bombs? What would that be?" Chance asked.

"I don't know. I like to think my father worked at a more cerebral level and not on the schemes hatched by Hitler's inner circle."

"Hmm. I agree. Otto wouldn't support mass murder."

Berlin, July 28

Karin wore the full-dress Russian uniform and was waiting when Zev arrived. The routine was well established, a silent drive to the conference in Potsdam. Except for today.

"You are no longer needed." He appeared nervous and spoke quickly. "The Colonel has new orders and must return to Moscow. Remove the uniform. I am to return it to the supply depot. You may be summoned later."

"This is strange. Will we be joining the Colonel in his new assignment?"

"For a smart woman you can be very stupid. We must hope we are not ordered to join him."

A few miles away, Duff Stewart was also confused.

"Tell me again," the US Army Intelligence officer ordered.

"My story hasn't changed. The woman asked for the translation of 'Tube Alloys' and I told her it might be a reference to the London subway."

"How much did Major Cooper tell you last spring."

"Cooper didn't tell anyone much of anything."

The intelligence officer grunted and studied a paper on his desk. "The story checks out. All kinds of agents were in the field this spring. That woman? Had you seen her before?"

"Only at the conference. I think she was an assistant to the fellow who appeared to be in charge."

"That's interesting too. We think the Colonel is Russian Secret police, the NKVD, probably a political officer or former Commissar. You saw him speak with Stalin. Was there an order? A simple request? Then a few minutes later the woman asks for help."

Stewart plucked a cigarette from his pocket, waited for the superior to nod approval and struck a match. "Maybe she was honestly struggling with the translation."

"But you said her English was excellent?"

"Tube alloys doesn't appear in most dictionaries."

"We'll let you in on a secret. American scientists have created a new weapon, a single bomb that can destroy an entire city. Americans use the code word 'Manhattan' but the British prefer 'Tube Alloys'."

"That doesn't help much."

"Ok." The intelligence officer grudgingly continued. "The Germans were working on the same idea. That's why the Berlin mission was ordered. At the Potsdam conference, President Truman told Joe Stalin about the success of our experiments. Truman was excited and expected Stalin would be too, except Uncle Joe didn't react, almost as if he knew of our secret. And then, this woman mentions Tube Alloys."

Stewart dropped the cigarette and ground it under his boot. "That's an interesting story. I can't wait to hear the next chapter."

"Don't get smart. That new bomb will be put to use in the next few days. The Japanese were warned as part of the Potsdam declaration."

"What does this have to do with me?"

"I'm not sure but we're bringing you back into the American Intelligence operation. The Control Commission can wait."

For Karin the hours passed slowly. Her few possessions were packed into a battered cardboard suitcase. Inside was the fur coat, a few other pieces of clothing and the medal, the Iron Cross collected from the Fuhrer's headquarters.

A shout came from the main portion of the cellar. "Don't come in here. We've no room."

A man's voice replied, "I am looking for Karin Werner."

"You must mean the Russian whore."

Angry, Karin jerked the cloth door open. "That Russian whore arranged for extra food for this shelter. I don't recall a complaint about that." The words were met by an icy silence from the other cellar occupants.

"Karin?" The stranger didn't appear to have washed in months. His clothes were a mixture of army and civilian castoffs and he carried a small sack. "Do you remember me? Heinrich Steinbergen, your grandfather's estate manager."

A flood of memories returned. Heinrich who found time for her and her cousins, willing to supervise their adventures and willing to forgive when other adults demanded punishment, and the man who kept the estate intact when her grandfather died. She threw her arms around him and spoke through tears. "I didn't think anyone was left."

He had aged, badly. Beneath the dirt were deep worry lines and eyes that had seen too much. "I had your address from when Greta came to visit. I haven't heard from her or Lotte."

"Both gone, I think. They were in Dresden, when the Allies launched the fire-terror attack. I've heard nothing."

For Heinrich, the words were another blow. "The three girls, so full of life. And only one left. Ahh…"

"Come and sit." She led him into her room. "A train ride in these days must be tiring."

"I walked." He pointed to his shoes. One was intact, the other a leather sole held to his foot with a thin cord. "Life is hard. The Russians came in waves. Our buildings were ransacked and what wasn't stolen was burned." Anger rose in his voice. "They are pigs! Murderers! Larissa was Russian, one of our foreign workers. She was raped, again and again until—they killed her. Aah. These are terrible times."

She shuddered but felt no real shock. "So, you came west?"

"Nothing to stay for. The Reds divided the estate. The land now belongs to the masses. And, I needed to find you. I tried to tell Greta but she wouldn't listen. Your grandfather left papers with me." He began to burrow in the sack until he produced a document.

Karin recognized her grandfathers handwriting, a big awkward scrawl, and over his signature the words, "*The bearer of this note, on presentation of the password, will claim the inheritance.*"

"What does this mean?"

"I hoped you would know." Heinrich sat on the mattress. "He had something hidden in Switzerland. He never trusted the Nazis, especially after the business with his prize horse."

"Horse? Oh, yes." A few words jogged Karin's memory. "The animal taken by a party official."

"Yes, and he didn't trust German banks so he borrowed money from a local Jew and felt he was treated fairly. The Jew had connections in Switzerland."

She saw his eyes begin to close.

"Rest," she told him. "We'll talk later."

It was several hours before he stirred. At first, he struggled to remember where he was but the sight of Karin brought relief. "I must go." He rose slowly. "A cousin lives near the Black Forest. I'll work with him."

"Stay until morning. Sunrise is an hour away. I've been thinking and have a few questions. When did Grandfather go to Switzerland?"

"Oh," Heinrich rapped his knuckles on his head. "The years blend together but before the war, maybe 1938."

"Did he tell you anything more?"

"No. His health was failing and he was often confused. He transferred ownership of the estate to Greta and her husband. Although, he didn't trust that husband, such a devoted Nazi."

Karin sighed. "In looking back, we all thought we were superior, exceptional. Afterall, we were the master race."

Heinrich shook his head in disgust. "I know what our men did. The Russians took revenge. Our people were killed or driven off."

"And those left, struggle to survive." She touched her battered suitcase. "I should go too."

"Come with me." The Heinrich she remembered; the faithful family servant re-emerged.

"That's kind. But no." Karin helped him to his feet.

"Be careful." He warned. "Hitler promised to bring order and look what we got. No one knows what will happen next. Ahh. Life can be a bitch." Gently, he touched her cheek. "Good luck, child."

Heinrich was gone only minutes when Zev returned. He wore a rumpled civilian suit, evidence of the end of a Red Army career. "I came to warn you."

The old fears instantly returned. At least with the Russians she was protected.

"The Colonel was sent to Moscow," he told her, "in handcuffs. Higher authorities believe him corrupted by western influence. An accusation is all that is necessary. He will be condemned as an enemy of the people."

"That's nonsense. He was dedicated to the revolution."

"He taught you well." Zev shook his head in amazement. "A German girl who bought the party line. Twice. First with Nazis and then the Reds. And both let you down." He paused and considered his next words. "The men who arrested the Colonel will look into his past and search for present associates. I'm afraid, the Colonel has no future."

"I've done nothing."

"That doesn't matter. Your role is minor but you may be a convenient target. They may ask—who was she really working for? Did she provide more than raw sexual pleasure? And then, they'll learn he never made the conquest."

"…Wait. You saw him that night."

"The Colonel was a bad actor. He had the desire but a German shell took away the capability. I knew the campaign wife, his woman during the war. He couldn't perform. They'll interrogate her."

"But I thought…"

"…And were wrong. But enough of this. I'm about to disappear. You should too."

CHAPTER 14

DUFF STEWART SAT on the edge of a bunk, one of a dozen beds in a makeshift army barracks. Under the canvass roof, the summer heat of Berlin was oppressive. And privacy did not exist.

"Why so glum?" Todd Aiken had arrived unannounced. "Not a smile. Nothing." The reporter bent to peer into his eyes. "It's no way to treat a friend with good news."

"Oh, I could use good news." Stewart rose abruptly, almost forcing Aiken off balance. "Talk to me."

"I've met a man with a line on accommodation. And, he knows you. Guy by the name of Murphy. He's in the transportation division and has fond memories of the two of you in action or to be honest— avoiding action."

"Murphy? In Berlin?"

"Yah. A bit of a wheeler-dealer. He's only been here a few weeks and already has his finger on the pulse of the city."

"That sounds like him. Tell me about this accommodation."

"He has a list of undamaged apartments. All you have to do is convince the present occupant to move out. He'll show you tomorrow. That's if you can cast off the depression."

"Ok!" Stewart brightened. "But I can't talk about my other problems. If I did, Intelligence might lock me away. Well, that's sounds more dire than it is but an issue has surfaced and I'm ordered to keep mum. Perhaps, in a few days I can explain. But not yet."

"Make it fast. I'm going home soon. Another few weeks and I'll be back in Canada."

"Aren't you lucky. What happens to the woman?"

"Hah! Inga and I have a good time but there's no long-term commitment. I'll give her something before I leave."

"Like what—a bun in the oven?"

"Duff. Don't be such a pessimist. Medics give out condoms, for free."

The next day Stewart, Aiken, and Corporal Tim Murphy stood in front of a small apartment building.

"I've a unit for myself and there's another at the back," Murphy told them. "Franz, who owns the building, wants to stay on good terms with the occupation army. He evicted a family this morning to open more space. The apartments are small but furnished. Move in tonight if you want. Although, first, I'd hire a woman to clean. The Russians were here before they moved to their zone and those men didn't understand indoor toilets."

"And we thought our farm boys and outdoor privies were backward." Aiken laughed.

Stewart grimaced but the chance to leave the tent was too good to pass up. "Let's take a look?"

"Hold on a minute," Murphy said and pointed to a man coming toward them, a former Wehrmacht soldier, who walked with the aid of a cane.

"Watch." Murphy whispered and stepped into his path. The man froze, unsure of what was to come. "I'm on the sidewalk," Murphy spoke in German, "Out of my way."

The soldier scowled but stepped off the curb. Only the skillful use of the cane saved him from a fall. "In the future, give way to an Allied soldier," Murphy warned before mounting the steps to the apartment building. "That's a trick I learned from Americans," he whispered. "Show the Krauts who is boss."

Inside, the hallway was dark. Heavy light fixtures hung from the ceiling but the bulbs were missing. Murphy pointed to the empty sockets. "Russians took them. Those peasants were impressed by steady light. Wait till they get home and find bulbs need electricity before they glow."

Despite the poor light Stewart could see the outline of a hall and stairway. The building appeared intact.

"Franz!" Murphy shouted. "Get your ass down here. Meet a new tenant."

"I'll move in a few days." Stewart decided. "It can't be any worse than living in a tent. I'll have more time when the conference wraps up and that's likely to be soon."

"The Potsdam conference isn't accomplishing much?" Murphy asked.

"Officially, there's minor progress, agreements on what to do with the Far East, Indochina and Korea. If I'm right, we'll never hear of those regions again. Of the other issues, a lot of talk. The Russians continue to press for a bigger share of reparations which appears to extend to anything they see."

Berlin, July 29

Karin spent a final night in the basement shelter but sleep was impossible. Waiting fearfully for the sound of Russian boots was as bad as the fretful nights of falling bombs.

"I will give up my room if anyone has something to trade," she quietly told the cellar dwellers the next morning.

"Who wants to live in a coal bin?" An older woman asked.

"The room has a measure of privacy. I've cleaned the dust. The mattress is soft."

"But stained with Russian semen."

Karin ignored the insult. "I've seen the butcher knife in your boot. Give me that and the China teapot. You get the room. I'll throw in a few Reichsmarks."

"Worthless currency won't do much. How many do you have?"

"Only a hundred but they're yours."

The woman could think of nothing else of value. "It's a deal."

Two hours later Karin bargained in the Tiergarten. All that remained of the statues, stately trees, and manicured paths in the once famous park were smashed pedestals and ragged stumps. The open areas were transformed to a bustling black market, frequented by the occupied and the occupiers.

Her battered suitcase was traded for a backpack and an army jacket. She convinced a British soldier the teapot was a rare ceramic treasure, worth at least at pound; sold the Iron Cross to an American before exchanging his dollars for a blanket and rubber groundsheet. Then, she repacked and began to move toward the rural areas in the west.

The road was filled with streams of people moving in both directions. East, in search of homes and relatives or west for the perceived safety of the British or American zones. Many carried a bag, or a suitcase and a few pushed baby carriages or wheelbarrows loaded with what little was left. Families and small groups stayed together and watched any stranger with suspicion or outright hostility.

The pockets of the new jacket held her small cache of food. To cope with summer heat, she stole a pair of athletic shorts from an unguarded clothesline, changed clothes, and carefully stored the woollen trousers in the backpack. That night she treasured the blanket and the ground sheet that kept moisture at bay.

The next day, a country priest took pity as Karin joined a line for soup and bread. "Do you have a place to stay?"

"No." She confessed.

"A parishioner needs help on her farm. A man would not be proper. Her husband may yet return from the army. She couldn't pay but would offer food and shelter."

Karin accepted. The women made few demands and provided a small shed for shelter. The work was outdoors, manual labour with a shovel and fork. A forest behind the cottage opened onto a small valley and a shallow river where she was able to bath at the end of the work day. Compared with the past few months, life was almost idyllic.

Near Berlin, August 4

With the end of the Potsdam conference, the official delegations left Berlin. There was no sign of the Russian Colonel or his interpreter and as the trail grew cold, intelligence officers found other work for the Canadian. The Americans kept Duff Stewart under their control as if afraid he might expose some well-kept secret.

"This is another stupid assignment." He kicked at the ground and sent dust flying.

"Quit the bitching." Captain James Quimby, the officer in command, dismissed the complaint. The squad was to search an open field and the burned-out shell of an army barracks. Under the occupation agreements, the Russians would soon take control of the area."

"What are we supposed to find?" Stewart asked. "The farmer up the road said this was a recreation facility."

"But we're not so sure." The captain unrolled a map. "It may have been a test site for poison gas."

"Any gas didn't hurt the bugs." Stewart swatted at a persistent fly. "And, the vegetation looks normal. Gas experiments should have stunted the trees." He lifted a set of binoculars to survey the property. "What kind of gas? Mustard, chlorine? Stuff from the First War?"

"No. Something more lethal. We collared a few scientists but haven't found actual supplies."

"Can't those men tell us where to look?"

"No. Their work was formulas and equations." Quimby rolled the map and stuffed it in his pack. "Dirty, dangerous production was relegated to lesser mortals, the slave labour. But we've got the brain trust. Eventually we'll learn the secrets."

"Captain!" A soldier yelled, "We've hit something." Quimby and Stewart cautiously walked toward the commotion.

"Ok, I was prepared for this." Quimby whistled and waved toward a van parked across the field. Two men emerged. Both were dressed in heavy rubberized suits, wore gas masks and carried rods and shovels. They approached slowly and tapped their rods into the ground before beginning to dig. "Cannisters, steel drums," one called, "I'll ease one open."

Stewart looked for an escape route and decided the open field facing a river was the safest option.

The specialist tenderly pried on the lid. Suddenly he rose, waved and shouted but the words were smothered by layers of protective shielding. He tried again after lifting the mask. "Shit! Human excrement. The cannisters must have come from a latrine. A recreation centre would have toilets."

"Ah for Christ's sake." Quimby threw his hands in the air. Stewart turned to hide his laughter but in facing the river saw a figure on the opposite bank.

He lifted the binoculars. "Captain. Better take a look."

Quimby took the glasses and in seconds began to chuckle. "Hah...Hah. A woman, a pretty blonde. Oh, she's turned her back, a shapely butt and fine muscular legs but she's getting dressed. Too bad sport, she looked better without the trousers." And, he passed the glasses back.

Stewart raised them in time to see the woman button a shirt and set a soft army forage cap on her head. Only as the hat settled around her ears, did he recognize the Russian interpreter. He began to run toward the river and waved his revolver. "Captain! That's the woman we've been looking for."

Stewart watched from a window as the prisoner was escorted from the cells the next morning. She was blindfolded, handcuffed and guided by the rough hands of a guard.

"Go sit in the corner and let me do the talking," Quimby ordered. The door opened and Karin stumbled into the interrogation room. The guard tugged at the knot to remove the blindfold. She was forced into a chair, her hands still cuffed, a harsh light aimed at her face.

"Name!" Quimby demanded.

For a few seconds, she was silent and then…"Karin Werner."

"Nationality."

"German."

"But you speak English and Russian and German."

"I went to school."

"Where…Moscow?"

"No. Berlin."

"An odd course of language study?"

"It was a good school." Her answers sounded flippant but she showed no sign of deceit.

"Why did you run yesterday?" Quimby demanded.

"A soldier was chasing me. He had a gun."

"Why were you watching our operation?"

"I wasn't. I went to bathe."

Quimby turned aside to savour the memory of her naked body and let it play in his mind before he spoke again. "We'd been looking for you and the Russian Colonel." Now, her face showed surprise. "We find it odd," Quimby continued, "…appearing with the Russian at Potsdam and days later posing as a common labourer. Care to explain?"

"I was trying to get away," she answered. "I was told I was in danger."

"From who?"

"Russians."

"Maybe we should ask the Colonel?"

"He'll be hard to find. He's been arrested and sent back to Moscow."

Quimby glanced at Stewart. Both were surprised by her answer and by her readiness to talk.

"And how did you know him?"

And in the next few minutes she told her story—of the fall of Berlin, Petrenkov's arrival, the reparation team, and the Potsdam conference.

"Do you remember me?" Stewart stepped from the shadows and saw her eyes shift from his face to the badge on his shoulder.

"Canada. At the conference. I asked for help in translation?"

"Why did you ask about Tube Alloys?"

"Because of the strange words. The Colonel wanted an exact translation. And, I had heard it before when the Russians were clearing the Kaiser Wilhelm Institute."

Stewart tried to contain his excitement. "When was that?"

"Right after the occupation. They spent hours at the Institute and collected boxes of files." She paused. "Is that what this is about?"

"I think…that's enough for now." Quimby cut the interrogation short. "We'll continue later." He turned to the guard. "Has she been thoroughly searched?"

"Oh, they looked everywhere?" Karin displayed a first hint of anger. "Up, down and inside, places in my body where I would never hide anything. And, I didn't need a delousing. I keep clean."

When she was gone, Quimby sorted through her belongings and gingerly lifted the knife from her pack. "Wouldn't want to tangle with her in a dark alley."

"She could be innocent," Stewart suggested. "She wasn't the only woman in Berlin who took up with a Russian to protect herself. But we now know the Russians were aware of this new bomb. In fact, they know more than I do."

"The whole world will soon know." Quimby glanced at his watch. "We're waiting for the President to make the official announcement.

The weapon has been used against Japan and the result is amazing. A single bomb destroyed a whole city. One gigantic bang has opened a whole new world of warfare."

Paris, August 6

Evers Chance glanced at the Canadian newspaper. It predicted the Prime Minister, Mackenzie King would win a by-election, allowing him to continue in office. The voters in the Eastern Ontario riding of Glengarry appeared certain to approve but Chance suspected the victory would be overshadowed by the announcement from American President.

He turned and leaned over the consul watching the radio engineer at work. "Can you find the broadcast? Truman is on a warship on the Atlantic, off Newfoundland."

"Don't worry. The quality may be less than optimal but we'll hear him."

"Relax." Maria laughed, "Besides, I suspect you've an idea on what's to be said."

"I've heard a few hints," Chance smiled. "After months of silence a few military leaders are starting to talk."

"It's coming through," the engineer adjusted the dials to fine tune the signal and the voice of Harry Truman broke through the static.

A few hours ago, an American airplane dropped one bomb, on Hiroshima an important Japanese Army base. That bomb had more power than twenty thousand tons of T.N.T.

Chance whistled and began to take notes.

It was an atomic bomb, a harnessing of the basic power of the universe. The source from which the sun draws power has been loosed against those who brought war to the Far East.

"So, the Japanese are finished?" Maria guessed.

"They were finished well before this bomb." Chance made another notation. "Tokyo sent feelers through Moscow asking for peace terms. I don't know how the Russians responded but as with Germany, the British and Americans demand unconditional surrender."

He studied the radio set as if he could picture the President and stiffened as Truman praised the co-operation of British and American scientists but hinted technical details would remain under American control. "The ultimate weapon," Chance said, "And, the implication is clear. The new bomb could be used against Soviet cities as it was in Hiroshima. I suppose that is why Truman appeared so cock sure at Potsdam. He has the upper hand in future negotiations with the Russians. He holds the big stick."

"Shouldn't we be pleased?" Maria asked. "The Americans are allies. British scientists were involved. Surely, we're in this together."

"I'm not so sure. The Americans like to throw their weight around. And, the Soviets won't stand idly by. Their scientists and Germans, recruited or forced into the communist operations, will work to create a Russian bomb. Plus, based on their past performance, the Russians will have agents inside Allied facilities. They may already know part of the secret."

Berlin, August 7

Duff Stewart watched as the prisoner was led across the courtyard. Again, a blindfold, handcuffs and the awkward march to the interrogation room, where the contents of her backpack were displayed on a table.

"Quite a collection," Captain Quimby ran his finger along the blade of the knife. "This weapon alone would lead to an arrest."

"I needed protection," Karin spoke softly.

Quimby shook the fur coat and unleashed a cloud of dust. "This must have been expensive?"

"No. The Nazi welfare office supplied it after the terror bombings destroyed my other clothes."

"Don't call them terror bombings." Quimby's voice rose. "Air raids were a legitimate act of war." Karin opened her mouth to respond but changed her mind. Instead, she watched as the American moved along the table and lifted the document written by her grandfather. "What's this? Money stolen by the Third Reich?"

"No…no. Before the war, my grandfather transferred something to Switzerland."

"Oh, come now. I'm not dumb. More likely Nazi funds or a secret stash from the Russian?"

"I'm telling the truth."

"Bull!" Quimby reached and cupped her chin. "Who was paying you?"

"No one. My grandfather was trying to keep the money for the family."

"I don't believe you. Maybe a few more days in the prison compound will improve your memory."

Her eyes showed first confusion and then a hint of fear. Stewart hadn't noticed the eyes before. A striking pale blue and misty as if she was near tears.

"Put her with the general population," Quimby ordered. "Give her a glimpse of the future."

"That's harsh," Stewart said after she was led away. "The yard is full of riff raff. Political dissidents are trouble enough but a few prisoners are outright criminals."

"Don't let her mislead you," Quimby warned. "The story about the funds in Switzerland doesn't stack up." He glanced through the window where the prisoner and escort were returning to the compound. "But we've been wondering about Nazi cash. Maybe we can find a way to use her."

That evening Karin sat on a rough bench against the stockade wall. Many of the other prisoners wore the striped pyjamas supplied in German camps. Food and medical care were a higher priority than clothing.

"The sun feels good." A young woman took a seat at the opposite end of the bench. In contrast to other prisoners, she obviously cared about her appearance. She smoothed her hair before she asked, "What are you in for?"

"I don't know." Karin answered, "I don't think there's a formal charge."

"The Allied talk of the sanctity of their justice system is laughable. Reality falls short. I'm Inga, by the way, as if names matter. I was arrested when I refused to put out for a French officer?"

"And what is the punishment?"

"Time in this rat hole. But I shouldn't complain. Others have it worse, like soldiers conscripted for labour. At least Germans sent to Great Britain are working on farms and will be fed. Thousands of our men in France or Russia have no shelter and little food. Compared to them we have it good. And, this barracks was disinfected. I wouldn't want to sleep in the straw used by vermin infested Jews."

"Was this a camp for Jews?" Karin asked.

"Weren't they all?"

"I...I...don't know? I never really thought much about them. Most Jews seemed to disappear."

"Oh, they disappeared all right. But don't play coy with me. I'm not an informer. Feigning innocence isn't necessary."

"But I don't know where they went."

"What? You didn't notice when Jewish-owned shops were closed, or men and women appeared with big yellow stars on their clothes, or when those same people...disappeared?"

Karin shook her head. "I didn't pay attention. I believed what our leaders said. Jews were to be relocated. I though perhaps to Poland."

For a moment Inga was silent. "An excellent ruse, I suppose. Was your head under a bucket? Was war a mere inconvenience?"

"We all suffered." Karin frowned. "The nightly air raids, friends and family killed, homes destroyed, the search for food."

"Ah, poor thing? Next, you'll claim to be part of the resistance. Did you paint Anti-Nazi slogans on walls at night? Did you hide a red sympathizer or save someone from the Gestapo? The British and Americans will eat it up until someone says no, she was a good little Nazi and faithful to the end." Inga shook her head in disgust.

"Don't you understand. We'll pay for our sins, including the sin of looking the other way or following orders or doing what everyone else was doing."

Karin abruptly rose to leave but Inga wasn't finished.

"Tough to hear, isn't it? I don't think our lives will ever return to normal. Is normal letting a soldier have his way? Is normal looking for a safe place to sleep? Maybe a 'holy joe' westerner will lead us to a promised land…maybe…"

Paris, August 11

Maria woke to a gentle nudge on her shoulder. Chance stood beside the bed, a broad smile across his face. "The war is ending. The Americans dropped another atomic bomb on the Japanese city of Nagasaki."

She quickly shook off the dregs of sleep. "We knew it was coming but I'm so glad the end is in sight."

"The Japanese were crushed these last few months. Fire bombing, atomic weapons and the Red Army has invaded Manchuria. Stalin wants his share of the Far Eastern booty. The formal surrender can only be days away."

She patted the bed and he sat beside her. "No more great cause," she said. "We can put our personal lives back together."

"Won't you find it dull?"

"If sleeping soundly at night and not fearing attacks by day is dull, bring on the boredom. But how will our lives change? We've been in this since 1939."

"A few things need to be done." Chance began to consider their options. "I'd suggest a war loss claim for your property at Le Havre. But a decision could take years. In the meantime, Europe will rebuild. That too will take years but with the right people, in the right places, we can speed the process. After I've trained new men, I can take a background role with the firm."

He brushed a strand of hair from her face. "Unless, you run the European office? A woman might have fresh insights."

"No." She didn't need time to think. "If we have the financial means, I'd like to spend the time with you."

"I hoped you would feel that way. Will we stay in Europe or return to Canada?"

"Canada would be much more comfortable." She rose and began to dress. "But you'll want to see what happens here and…" Her voice trailed off and she shook her head. "Listen to us. We've talking about the private concerns of two people when thousands of souls have just been wiped from the face of the earth. We only think of them as the enemy, as if they had no value, no wives or husbands, no children, no friends. What have we become? We're no better than a pack of wolves."

Chance reached and took her hand. "You are right. Compassion was another casualty of the war. Six years has hardened everyone. I wonder if we'll fully recover our humanity."

CHAPTER 15

TIM MURPHY PROVIDED the alcohol for a victory party in his Berlin apartment. His army friends overflowed the rooms and spilled down the hall to Duff Stewart's recently acquired lodging. Electricity had not been restored but a wind-up phonograph produced music. Couples danced or drunkenly swayed in a make-believe ballroom.

"That boy knows how to have a good time." Todd Aiken watched as Murphy lost his balance and fell to a couch, taking his latest partner with him. The woman recovered and lifted herself across his legs while she drank from the neck of a champagne bottle.

Aiken laughed. "Ottawa will seem very provincial after this."

"When do you leave?" Duff Stewart asked but saw the reporter was distracted. The woman had tossed the bottle aside to give Murphy her full attention. "Murph," Stewart hissed, "The bedroom would offer a bit of privacy."

"Yah. Ok." Murphy lifted her in a bear hug and staggered across the room. "Won't be long," he called and slammed the bedroom door.

"We missed the Victory in Europe party," Aiken poured a measure of whiskey. "We'll make up for it tonight. V.J. Day, Victory over Japan, will be a grand old time."

"When do you leave?" Stewart asked again. He was now torn between waiting for the answer and watching an army nurse dance on a table.

"Next week. I'm to do a story on one of the first ships to carry the troops home plus a series on the occupation. It will be an eye opener. But don't worry. I'll change the names to protect the innocent. If I'm right, the story will cause a sensation."

"What is happening in Canada?" Stewart asked. "I haven't paid much attention."

"Ha. The latest is a communication foul up. The Prime Minister recorded a message for release when the Japs surrendered and someone messed up. King's broadcast went out a day early. The man responsible will be looking for a new job."

The dancing nurse had attracted a growing audience of male admirers as inch by inch she raised her skirt.

Murphy sheepishly returned, alone. "My strumpet passed out. What a waste of good booze." He lurched across the room, found an opener and snapped the cap on a bottle of beer. "Gentlemen. This is a party. Behave accordingly."

"Are you expecting to be transferred home?" Stewart asked him.

"No rush." Murphy tipped the bottle to his mouth. "The government promises to cushion the return to civilian life but I'm in no hurry to find a paying job."

"Assuming jobs can be found," Aiken cautioned. "The big thinkers fear a return to depression, a repeat of the dirty 30s."

"Another reason I'm in no hurry." Murphy lit a cigarette. "And, government programs sound good until we read the fine print. I'll make extra cash here and now. I learned the basics in Holland. I'll perfect the game in Berlin."

"I wonder how front-line soldiers will adapt to civilian life." Aiken's eyes returned to the nurse. The dress had reached mid thigh.

"A lot of our boys knew only their local society before the war. They've seen a whole new world."

"Yah." Stewart topped up his glass. "European culture is certainly different and some of their new acquittances, the DPs, don't leave a good impression."

"An eye opener for sure," Aiken nodded. "Most of the rank-and-file will be fine when they get home. Although, how can we expect men to flip a switch and return to the role of a peaceful, God-fearing civilian overnight? Or, for that matter to think for themselves. The army will no longer be telling them what to do. And some have untreated and unseen wounds…psychological damage."

"Is that what this expose will tackle?" Stewart was curious. "The dark side of victory and occupation? The black market? The good, the bad and the ugly? And don't worry Murph. He's assured me he'll change the names…"

"…I doze want my name in any newspaper." Murphy's words had begun to slur but his intent was clear.

Aiken smiled. "You've been a big help. I won't forget. I'll protect Duff too. Although, I'll bet he knows more than he lets on. He spends a lot of time with those intelligence officers."

Berlin, August 16

Karin sensed the change when the guard failed to produce a blindfold and for the first time, she crossed the compound without handcuffs. In the interrogation room, Captain Quimby smiled as if welcoming an old friend. "Take a seat. I've ordered coffee and thought we'd chat before Stewart arrives."

She walked slowly to a table where three chairs had been placed.

"Cigarette?" Quimby placed a pack in front of her. As he turned aside, she slipped one into her mouth and several more into her pocket. She struck a match and took a slow drag before Quimby turned to face her. "The prison compound is full of seedy characters.

We wondered if a communist agent might try to reach you. But the Reds have lost interest, probably bigger fish to fry."

She waited silently, wondering what was to come.

"Lieutenant Stewart believes you did nothing any other young woman in Germany might have done. The Russians were...well... beastly...when the Red Army first arrived. Hospitals need assembly lines for abortions and female complications. We'll also see a bumper crop of Russo-German babies in a few months. I shudder to think of what's ahead for those poor little bastards."

Karin maintained her silence. Eventually, like the Russian, he would get to the point.

Quimby lit a cigarette, held the match and stared at the flame. "And, no one cares about 'Tube Alloys' anymore. That secret is out. I'm sure you've heard of the Atomic Bomb. The explosions in Japan make what happened here look like child's play." He gently waved the match until the flame died.

Word of the new weapon had caused barely a stir in the prison compound. She had decided death and destruction were the same, from one big blast or from thousands of smaller explosions. And, she had never been sure what to make of Hitler's eastern allies, what he had called 'Honorary Aryans'.

"We do have another project." Quimby was coming to the point and Karin wasn't sure whether to be pleased, frightened, or merely suspicious.

"That mysterious deposit in a Swiss bank. We're interested in that." He signalled to a guard. "Send the Lieutenant in."

Stewart arrived a minute later and slipped into the chair beside Karin. Quimby cleared his throat before he continued. "Lieutenant Stewart will escort you to Zurich to search for this account. We'll provide a list of major banks and arrange appointments. Many Germans have been making the trip in recent months so it won't appear out of the ordinary. But we'll want to know everything you learn."

"That's it?" It sounded much too simple.

Quimby offered a thin smile. "A measure of trust will be required. In exchange for co-operation, we'll drop all charges."

"I didn't know I was charged with anything."

"You will be if you don't co-operate. And don't get the idea of disappearing. The final bargain won't be sealed until you return to Berlin."

"And then?"

"Up to you. We could seize assets obtained by criminal activity. However, you claim this…inheritance…is legitimate so eventually it would revert to you."

"Eventually?" Her eye brows rose.

"War time conditions, the occupation, a backlog in the courts. Everything moves slowly. We might arrange a job with a small stipend while you wait."

"And what does he do?" She pointed to Stewart.

"Not a totally unpleasant assignment. He watches you."

"And if I refuse?"

"Winter will be very cold."

CHAPTER 16

CAPTAIN QUIMBY HAD been unable to arrange air transport so Karin joined Stewart and an army private on a long drive across southern Germany. She tried to avoid conversation and instead starred silently at the passing countryside. Only a few farmers worked the fields and she suspected the country would be desperate for food in the months ahead.

At one point the car slowed where a road repair crew worked to fill bomb craters. "The autobahns were the best highways in the world." Karin broke her silence. "And look at the damage."

Disarmed German soldiers in faded Wehrmacht uniforms worked in the hot sun. Cars and jeeps with American markings were parked nearby but there was no heavy mechanized equipment. Instead, former soldiers worked with shovels and wheel barrows and Karin watched in shock as a 'coloured' supervisor waved their car forward.

The driver began to snicker. "For those Germans the face of the master race is now black. The Yankees are sticking it to them by putting a coloured in charge. The Krauts are too dumb to know

Americans will only tolerate the Negro for certain jobs. The US army is segregated. Mixing races is verboten."

"Is that true?" Karin whispered to Stewart.

"In most cases, yes." He told her, "Their constitution says all men are created equal but white men rule the roost."

"What about the British and the Canadians?"

"The Brits see coloured, of any hue, as what's called 'The White Man's Burden'. British officials must steer them on the right course. That may change though. The colonies could become independent as Canada already is."

"In Canada, do you have segregation?"

Stewart thought for a moment and studied the tall black soldier on the roadside. "Not officially but I suppose we do. Black soldiers served in our army and native Indians were in the ranks. Probably they faced great risk. Your Nazi friends had a special hate for non-whites. But with the end of the war things are likely to revert to the old ways back home. Anyone who isn't white has a hard road to travel."

"So, Germans weren't alone in seeking racial purity?" Karin too studied the guards. "Perhaps the west isn't as perfect as we're led to believe."

"That's probably true. But I like to think we're more subtle in dealing with the issue."

Hours later the driver stopped outside a small, well-kept Zurich Hotel. "This is the address, Lieutenant. My billet is a few blocks away but I'll be available if needed." He set two suitcases on the sidewalk and pointedly turned his back on Karin.

"Thank you, Private." Duff Stewart nodded. "We'll manage."

Karin found herself staring at the surroundings. Ordinary people were going about ordinary lives and there was little sign of the damage that scarred Germany.

"The war only came to Switzerland, by mistake." Stewart tried again to make conversation. "The Battle of Zurich. American bombers were off course, way off course, and dropped a payload on the city. Aside from that, it's been quiet. A perfect climate for the spies and secret agents who took advantage of Swiss neutrality during the war."

She didn't respond and instead thought of what lay ahead. Makeup, new dresses, a hat and shoes, material that would have cost a fortune for a refugee, had been supplied by the Americans. Two pair of nylon stockings were already packed away and would be sold when she returned to Berlin. "I prefer bare legs," she had lied to Stewart, "Nylon irritates my skin."

"Private Sadler." Stewart stepped to the driver's door. "I know Murphy assigned other chores but Miss Werner's mission takes priority. Keep that in mind."

"Oh, I will Sir. And do be careful. I've had my fill of Krauts since we landed in Normandy. I lost a lot of friends fighting in the Schelte. No German can be trusted."

As the car moved off Stewart returned to Karin. "The private had a bitter experience. His unit was shot up pretty bad in Holland. I've an old friend in the motor pool who is trying to help. He thought a change of scenery might do some good."

"Isn't that noble." Karin showed no sympathy but as they moved toward the hotel began to regret her tone. The Lieutenant couldn't be blamed for all that had happened.

Stewart grabbed her shoulder and spun her to face him. "The ground rules. Adjoining rooms and I'll have the key. I'll lock you in at the first sign of any trouble."

"I understand."

"And tomorrow, we'll start with the banks. From the length of the list, it will take a several days. For my benefit, all conversation in English. I'll be in civilian clothes. You might introduce me as…"

"…Don't worry Lieutenant. I'll think of something. And, I'm sorry. I don't mean to always sound rude."

By the next morning she had become a refined woman of postwar Europe.

The short blonde hair was neatly curled under a broad summer hat. Light red lipstick supplied a touch of colour while a hint of mascara accented the blue eyes. The knee length dress revealed shapely, if bare, legs.

"Miss Werner?" The bank clerk was impressed.

"I am." She extended a hand. White silk gloves covered the bruises and cuts from her summer work. "This is my cousin, Hans. He's from Canada, just demobilized." She glanced to see Stewart tug at his tie. "He's not yet comfortable in civilian dress."

He acknowledged Stewart and guided Karin to a chair. She primly folded one leg over the other while the banker returned to a seat behind the desk. "This concerns your—grandfather?"

"Yes. He passed away before the war and the record of a deposit only surfaced recently. Our property was in the Russian zone. I fear the land is lost."

"Ah, the Communists. We hear similar accounts. Is there any chance, your grandfather or his executors, made other deposits? Germans have brought considerable sums in the last few months."

"No. I believe this was a single transaction."

"I must ask and I apologize in advance but do you have Jewish relatives?"

"Oh no! Definitely not."

"I only ask because we did open accounts for..." He paused, searching for the right word, "...Hebrews. The Nuremberg laws made it difficult for them to function in Germany. Funds were left with us as families waited for foreign governments to approve emigration. That rarely happened and many of those families have...uh...well... disappeared."

"What does this have to do with me?"

"I mention it only to illustrate the complications facing a bank. It's difficult to establish proof of identity, determine next of kin, that sort of thing. We can't hand over funds without proper documentation. However, in your case, it won't matter. I've checked. We have no record of any account."

"I see." Karin contained her disappointment and rose to leave, "Thank you for your time."

"Excuse me?" Stewart spoke for the first time. "What if no one claims the money or a claim is denied?"

"That's unlikely but we'd keep the funds under administration."

"The bank would keep the money?"

"That's a bit harsh…but…yes."

As they walked toward the next meeting, Stewart asked a question. "Does it strike you that banking is extremely profitable? Millions of dollars could be hidden in their vaults."

"Be careful, Lieutenant. Questioning banks makes you sound socialist or worse yet, communist. I'm not sure you would progress in the army if word got out."

"I must learn to keep my theories to myself." Stewart smiled. "I was impressed by your…performance. Maybe we'll have more success at the next appointment." But they didn't.

Later, a quiet lunch at an outdoor café passed in silence. Karin picked at her food while Stewart made a series of notes. "Intriguing," he said when the coffee arrived. "The Nazi hierarchy were trying to protect their booty and what better place to store it than Switzerland. And, not only cash. Gold or other valuables are likely hidden and protected by a wall of secrecy. Think of the artworks looted from across Europe."

"My grandfather wasn't the type to collect paintings."

"No, I suppose not." He folded his notes. "We should move on. Bankers end their day at mid afternoon."

The executive at the next meeting, wasted no time.

"I'm sorry, Frau Werner. We have no record of any deposit. Could it have been mixed with National Socialist funds?"

"Oh no," Karin answered. "Grandfather always supported the Social Democrats. In fact, he used to say the Nazis shouldn't be called Socialists. There was nothing Socialist in their policies."

"But what if there had been a link to the Nazis?" Stewart interrupted.

"Today that could be a problem," the banker admitted. "We're being very cautious. But normally we didn't ask the source of funds. That's a government or a police function."

"Even if money came from criminal activity?"

"Define criminal? A year ago, even a few months ago, any German could open an account, a normal business transaction. We weren't equipped to assess a client's background."

"What now?" Stewart asked as they left the meeting. "Do you want an early dinner?"

"No. This will sound odd but I saw a brochure at the hotel advertising a local beach. I would really like to swim and enjoy the sun. I avoided beaches in Berlin this summer. Too many people were finding bodies in the water."

"Humm…I'm not a swimmer but I'll see what I can arrange."

Karin laughed as she left the water and returned to where Stewart waited. "Wonderful, thank you."

"I'm glad you enjoyed it." A quick word with the hotel concierge and the swim suit and towels had appeared. A tight-fitting suit showed her body to perfection.

"I'm like an old farmer." She rubbed a towel through her hair. "My face, and hands are tanned but the rest of me is as white as snow. It wasn't always this way. Summers were spent outdoors at Grandfather's estate and in the BDM, we were often biking or hiking."

"What's the BDM?"

"Oh, of course you wouldn't know. The League of German Maidens. I suppose it might be described as a female wing of Hitler Youth." She smiled at the memory. "I shouldn't reminisce of those days but it seemed innocent fun at the time. The young men stayed at a separate campground a mile or more away. We Germans are very proper."

"Did you live with your grandfather when you were younger?" Stewart asked and spread a towel for her to sit."

"In the summer and at the holidays. The rest of my time was spent at a boarding school. My parents died when I was very young but I was close to my cousins."

"And where are they?"

Her smile faded. "Dresden. I've heard nothing since the fire raid."

"I'm sorry. Perhaps we should concentrate on good times."

After a moment, her tentative smile returned. "Well, at school, we had parties and dances. With boys."

"And, you studied languages, in addition to boys?"

This time she laughed, a gentle, pleasant sound before she grew serious. "I worked at the Foreign Ministry for a short time, until there was a problem, a boy problem or, actually a man, an SS officer, very efficient and very officious. He wanted me to produce a baby for Hitler and when I refused, I was moved to another job. The party encouraged those unions, especially for those of us with a Nordic appearance. The children were to grow to manhood and fill the ranks of future Aryan armies."

"We've heard similar stories," he told her. "Blonde, blue eyed, Nordic boys were kidnapped in the occupied territories and brought to Germany to be raised by a local family. Again, men for the armies of the future. Unfortunately, if the boys didn't adapt to their new homes they were euthanized." He saw the shock on her face and she turned to stare across the lake.

A full minute passed before she spoke. "We hear so many rumours and so little proof. I've reached the point where I only accept what I know to be true. It was the same during the war. I had to concentrate on my job. I worked outside the home even though the Fuhrer believed in 'Kinder, Kuche, Kirche."

Stewart shook his head in surprise. "The KKK?"

"In English—children, kitchen, church," she explained. "A woman's place was with children in the home and the party was the religion."

"In North America KKK has a much different meaning." Stewart rose and shook the sand from his towel. "So, Hitler wanted women domesticated. Our armed forces found work for the fairer sex. And not making Churchill babies."

This time her chuckle was deeper and the evening sun bathed her face.

"You know most of my story," she said. "What about you? Did you always plan to be a soldier?"

"Oh no. I'm a lover not a fighter, a dedicated civilian." He spread the towel and sat beside her. "I'm supposed to be a civil administrator, making arrangements for reliable electricity, clean water, and so on. Somehow, probably because of my rudimentary German, I was moved to an intelligence unit. But for the life of me, I don't see how army service will help when I'm demobilized."

"Will that be soon?"

"Not soon enough."

"Is someone waiting?" she asked.

This time Stewart laughed. "No. I had friends but nothing serious." Images from that past flashed though his mind. The woman beside him would put them to shame—if it wasn't for her Nazi past. "What about you?" he asked, only mildly curious. "Anyone special in your life?"

"No." She shrugged. "And, no burning ambitions."

"Hmm…well…that makes two of us. And we should go. We've another full day tomorrow."

Ottawa, August 24

"Aiken, welcome back." Despite the greeting the managing editor appeared tense and annoyed. "The publisher wants a few words. He's taking a bigger role in editorial policy." Aiken was surprised by the quiet of the newsroom. More desks were empty than when he left for Europe. "Where is everyone?"

"The boss fired a half dozen reporters," Bert Thompson told him. "He didn't want to appear cheap during the war but now he's decided to retrench. This city, for example, is awash in public servants. If those jobs were to disappear fewer men would buy a daily paper. He's prepared."

"Did he consider spending more? With better writing and more aggressive reporting the *Sentinel-Guardian* could become indispensable."

"Too much competition for that to work. Years could go by before we catch up with other papers. "

"I thought with the articles from Europe, we might step up our game."

"You thought wrong. Our publisher believes local stories are the wave of the future; society columns, charity events, features on gardening, positive reports after years of bad news. And brace yourself. He's not happy about what you wrote."

"Ah, the prodigal returns." The publisher greeted Aiken with a sour smile. "Lots of copy to justify the expense of the trip but frightfully negative."

"I'm not sure what you mean."

"What about the contribution of the brave men and women in the armed forces? Hundreds of thousands fought to create a better world. No one would know that based on these articles."

"That's not fair." Aiken tried to keep the anger from his voice. "I gave full marks to the fighting men."

"Fighting men. Fighting among themselves. I felt the V.E. Day riots in Halifax last May were given far too much play. And so, I don't need to read of our boys rioting in England."

"Soldiers are upset over slow demobilization. Wives can see the war has ended and the children are asking—when can daddy come home?"

"Balderdash!" The publisher's voice rose. "The army is speeding the process. The shortage of shipping space will disappear with the Japanese surrender. A few drunken malcontents, who took to the streets of England's Aldershot, should be ignored."

"Those men have legitimate grievances…"

"Those men will live like kings when they get home. I don't agree but the Liberal gang on the Hill are moving toward a socialist utopia. Special grants, housing incentives, money for higher education—despite the fact that a whack of those veterans didn't pass grade eight."

"Did you read all the articles?" Aiken asked. "I wrote them as a series."

"Parts of it work. That victory parade in Berlin, with our swashbuckling heroes marching in triumph. That's the tone I expected. And, keep the story on that little German wench, that uh…" He glanced at the typewritten page for the name "…Inga. Let people see what comes from following the wrong leader. You were quite sympathetic to her, the hardship, looking for food, flaunting her body." The publisher tapped his fingers on the desk. "I hope the expenses don't include a hidden bill for personal services."

"No, Sir. They do not."

"Good then. Now, this army of occupation. I was taken aback by the references to the black market and corruption. I ran it by a friend, a retired staff officer who assures me, the situation can be nothing like what you describe. We might have an odd bad apple but don't implicate the whole army."

"I understand that. Most men are following the rules. Regulations like no fraternization made their lives difficult. They aren't supposed to get close to the Germans and most don't. But not everyone follows the rules."

"People don't need to read about that. At one point, I planned to syndicate this series but other papers won't touch it. Too damn negative. Re-write."

"And if I refuse?"

"Lots of reporters are looking for work. The door to the street is across the newsroom and down the stairs."

Zurich, August 25

"We saved the most impressive for last." Stewart gawked at the marble arches and vaulted ceiling of a bank reception hall. "I should have worn formal attire."

Karin went to find a bank employee. "We're to wait," she said when she returned. "I don't have high hopes. I'm afraid this trip will end in failure, at least for me. Did you get what you wanted?"

"I have uncollaborated suspicions. Millions of dollars flowed into these banks but a brigade of accountants with full access to the books would be hard pressed to prove much. Although, I'm sure the Allies will try."

"Frau Werner." A secretary approached. "Mr. Hofstetter will see you." She led them to a private office and made the brief introductions.

"I've reviewed your letter." Hofstetter didn't stand and instead rudely remained seated behind a large polished wooden desk. "We're a large institution, dealing with influential clients and very large accounts." He scratched at a note pad and pushed the paper across the desk. "Unless, you believe the deposit is in this range, we wouldn't have dealt with it."

The figure was enormous. "No," she told him, "Grandfather didn't have that much money."

"To be thorough, I did order a review of our records. We have nothing connected to this man."

"I had to check." Karin's face showed her disappointment.

"And I won't make suggestions on where else to look. Our banks have been reviewing policies and will be much more discrete discussing business in the future." Hofstetter turned to Stewart. "The Allied governments are obviously interested in our activity. My fellow bankers tell me you raised many questions about the operations."

"What are you suggesting?"

"That the Allies shouldn't be snooping in Zurich." He turned back to Karin. "The questions this 'cousin' raised were a little obvious. He was fishing for corruption. I wonder if this 'grandfather' existed."

"Oh, I assure you he did!"

"Well, he never did business with this bank. My secretary will see you out."

When they reached the main entrance, the secretary spoke quietly. "Mr. Hofstetter can be difficult but I know of another place to look. There's a man who runs a small investment firm. He had German clients."

Unlike the banks, the entrance to the next office was up a dingy stairway to a room littered with books and papers. A single table lamp illuminated the workspace.

The lawyer, Conrad Levine, listened patiently and Karin presented the document from her grandfather. He studied the note before rising, moved to a cabinet and thumbed through files. "1938 was a difficult year. Business was bad." He retrieved a file and returned to the desk. "But I remember that man."

Karin took a deep breath.

"Gentiles didn't often do business with Jews," Levine explained. "But your relative was referred by a friend, who, like me, was Jewish. I remember the conversation. Your grandfather didn't trust Nazis or their banks. We came to an agreement and I collected a fee that probably saved my business. The money was invested overseas. At that time, the best returns were in Canada."

Karin gasped. "So, it's real. I don't mean to sound greedy but... what's the value."

"I'd have to contact an associate in Toronto but the amount should be substantial. However, we're getting ahead of ourselves. Your grandfather suspected attempts would be made to seize the money. He believed the world was full of dishonest, disreputable people and created a special code, a password."

"Yes, that's in the note."

"And do you know what that is?"

"I think I do. He had one possession that he lost and talked about—a lot; a prize animal taken by a party functionary. A horse, a magnificent and valuable stallion. Stallions can be very temperamental but that horse was gentle. I rode him bareback."

"Obviously, a pleasant memory." Levine leaned back in his chair. "But I haven't heard the proper words."

Karin began to smile. "Opa, Grandfather, named the stallion after a Prussian King, Frederick the Great. The horse was called Old Fritz." She leaned forward. "Is that the password? Old Fritz?"

"Frau Werner." Levine too shifted forward. "You are to become a wealthy young woman."

Karin beamed. She heard Stewart whisper, "Congratulations." His hand rested lightly on her shoulder and she reached to pat his fingers.

"There are legal steps," Levine told them. "And these things take time. If you give me an address, I can forward the details."

Her joy evaporated. "I don't have a home or an address. Berlin is in shambles…"

"I have an address." Stewart began to scratch out the details. "Send a message to me. I'll keep in touch with Karin."

"Will that work?" she asked.

"It's unusual," Levine answered. "But these are unusual times."

The next morning Private Sadler met them at the hotel and saluted Stewart, now back in army uniform. "Sit in the back. I'll put the bags up front. The trunk is full of Murphy's supplies." Sadler had spent the days in Zurich haggling over the value of jewellery brought from Berlin and with cash in hand filled replacement orders for luxury items that were almost impossible to obtain in Germany.

"You should be pleased," Stewart whispered to Karin as the car moved into traffic. "And if the inheritance is in North America, the authorities in Berlin may not have a claim."

Without thinking she squeezed his hand. "I am pleased but the inheritance is an ocean away and as the lawyer said, everything takes time."

Sadler was intent on making speed and the Mercedes flew toward the border. Karin dropped off to sleep, her head slipping to Stewart's shoulder. He shifted to give her full support and closed his own eyes. They both woke as the driver stomped on the brakes for the border checkpoint.

"I'll handle everything." Sadler glanced at his watch. "One of Murphy's associates is on duty." He sprang from the car and approached an armed guard. The border routine, the review of documents and the search of the car were replaced by a nod when Sadler presented a thick envelope.

CHAPTER 17

"**T**HOSE LITTLE JAPANESE fellows are nicely dressed." Todd Aiken pointed to the picture of the Tokyo surrender ceremony in the previous day's newspaper. "All decked out in formal wear. With the Americans in army and navy garb, a fellow could be forgiven for wondering which side was more militaristic. A big story though. I'm surprised there was no special edition."

"The boss wasn't going to spring for overtime on Labour Day," the managing editor grumbled. "The story may be a day late but it's important. The dawn of a peace." He slashed a line from the copy destined for the next edition. "The Allied armies have the power to snuff out any future conflict before it starts."

Aiken began to flip through a newspaper. "That's assuming the Allies agree. Russians are hard to deal with. I had that in one of my articles from Berlin, another story that was killed."

"That wasn't my decision. And, I went to bat to save your job. The publisher was ready to show you the door."

"I do have to thank you. Reporters are not in as much demand as

I hoped. The other papers have no openings so the *Sentinel-Guardian* will continue to be my home. I'm looking for a new apartment and have a line on a place on Somerset. That's walking distance to the office so I'd be available on short notice."

Aiken's new home was a small apartment. A single bedroom, bath, kitchen and a tiny living room. "It's small," the building manager, Billy Preston, confessed. "But better than a rooming house. And the natives are friendly. Every week the men play cards. You should join us."

Aiken inspected the rooms, flushed the toilet, opened the cupboard doors, ran a finger through the accumulated dust and walked to the window to look to the street below.

"Everyone knows everyone in the neighbourhood." Preston joined him at the window. "That fellow coming up the street is a rarity, a Russian, who works at the Soviet Embassy. Nice enough fellow for a foreigner, I guess. Name is Igor. His English isn't that good so we don't talk much."

Aiken turned from the window and surveyed the living room. "These rooms will do nicely. I've been in Europe the last few weeks. Soldiers and DPs raise all kinds of hell. I could use peace and quiet."

"Well, this is Ottawa. You're in the right place."

Saturday night the men gathered for poker. The conversation was as Aiken expected. A man complained of his wife's spending. Sports fans were pleased with the recent performance of the football Rough Riders and a civil servant fretted over his salary. Only when the landlord began to speak did Aiken pay attention.

"So, Igor Gow…zink…cow, I can't pronounce those foreign names, apparently wants to defect from the Soviet Union," Billy Preston said and shuffled the cards. "The other day he comes out of the embassy loaded down with secret documents. He should have gone to Aiken's paper. They'll print anything." He chuckled and winked, "But no, he goes to the *Journal*. Reporters are on deadline and don't give him the time of day. He goes to government offices, wants to see a senior minister, St. Laurent, but Louis is too busy." The players arranged their cards as Preston continued. "So, he comes home to the little apartment on Somerset, collects the pregnant wife and kid and wanders the capital to find anyone who will listen. Finally, he finds someone who believes him. A few hours later, Russians break down the door of Igor's apartment but the family is gone. I think the Royal Canadian Mounted Police took them."

"Two cards," a player called. "Sounds like a movie plot."

"Three." Aiken grimaced at his hand. "What about the documents. What were they?"

"Nobody knows." Preston took a pair for himself. "Maybe a reporter could find out more? What do you say Aiken?"

"I'm folding." He tossed the cards on the table. "As to this... Russkie. I'll make a few calls."

It was several days before he found time to chase the story. The enquiries met official silence until he talked off the record to a senior civil servant. "The censors have the story locked down. I'd be careful, the guy could be a simple nut case."

"But he wants to defect?" Aiken grasped for anything.

"I guess. He was going to be sent home and didn't like the thought of returning to Moscow, especially after sampling the good life in the west. I gotta go."

"Wait. What about the files?"

"I didn't say anything about files."

"He must have brought something to bargain with. I saw him on the street a week or so ago. A neighbour pointed him out. We don't have many 'Reds' in Ottawa."

"Maybe more than we know. I'm guessing but maybe he had something about the A bomb."

"The files must be important if the RCMP grabbed him and..."

"Sorry pal. Can't help on this one."

Berlin, September 7

The return journey from Zurich had been extended by a car breakdown and Stewart had been a perfect gentleman as they waited for repairs. Once back in Berlin he gave Karin permission to keep the new clothes and repeated the hint of a future job with the occupation forces. But he'd been distracted by the arrival of the Transport Corporal Murphy and a hurried conversation over the goods packed in the car. "Be careful, Murph." She heard him say. "Don't get in too deep and keep me out of it."

When Stewart left Murphy turned to Karin. "No where to go?"

"No." She felt Stewart might have helped but had been reluctant to ask.

"I know a place but lodging can be expensive."

She shivered as Murphy silently appraised her body. "Not that!" She told him, "But I have two pair of nylon stockings. What are they worth?"

He did a quick mental calculation. "Maybe a week."

The room had a rickety bed, a dirty mattress and the view through a cracked window was of skeletal facades of bomb-damaged tenements. But the door was strong and the roof appeared intact. She changed into her Russian workpants and shirt and began an inventory of her possessions.

She'd keep the best clothes and shoes and thought Murphy might exchange the other dresses for a few more weeks of shelter. As her hand swept across the soft texture of the fur coat, she feared it too might have to be bartered. Her fingers traced the outline of an earlier patch where the lining had bunched into tiny hard pellets. A minor repair would increase the value.

She pulled at the yarn, working with her teeth until the thread broke and several small stones spilled to the floor. When she re-examined the collar, she saw someone had inserted a thin sleeve and filled it with what appeared to be gems. Carefully she counted, adding each precious piece to the growing pile and counted again. The total came to twenty-five.

An hour later, in the frenzy of the black market at the Tiergarten, Karin moved slowly, finally stopping by a man with a half dozen watches displayed on a foot stool. "I need a jeweller," she told him.

"Jeweller? Watch maker? All the same. Want a great deal ?" He reached under the stool and added another time piece to the display."

"No, I have a gem. I need to know what it's worth."

"I'd have to see it?"

Karin hesitated but unwrapped a single stone from a handkerchief and only then thought how small it looked.

"Probably a glass trinket," the watch maker offered a quick opinion. "Not worth much, maybe half a cigarette."

"I hoped for more."

"Doubt it." He raised the stone for a better view. "These things look like diamonds but shatter at the slightest blow." He reached under a makeshift counter and lifted a hammer. "I'll hit it but if breaks it's not worth anything."

But as he raised the tool someone yelled, "Stop!"

Karin turned to look for the speaker.

"Take it elsewhere, Gretchen. The hammer would smash a diamond. He'd steal the fragments." A thick beard covered the speaker's face. The hair was dirty and dishevelled. Only the eyes were familiar. "Zev?"

"Collect the bobble. I know a real jeweller." Taken by surprise, she followed him to the street. "I didn't recognize you?"

"The Russians were looking for me. But while I've been hiding you appear to have lived well."

"I was picked up by the Americans. There were questions about Colonel Petrenkov."

"Questions the Colonel can no longer answer." His voice was flat. The implication was clear. "Since you are free the Allies must have lost interest?"

"I guess." She hesitated for a moment. "No one asked about you. Maybe the Americans didn't realize you were involved?"

"Then leave it that way. I have an associate, a real jeweller, who has just arrived from Paris. He was lucky. He found a building that wasn't badly damaged."

Inside the shop, a clerk waved a greeting. "Zev forgets his manners. We should be introduced. I'm Saul Bornstein."

"Call her Gretchen." Zev cut the conversation short. "She has a jewel to appraise."

Again, she unfolded the handkerchief. Bornstein reached for a small eye piece and slowly examined the gem. "A delicate cut. Done by a master." He examined it again under a lamp. "It is a diamond. It might have been dismantled from a necklace, or a broach. I'd need more time to determine the value. Can you leave it with me?"

"He can be trusted." Zev assured her. "He works with a Jewish relief organization but has long experience as a jeweller."

"How long would it take?" Karin asked.

"I have other jobs. Probably a couple of weeks."

Ottawa, September 10

"Aiken, give it up. You're flogging a dead horse. That's an order from the managing editor."

"But isn't it odd?" The reporter leaned over the desk. "Igor Gouzenko has vanished."

"People disappear all the time." Bert Thompson flipped through the morning edition of a rival paper. "Maybe the Russian wanted to ditch his family."

"No. The wife and kid are gone too. The Mounties have them… somewhere. The Prime Minister would be informed of a diplomatic defection. And, senior staff should have been told but for some reason, King is dealing with this himself. The police, by the way, have warned my neighbours not to talk. No one wants to admit the Red existed."

"Find another story."

"But aren't you curious?" Aiken lit a cigarette before he answered his own question. "The atomic bomb. That must be it. Maybe the

Russians are trying to find how it works. Or maybe they have spies digging into…"

"…Oh, get a grip. We love the Soviets, gallant allies and all that. King thinks Joe Stalin is his best friend. A few years ago, I might have followed your line of reasoning but after their war effort? No. We're allies. We're buddies."

"But what if…"

"Aiken drop it." Thompson rose to check the latest headlines from the national news wire teleprinters. "The big story this week is going to be jobs. President Truman has been on American radio. He won't propose a 'New Deal' in the FDR mode, instead, a more modest 'Fair Deal'. But, anything to do with jobs could affect Canada. We need new employment as war time jobs end."

"What if they don't end?" Aitken stepped closer to be heard over the clatter of the teletypes. "The military contractors have tasted prosperity. Business can use those rich tax relief schemes as they've done for the last six years. The more men kept in the forces the fewer the number of unemployed."

Thompson ripped a sheet from the wire and returned to his seat. "I think you're wrong. Canada eliminated a whole raft of positions when programs like the Commonwealth Air Training Program ended. That affected servicemen and civilian contractors. And women, who kept factories humming, are being let go. Unemployment, my friend, can be cruel. No jobs, no money."

"But the government has money. Taxes have been high over the last few years and government borrowing has become acceptable. The way to avoid another depression is to spend like hell. Consumers cash their victory bonds and the government borrows. I'll bet the civil service mandarins have learned how to spend."

The St. Lawrence River, September 16
The strains of a hymn from a small church carried in the late summer

air and mixed with the soft murmur of waves on a breakwater. A tiny village was in Sunday repose.

"Blissful, isn't it?" Vincent Russel lifted his hat and let the breeze stir his hair. "But if the seaway project goes ahead this village will disappear, swamped by an economic tidal wave. Still, look at the plus side. An expanded seaway will mean larger ships and as important, abundant hydro electric power, a Godsend for Northern New York and Eastern Ontario. A battlefield from the War of 1812 will be flooded along with villages like Aultsville but only local people will care."

"Have you decided who will pay for this economic miracle?" Bert Wiley had opened his army tunic to counter the heat from the sun. "Truman is in the White House. Unlike FDR, he's not likely to jump on huge projects. Canada might have to go it alone."

"Washington and Ottawa have bickered over seaway financing for years," Russel reminded his American associate. "Everyone agrees on the benefits. Both countries are starving for electricity and everything from iron ore to grain could be shipped from the Great Lakes and across the Atlantic. Washington does want a bigger share of international trade."

Wiley yawned. He hadn't slept well on the train and felt the journey was a waste of time. "Don't expect America to cut a cheque," he warned. "We've bigger issues. Europe is a basket case. And the first of our people are only now assessing the situation in Japan. Plus, we've entered the atomic age. Scientists may have new ideas on power production. Maybe we won't need hydro."

"Be a shame if there were more delays." Russel pointed to the river and the line of ships waiting to enter the aging locks. "The locals have heard so much about expansion that property values near the river have dropped. No one buys land that will be flooded. But imagine those bigger locks and bigger ships. And, think of the commissions for people like us who set up the contracts. Could be a whole new line of business for you and me, maybe a new company?"

"It may come but not as fast as you might like. The United States controls the bomb. It will be ten years or more before any other country can duplicate that achievement. In the meantime, America calls the tune." Wiley paused. He wasn't sure how much Russel knew. "Unlike our allies we're careful with secrets. Washington has asked the news industry to back away from stories dealing with atomic energy. And, these rumours of a network of spies makes us wonder if Canada shares our concern over secrecy."

"It's one man and he's not really a spy or so I'm told."

"Spy, defector, turncoat. It reflects badly on national security. And, for the record, sharing the details of the atomic process with other countries is not going to happen."

"But American scientists are pushing for open access."

"Not going to happen!" Wiley repeated and fastened his tunic. "Besides, we've more to learn. The A bomb killed thousands and destroyed Hiroshima and Nagasaki but we're only now learning of something called residual radiation. The Japs who arrived after the blast are coming down with a sickness our scientists didn't expect. The Japanese will be unwitting lab rats."

"I'm not sure I like the sound of this," Russel shook his head.

"Vincent, best if everyone accepts American leadership. We're the only ones capable of making the changes the world needs." He began to leave but suddenly turned back. "I almost forget. My army contacts say that Stewart fellow is doing an admirable job. As I recall you weren't impressed by his earlier work. Just shows how people can change when given a challenge. Of course, if you're thinking of a creating a new business, he'd be out in the cold."

"I was only thinking out loud. It's too early to make any hard and fast decisions."

Berlin, September 17

"My God, she's back in fatigues." Captain Quimby shook his head in disgust. Karin had been summoned for a meeting and sat in the waiting area dressed in rough army clothing. "We spent good money on the wardrobe."

"Maybe she sold the dresses," Duff Stewart suggested. "Living conditions for civilians leave a lot to be desired. Most Germans have no steady income. That's why I suggested taking her on as a translator."

"And that's not going to happen until we know more about her past and she's gone through the whole de-Nazification process. She's an excellent candidate for this new questionnaire, on her life story, what German's call—the Fragebogen."

"That survey has over a hundred questions." Stewart shook his head in disgust. "She might fill it out but weeks will pass before the answers can be assessed. We need translators now."

"Lieutenant, we did not fight a war to reward the enemy with government jobs. That survey will identify problem cases. But I may cut her some slack. She did co-operate on the Zurich trip. Shame you didn't learn more. We're hearing amazing stories of Nazi loot. But, let's get this started. We'll go to the projection room."

Karin smiled as Stewart entered the room but her face tightened on the appearance of Quimby. The captain took a seat and began the interview. "A few questions before we can consider a security clearance. For a start, were you a Nazi party member?"

"I was part of the BDM, the League of German Maidens, but I never joined the party."

"And why not?"

"I didn't feel it my place. Men belonged to the party."

"Do you still support the Fuhrer and his policies?"

"Of course not. He's dead."

"What if I told you, he was alive," Quimby said and watched for her reaction. "That he escaped by submarine to South America."

"I'd say you were wrong. He's dead."

"How can you be so sure?"

"I was there when the Russians recovered his body."

Quimby's jaw dropped as Karin continued. "Hitler Kaput. That's what the Russians said. The remains were in an ammunition box. I didn't see the body only the box."

"Why haven't you told us this before?"

"No one asked. Besides, the Russians claimed I didn't see what I know I saw. They want the world to believe he survived but I don't know why. Maybe to keep the west on edge, the fear of a Nazi resurgence?"

"Let's take a break." He signalled to Stewart and the two men left the room. "Had you heard that?" Quimby demanded.

"No."

"Does she lie…much?"

"I don't think so."

"Leave her for a few minutes. I'm going to make a phone call. Men above my pay grade may be interested in this."

A full hour passed before they returned and Quimby began to thread a projector. "We may have more questions later but my superiors believe Hitler is dead and like it that way. So, first things first. Kill the lights and start the film, Lieutenant."

Images of a political rally flashed on the screen with Adolf Hitler cheered by ardent supporters before the scene shifted to what the narrator described as Ukraine. Men and women were forced to the edge of a pit, where a German soldier fired a bullet into the back of each head and the body was kicked into a mass grave. Over the next hour the screen erupted with graphic battle scenes, grainy images of executions, bodies in the snow and eventually the liberation of the camps. The camera lingered on closeups of the dead and of the living who were all but dead, until in the final scenes a bulldozer pushed bodies into a pit.

"Well?" Quimby asked and switched on the lights.

Karin took the time to consider her answer. "During the war we went to the movies and had to watch the newsreels. I wondered if we were told the full story. And watching this, I see skillful propaganda. The film maker obviously learned from the work of Dr. Goebbels."

"Propaganda? Do you think this is Allied propaganda, that the scenes were staged?"

"I see the work of a skilled film maker and the picture failed to answer a number of questions. Why were people sent to the camps in the first place? Or, what if many deaths stemmed not from execution but from a lack of food or medicine. We had very little at the end. Ask anyone. Perhaps that's why so many died."

"That's preposterous!" Quimby was on the verge of rage. "The film was the truth. Innocents were victims of outright murder. Your countrymen are murderous bastards!"

Karin took a deep breath. "We all suffered. But prison camps are created for a reason."

"What about the ovens and mass cremations?"

"For health reasons, bodies had to be disposed of quickly."

"You don't believe that crimes were committed?"

"Oh, there may have been crimes but most of us didn't see the camps."

"Nonsense. You must have known what was happening." Quimby clenched his fists in frustration. "Prisoners on the streets in every city were literally worked to death. Did you look the other way?"

"I suppose I did. I'm not proud of that. But, don't be too sanctimonious. German soldiers are being held in camps today or are being used for forced labour, for slave labour. Is that Allied decency? And what about the Japanese who were imprisoned in Canada and the US?"

"Karin." Stewart slipped into a chair beside her. "Our internment facilities provided ample food and shelter. I saw the camps in Europe. Thousands of men and women were dead or dying."

"That may be but many of us did not know. Do all of you know everything your leaders ordered?"

"Do they all think that way?" Quimby asked when Karin was gone, "An entire nation with its head in the sand?"

Stewart began to rewind the film. "Maybe she needs time. These revelations must be a shock for those not intimately involved."

"Bull shit!" Quimby shook his head in disgust. "They knew! It shows how much work we have to do. Call it de-Nazification or re-education. Years will pass before we root out this poison."

The film had a greater impact than Karin admitted. Too many soldiers had whispered of the horrors of the war. Too many prisoners clearing streets had been little more than walking skeletons and too many Germans who opposed the regime had, like the Jews, disappeared.

The film was fresh in her mind when she kept her appointment with the jeweller. "Welcome." Saul Bronstein smiled a greeting. "I've had time to study the diamond. The gem is high quality. I assume you want to sell it."

"I do need money. And there is more than one stone."

"Hmm. I wondered. The diamond appears to be from jewellery, a piece that was dismantled. The complete set would be very valuable. May I ask where you found them?"

Karin made the instant decision to trust him. "In a fur coat, sewn into the collar."

Bronstein showed no surprise. "Expensive jewellery might be confiscated—stolen. A piece could be taken apart and individual stones would be easier to hide. A woman could carry a small fortune and escape detection."

"But why give up the coat without removing the diamonds?"

"Where did you get it?"

"From the welfare office. After the bombings, I needed clothing." Karin's mind flashed to the day in the shop. "The attendant said the coat was a shipment from somewhere in Poland…ows…something…"

"Auschwitz?"

"Yes. That's it."

Bronstein turned away and a full minute passed before he was able to speak. "It was one of the death camps where Jews were sent—by the train load. Imagine the scene. Days crammed in a cattle car and at the destination guards and dogs divide passengers into two lines. One group, perceived as the strongest are selected for labour…for slave labour. Like animals they were tattooed for identification. The other passengers, the old, along with many women and young children were marked for immediate death. No tattoo would be needed. Whoever wore the coat was probably ordered to a shower."

"A shower? For cleanliness?"

"Or so they thought. They would be ordered to undress and hang their clothing. Fresh, clean clothing would be promised. But in the shower room was poison gas instead of water. The guards claim it was humane because death was fast. I prefer not to dwell on the process."

Karin fought a cold chill and steadied herself on the counter.

Bronstein took a deep breath. "The bodies were sent to the ovens while the clothing left behind would be inspected and sorted. It must have been a busy day since they missed those jewels. Still, a coat had value. A warehouse at Auschwitz was called Canada because of the bounty inside. Clothing, rings, bracelets, gold fillings from teeth, shoes…a fur coat."

"How do you know this?"

"Witnesses, survivors from the camps. The guards, as you might guess, don't seem to remember much. We hope eventually their memories will improve."

"Records?" She thought of the papers processed for party officials. "Germans kept good records. What do they show?"

"It's really quite surprising. The few records we've found so far indicate a veritable epidemic of heart failure. But of course, we are collecting affidavits from prisoners who survived. The truth is slowly emerging."

"Are you sure it is the truth?"

"Oh yes. I admit documentation is difficult. An autopsy is impossible when only ashes remain. But the survivors are willing to speak, willing to tell what they saw. We'll eventually have an extensive archive."

"I didn't know. I didn't want to know," Karin said softly. "I wanted to believe only criminals were sent to the camps."

"The Jewish crime was to be a Jew," Bronstein said. "Few ordinary

Germans are willing to admit the full scope of the slaughter. I was sent to Berlin to help those who survived."

"Our Gretchen is naïve." Zev had silently slipped into the room. "And she is easily manipulated. Nazis. Reds. She fell for their lies."

"Many people didn't want to listen," Bronstein said. "During the war, Jewish leaders learned of what was happening. We suggested bombing the camps. Air raids might have killed or wounded prisoners but others could have escaped in the confusion. Yet, nothing was done. Instead of bombing Auschwitz, the Air Force hit a synthetic oil refinery only a few miles away."

"When did you learn of what was happening?" Karin asked the Russian.

"As the Red Army drove west. We found the camps but had seen so much death and suffering we hardly noticed."

Karin silently hung her head.

"And, today," Zev continued. "Prisoners are released from the camps, classified as Displaced Persons, considered stateless and herded back behind the wire. And not only Jews, millions of other refugees have no where to go."

That night Murphy was waiting in Karin's room. "I've a pass key." He smiled. Her meagre wardrobe lay on the bed and she suspected he had completed a full inspection. Silently, she praised her caution in hiding the diamonds.

"Are you planning to stay?" he asked. Again, she felt his eyes assess her body.

"Those two dresses." She pointed. "They're worth something."

Murphy ran his hand across the fabric. "Nice feel but only good for a few nights. I do however have a proposition." His smile became a disconcerting leer. The thought of quick sex made her stomach churn. "I've an associate who needs a place to stay. Share the rooms and I'll give you a few weeks longer."

"Who is it?" Karin asked.

"A lady who works for me. She'd be out a lot but needs a safe place to rest."

"A prostitute?"

"Beggars can't be choosers. If you don't agree, move on."

She thought of the diamonds. The gems should be worth something to him. But she wasn't ready to share the bounty.

"Is she clean?" Karin asked.

"Very. A high-class broad." A smirk played across his face. "She might teach you some tricks. Maybe you could work with her."

Karin shook her head. "I won't need that kind of skill but she can move in. Let's say our agreement is extended for another month."

"Oh! A negotiation. Have you now become a capitalist?" He thought for a moment. "Yah. Ok."

Ottawa, September 23

"Is there a press pool for Mackenzie King and the Washington trip," Todd Aiken asked. "I'd like to go."

"Forget about any expense paid junket." The managing editor shook his head. "The Prime Minister is holding private meetings. No reporters."

"Oh, a private session, President and Prime Minister. And what do you think the subject will be."

Bert Thompson shrugged. "Tell me, oh great, hot shot reporter."

"The Gouzenko revelations!"

"Oh, come on. No one else sees anything in that story."

"Persistence pays off." Aiken pulled his chair closer. "I've been digging. Igor did have information on spies. Communist sympathizers in the US and Canada are feeding secrets to Moscow."

"Why would they do that?"

"Pretty obvious. The Americans are keeping atomic secrets for themselves. The Reds want to know what's happening."

"What is Mackenzie King going to tell the Americans?"

"Maybe where the spies were working or what they might have

learned." Aiken decided to share his speculation. "The British and Canadians had research facilities in Montreal. That's one potential source and if there's one, there are others. The Russians may have agents inside government or at the sites where the bombs were made. King could warn of the danger."

"That's all you have? Rumours and conjecture?"

"Oh, there's more. The Mounties are taking a closer look at our home-grown leftists, peace-loving Canadians or so we thought. I hear that a member of Parliament has been fingered."

"Proof?" Thompson demanded.

"No."

"If we print what you peddle, we'll be accused of everything from character assassination to treason. And we'd be guilty. Give the story a rest."

"King isn't coming back to Ottawa." Aiken pushed on. "Did you know that? After Washington, he's going to England. He'll take his fears to the British."

"You like theories. Try this one. King wants to meet Truman to get to know the new President. He'll see the new British Prime Minister for the same reason."

"Excellent cover story." Aiken nodded. "But there's more to it."

"You need a rest." Thompson reached into a drawer and began to count out cash. "Take a few dollars and write a nice feature on the fall fairs of the Ottawa Valley. That story has more chance of making the paper than a spy saga. Millions of Russians died in the war. We can't turn on our friends now."

CHAPTER 18

"**Y**OUR WISH COMES true." Captain Quimby offered a half-hearted smile. "We're sending you back to the Canadian operations. All for the best, I'm sure."

Duff Stewart frowned. "I don't understand."

"Something has surfaced that may be embarrassing. If the story explodes, we'd rather the dust settles where it belongs, on Canadians. Fellow from your legal affairs department will fill in the details." Quimby awkwardly shook his hand. "Had some interesting times together, didn't we?" And before Stewart could reply motioned to the hall. "Office D43. You are expected."

D43 was an austere cubby hole. A desk, separated two chairs with one already occupied. The introduction was brusque. "I'm Captain Andrew Potter. What do you know about war crime investigations?"

"Only that they happen and the Nazis face the courts." When there was no immediate response Stewart continued. "Take the commander and the female guard on trial from Bergen-Belsen. Murdering bastards, both of them."

Potter opened a folder. "It's hardly a surprise that the German population sees *any* investigation as Allied vindictiveness. Ever heard of Kurt Meyer?"

"No and I haven't heard why I'm here."

"Bear with me. Meyer was in command of a German SS unit in Normandy after D-Day. A bunch of Canadians surrendered to his force and disappeared. We found them a few days later—murdered. Meyer didn't pull the trigger but his orders could be interpreted as take no prisoners. He'll face a court martial and maybe a death sentence. Now, you must understand, our armed forces have mixed feelings on this. Verbal orders in war time can be misconstrued. Perhaps a few of our soldiers believed they could kill prisoners. It could happen in any army. No one would mount a case against Montgomery or Eisenhower so they look for smaller fish and found you."

"What?"

"A prisoner claims you killed men who had surrendered. I pulled the record and you were in the Rhineland."

"Yah, but I didn't see much action, mostly grunt assignments."

"Uh huh. The German says these men were shot during transfer to a prison stockade."

"This is bull…unless…" And a mental image returned of dead prisoners, of men shot in the back. "We were ordered to collect a few POW's and the officer in charge said he'd thwarted an escape. Three Germans had been shot…dead. We took the rest to the cage."

"Who is we?" Potter began to take notes.

"Murphy, my second in command. He's here in Berlin. He can tell you what happened."

"I'd like you to tell me."

"Ok, sure. Record keeping at that point wasn't a big deal. The officer who handed the prisoners over had a thick English accent… at first, I thought he was a Brit, but he said he was with the Fifteenth New Brunswick."

"Anything else?"

"Krauts were all over. No one had time for idle chatter. His troops had been through hell and looked it. He said division headquarters would handle any paper work. And then, he took his men back to the front."

"Are you certain, it was Fifteenth New Brunswick?"

"That's what he said."

"And the dead?"

"He said the pioneer corps would dispose of the bodies. Pioneers always got the dirty work. But look, we were close to the front. All hell could have broken loose."

Potter opened a thick journal and silently began to read. Several minutes passed before he set it aside. "Are you sure the troops were Canadian? Order of battle shows no Fifteenth New Brunswick with Montgomery. In fact, it doesn't appear to exist in the Canadian army." He raised his eyebrows. "It will be hard to find witnesses from an outfit that didn't exist...but uh...this Murphy. He's in Berlin?"

"Yah...with a transport unit. He'll back me up. But look, I don't shoot prisoners...hell...I didn't shoot...period. As to the other troops, everyone was dirty. I don't remember any insignia."

"Could be a mix up or an attempt to make us look bad? The Nazi hierarchy have been moved to Nuremberg for war crime trials. Everyone expects death sentences. Maybe, this guy is trying to muddy the water."

"Yah." Stewart laughed nervously. "That's probably what's going down."

Potter closed the file. "I'll need your sidearm, belt and uh, better remove the shoelaces."

"What?"

"We can hardly send an armed prisoner to the cells and we don't allow anything that could be used for suicide."

"What?"

"It's only until we find this Murphy and hear what he says. If you're lucky you'll only be in the cells for a couple of days...unless..."

"Unless…what?"

"Unless there's more to the story."

Berlin, September 27

The hint of fall deepened with a cold wind and Karin pulled the fur tighter. The coat prompted stares but as night set in she welcomed the warmth. Returning to her rooms she saw Murphy's army jeep outside and once inside heard a woman's laughter.

Murphy sat alongside a slender young woman. "Look who's back," he called. "Time for introductions. Inga-Karin. Karin-Inga." The two women recognized each other from the brief encounter in the stockade. Their eyes met but neither gave a sign of knowing the other.

Karin hung her coat on the back of a door. "That looks warm," Inga said, "but be careful. People are robbed for clothing. Murphy would buy me new clothes but my old coat attracts less attention."

"It's what's underneath that demands attention." Murphy laughed and pointed to an open bottle. "Have a drink, Karin. On the house. Inga is your new roommate. You have things in common. She too had a Canadian friend. What was the name of that reporter? Atkins?"

"Aiken," Inga corrected him. "A nice man."

"Aren't they all." Murphy laughed. "Karin spent time with a Canadian. And, by a quirk of fate, Duff Stewart needs my help. He got himself locked in the cells."

"The Lieutenant?" Karin was shocked. "He's not the type to cause trouble."

Murphy refreshed his glass. "Damned if an incident last winter didn't come back to haunt him. If you ask me, they're making too much out of a few dead prisoners. A war crime accusation is a bit much."

"War Crime? What did he do?"

"Nothing. Typical Duff. Wrong place. Wrong time. I'll straighten it out but let him rest in the cooler for a few hours…" He stopped at mid sentence. "Are you worried about him? Did you fraternize in a bedroom in Switzerland?"

"Don't talk like that." Karin's face flushed in anger. "We didn't do anything. A true friend would work to free him."

"I'll get to it but Inga and I have a job first. I'm going to introduce her to an American colonel." He winked at Inga. "And, don't worry old Murph will be close by."

Inga turned back to Karin. "Thanks for letting me stay. A warm, safe room is hard to find."

Murphy began to laugh. "Aside from the hair colour it would be hard to tell the two of you apart. Like two cuddly little kittens. Karin, don't wait up. We'll be late."

"What about the Lieutenant?" she asked.

"Ah, I'll get to him. Don't get those knickers in a knot."

Captain Potter peered through the prison bars the next morning. "Are you cozy?" Stewart's scowl was the only reply. "Murphy didn't show," Potter said, "Maybe he'll come today. In the meantime, my witness is here," and he led Stewart to an interrogation room.

"That's him!" A man in military cast offs leaped to his feet. "I'd know him anywhere. He killed my friends." He lunged toward Stewart but Potter stepped in his path. "Easy fellow. I need a witness, not an executioner."

Stewart stepped back. He didn't recognize the man. What he saw was another nondescript former soldier.

"The British had dropped leaflets promising fair treatment if we surrendered. But that one." The German pointed to Stewart. "Separated three men from the group and shot them...in the back."

"It wasn't like that." Stewart countered. "Those men were dead before I got there. Find Murphy. He'll back me up."

Potter scratched at a notepad. "Confirm your name, soldier."

"Meisel, Johan, Sergeant in the Wehrmacht."

"Lieutenant Stewart thinks you made a mistake, says he didn't do it."

Meisel's face twisted to a sneer. "The Allies refuse to admit the presence of animals in their armies."

"This could be a mess." Potter shook his head. "One story against another."

"Whose side are you on?" Stewart demanded. "Find Murphy. We'll straighten this out."

Potter ignored him. "Johan. Where have you been the last few months?"

"Starving in a prison camp, watching other soldiers starve. Those who say Germans were monsters don't admit to the suffering at the hands of the Allies."

"How is your eyesight?" Potter asked. "Any chance of a mistaken identity. A lot of Canadians look like Stewart. They lack a manly German profile." He offered a quick smile.

Meisel failed to see any humour. "He should face the same justice as our people."

"Don't go too far down that road," Potter warned. "Be damn glad we aren't demanding more punishment of ordinary Germans."

"But you are. Look at how my people are forced to live."

"Excuse me, Sir." A private appeared in the door way. "A Corporal Murphy is here."

"Finally!" Stewart exclaimed.

Murphy winked at Stewart but gave Potter a smart salute. "Sorry I'm late. I've had a busy day." Potter returned the salute and repeated Meisel's story. "Do you recognize this one?"

Murphy made only a passing glance. "Can't say that I do."

"And Herr Meisel?" Potter asked. "Do you know this soldier?"

"Yes. He was there. He went through the pockets of the dead and stole their money."

"Oh, that's bull." Murphy took a step toward Meisel but stopped and instead faced Potter. "Those prisoners had been captured a couple of days earlier. Any valuables would have been seized on surrender. Somebody else took the cash. Besides, Germans were not above stealing from the men they captured."

"I'm not sure that is a help." Potter sighed. "Makes it sound like stealing from prisoners was a common occurrence on both sides."

Murphy stepped closer to Potter and dropped his voice. "I've been dealing with these people. I can straighten this out in a hurry. Take Stewart and leave me with the Kraut for a few minutes."

"I won't condone a beating," Potter warned.

"No bruises, no beating." Murphy promised.

Murphy waited for them to leave before he spoke. "It takes a liar to know one. I know what happened and I can guess where you heard about it. Probably from another prisoner in the cage. But you don't have the right story."

Meisel scoffed. "And what will you do?"

"I'll offer a choice. I need men who know Berlin. I don't have to trust them. If something goes bad, I find a way to settle a score. Come work with me. Make some money. Or, we go through the justice system. You won't like it. Our judges hang Nazis."

"This is intimidation. Where are the principles of western justice?"

"For you, they don't exist. I did more checking than Potter. You weren't in the Rhineland or the regular army. You were in the east— with the SS. False accusations could bring years in prison. Or, work under my rules and grow rich. I'll count from ten and then I need a decision. Ten…nine…eight…"

"What would I have to do?" Meisel asked.

"Admit the mistake. It wasn't Stewart. Later you work the streets. I'll give you instructions. Seven, six, five…"

"How do I know I can trust you?"

"You can't…four, three, two…"

"Ja. I'll do it."

"I knew you were smart. Now sound contrite when you apologize. An unfortunate mistake and you are sorry for wasting our time."

"How did you do it?" Stewart asked later. "We didn't do anything but he could have made our lives miserable."

"I've made his life easier." Murphy grinned.

"There's still a matter of dead prisoners." Potter reminded them. "Of course, my inquiry was preliminary, presumably my superiors will let it die. A bit of an embarrassment as it stands. Might be best to let it go."

"There's the answer." Murphy smiled. "Drop the file in a drawer and forget it."

Ottawa, October 10

"Like the feature on the fairs?" Todd Aiken sidled into a chair beside his managing editor. "Nothing like fall in the Ottawa Valley."

"Wonderful," Bert Thompson muttered. "I felt I was there."

"Bet you wish we had a spread from Washington on the King-Truman meeting?"

"No, I prefer riveting articles on carnivals. As to Washington, I'm sure there was a frank exchange of views. We'll hear the same description of King's meeting in England."

Aitken nudged closer. "I've got the name of an MP. Fred Rose, the so-called Labour Progressive—his detractors think he's a commie."

Thompson shook his head. "We're not going to print anything until we have confirmation and our government has yet to confirm the spy exists."

"Oh, he's out there somewhere. He and his family are under RCMP protection."

"And again…no confirmation."

"Intrepid was involved." Aiken continued. "The Canadian super spy, Bill Stephenson, had a chat with the Prime Minister. Stephenson has excellent intelligence connections, with the British and the Americans. He'll know how to deal with Russians."

"I'm relieved. The situation appears in hand. Enough said."

"What is it going to take to get you interested?"

"When there's something solid."

"Another news agency may beat us."

"Let's wait to see what that other outfit comes up with."

CHAPTER 19

THE PIANO COULD barely be heard above the chatter as the two women entered an unauthorized club in the American occupation zone. The room was a recent addition to the Berlin nightlife. Tables and chairs were hastily scavenged from damaged buildings, a stand-up bar made with a slab of unfinished lumber rested on metal barrels and lighting came from several single lamps dangling from the ceiling. Most customers were in American or British uniforms. Several called out, whistled or winked as the women entered. Karin ignored them but Inga smiled back. When they found a table, Inga whispered, "Murphy pays for everything so order what you want. Sometimes I come to eat but mostly I look for big spenders."

"Doesn't it bother you?" Karin asked. "Selling your body for a few drinks or dinner."

"Plus, a little cash." Inga showed no remorse. "In today's Berlin we all sell ourselves, one way or another."

"I'm not a sellout."

"Some of us don't have a gift for languages. And, don't think my work is easy. Murphy gave me a new pair of nylons and an American tore them before I could get them off...wait a minute..." She stood and beckoned to a civilian. "This is the new guy who works for Murphy. His name is Johan, Johan Meisel. He's ok. He's German."

"Murphy will be late," Meisel announced as he joined them. "We should eat." He barely glanced at the women, more interested in what was happening around him. "Can't you find German men? Why associate with the enemy?"

Inga patted his hand. "Karin and I need a good meal."

"I fought to protect our women." His words had a harsh edge.

"And failed." Inga smirked and watched his frown deepen.

"The Wehrmacht was overwhelmed." Karin tried to ease the tension. "Our men fought to the very end but it wasn't enough."

Meisel signalled for a waiter. "Seeing the aftermath, I would gladly return to the front line."

"That's dangerous talk," Karin warned. "Those words could be used against you."

"Do you think I care? I'll only work with Murphy until I find something better. The French would accept me for their Foreign Legion but I don't see myself in Algeria or the jungles of Indochina. The Middle East would be more interesting. The Grand Mufti of Jerusalem needs expertise to deal with Jews in Palestine. I'd have no problems putting Jews in their place. Again!"

"Keep your voice down." Karin warned.

"Don't lecture me," Meisel answered but dropped his voice as a waiter brought his drink. "I won't sell out for a plate of food or a few cigarettes."

"No. You'd expect a couple of cartons." Murphy had arrived without anyone noticing and added his own wisdom. "Everyone has a price."

His arrival stopped their conversation and for a few seconds they were silent. Murphy glanced at movie posters tacked above the bar. The few Berlin theatres that survived were under occupation orders to show only approved western productions. Films made in Germany were restricted for fear of latent Nazi propaganda. He turned to Karin. "I understand you know Potsdam?"

She was instantly suspicious. "I've been there."

"Ok. Filmmakers lived in that area. I'd like to find a movie print." He leaned closer. "Before the war, a Hollywood starlet performed in some racy scenes. Hitler was a prude and blacklisted the film. But, today, American GIs would pay good money to see Hedy Lamar in the buff."

"I wouldn't know where to look."

"If you hear of anything, let me know. I'd pay a finder's fee. Soldiers would rather see her tits than watch 'Bonzo' movies. That actor, Ronald Reagan is paid to act with a monkey. There's nothing in his future but 'C' grade flicks."

By her silence, Karin indicated she didn't care. Murphy gave up and motioned to Inga. "We should go. Johan can make sure Karin gets home safely. And Karin, I almost forgot, Duff Stewart wants you at the office tomorrow."

Outside the club Meisel matched Karin step for step and the sound of army boots striking cobblestones echoed across the ruins. Eventually, he began to speak. "The Canadian, Stewart, is weak. You should find a real man, like me. I was on the Eastern Front. We eliminated the lesser races and I found the work…satisfying. Jews, Russians, Poles. It didn't matter. The world needed cleansing."

Karin froze, shocked by what she was hearing.

"Don't act surprised." Meisel smiled. "Everyone knew what was happening. It was government policy."

"I didn't know. I must have been blind or stupid."

"Yes, on both counts, a real 'Dummkopf'. I, on the other hand, followed orders and did my job. I'm proud of what I did."

She felt the urge to run, from him and the Nazi record. Instead, she spoke hurriedly. "My rooms are up this street. I'll be fine from here."

"I could come up?"

"No!"

For a moment she feared an angry outburst or a blow but he took a step back. "I see. Saving yourself for the enemy." He squared his shoulders and raised his arm. "Heil Hitler."

"Hei—…" Her response was automatic but she caught herself before returning the full salute.

Duff Stewart offered Karin a broad smile the next morning and directed her to a small corner office. "This is my new home. I'm finally working to rebuild essential services, everything from water and electricity to a functioning police force. My language skills aren't the best so I'd like to hire you but until your security clearance is approved, I can only offer temporary work." He opened a desk drawer and removed an envelope. "And, a letter came from that lawyer in Zurich. I'll leave you in private for a few minutes."

Her hands shook as she broke the seal. The letter from Conrad Levine told her the funds were safe but the stipulations of her grandfather's legacy demanded a recipient appear in person. Stunned, she reread the letter. She was no further ahead and Toronto was far away. Her face was wet from tears when Stewart returned.

"What is it?" He dropped to his knee beside her.

She sniffled and passed him the page. "I have to go to Canada to claim the money. How much would that cost?"

He opted for brutal honesty. "Probably more than you have and there's a problem with any form of travel. The Canadian government is well aware of the millions of displaced people in Europe. Ottawa can't decide who should be offered refuge, even temporarily. So, for now, the answer is no one."

"I can't stay here. I'm not going to spend my life negotiating with Tim Murphy or his associates." She thought of the diamonds. For an instant, she considered telling Stewart, yet as part of the occupation army he might be required to confiscate the gems.

"You've been decent," she said. "But this is something I must sort out myself."

Later, at the jewellery shop Karin waited until other customers were gone.

"I need to sell the diamonds." She slid a small cloth bag across the desk, "Twenty-five of them."

Saul Bornstein merely nodded. "I'm not surprised. It will take a few weeks to arrange full payment."

Karin made an instant decision. "I can wait. Make the payment in America funds. And something else. I want to know what's happening with the Jews, the ones who survived."

"I'm closing in a few minutes. Come with me."

Their route took them along a street where rubble women continued to clean and pile bricks as potential building blocks for the future. Entrances to many cellars had been cleared and a steady stream of people moved toward rough, underground homes. A few tin chimneys sprouted from the debris with puffs of smoke rising against the evening sky. "The lucky find scraps of wood for heat," Borstein said as he watched a man sifting through wreckage. "And, women walk the railroad tracks looking for any lumps of coal that might fall from a locomotive."

"I know. Food and shelter are hard to find and each day more refugees arrive."

He led her down a side street and to a tall barrier of barbed wire, a single guard and a gate. Bronstein was obviously well known since they were waved through quickly. Inside, he approached a group gathered by a bonfire. "Any news?"

An older man warmed his hands before he answered. "David Ben Gurion is coming from Palestine. We'll see if a prominent Jewish leader has any influence. North Americans don't appear to want us. Their immigration laws demand agricultural experience and few Jews have a background in farming. We're more often lawyers or bankers or craftsmen, like tailors or writers."

Bronstein dropped his voice so only Karin could hear. "Immigration is very difficult. Palestine would be an ideal home but the British control the region and keep us out to keep the Arabs happy. Next year in Jerusalem has a hollow ring."

Karin glanced at the faces close to the fire and men standing deeper in the shallows. "Is everyone German?"

"No. They come from all over Europe. Men who returned to places like Poland found relatives missing, homes confiscated, virulent anti-Semitism, and the constant fear of another pogrom or blood bath. In short, conditions were worse so they returned to these camps. Millions of our family members are missing and with each day there is less hope for a reunion. For my people, the last few years have been a disaster. A Jewish Armageddon, a Holocaust of biblical proportions. But, no one yet can agree on a proper description."

"I've learned more about the war in the east and know the Allies believe all Germans share a collective guilt. A few weeks ago, I rejected that idea but now…"

Bornstein let the silence linger before he spoke. "Many Germans refuse to admit what happened to their own people, like the mentally or psychically handicapped. They needed special help but instead many were euthanized."

Her face paled. "I didn't know of that either. I trusted our leaders, our doctors, all the professionals. I was such a fool. But," she hesitated, "I'm not sure what I could have done to stop it."

"At least, you are thinking…now."

She thought of what Meisel had said. "Did you know former German soldiers are being recruited for the Grand Mufti of Jerusalem?"

Bronstein's expression showed surprise. "You are well informed. We hear the same story. A few men, even Russians like Zev, men who have forsaken Stalin, will be smuggled into Palestine to train with our defence forces. In a few weeks, they'll return and recruit survivors from the camps. Those men had to be strong and will be the best choice to defend our people."

"Is there a peaceful solution?"

"I leave that to others. For now, we appeal to the British to allow more immigration. If it comes to a fight, we must be ready. We'll call-in favours, perhaps play on the rhetoric of the United Nations and push for self determination. With friends and money anything is possible."

Ottawa, October 17

"A sad sight on an Ottawa street." Todd Aiken stood in the door to the managing editor's office. "I saw the Prime Minister walking his dog last night. He looked terrible."

Bert Thompson didn't raise his head. "King or the dog?"

"Aren't you clever. The dog was fine." The reporter smiled. "But King carries the weight the world on his shoulders. Or, I should say, the democratic world. War time allies are waking to the communist threat."

"Are you setting the stage for World War Three and worrying about secret Soviet agents?"

"We've reason to worry. If the Russians and Americans come to blows Canada would be in the middle. Any war in the sky could be fought over our country. King actually considered a private meeting with Stalin, a face-to-face session, a bid to preserve world peace."

"Oh God no. He tried that with Hitler and failed miserably."

"Don't be alarmed. His staff talked him out of it."

"That's a relief." Thompson tilted back in his chair. "Tell me the latest on the other fairy tale, the mystery man."

"I don't have much more, at least not yet, but I've learned Canada was deeper involved in the atomic bomb project than I realized. The Federal Minister, C.D. Howe admitted as much after the attack on Hiroshima. He put out a statement praising Canada's role but no one paid much attention."

"We do miss the odd story every now and again. Anything else?"

"The fuel for the bombs," Aiken continued. "Uranium is mined in the Belgian Congo and wait for it…in Canada. Mid war, the government took over an outfit called Eldorado Gold. No one cared about gold, the target was a uranium mine way up north at Great Bear Lake. The ore was shipped south and refined for atomic testing."

"Oh good. Our readers will be captivated by the process of uranium refining. I can hardly wait to read the titillating details." He threw his hands in the air. "Aiken, face it. You and this so-called spy are the only ones who care."

"Yah, well in the Ottawa Valley research continues as we speak. The work is being done at labs in Chalk River. And, uranium deposits are rare but there may be more in Ontario, near Bancroft or Elliot Lake."

"Maybe we could send you north this winter. I'll pay for the pick and shovel."

Aiken refused to surrender. "How about the National Research Council? That agency had to be involved. The story is there. What can I do to get you interested?"

"I don't think you can." Thompson shook his head. "Everything is protected by Official Secrets and the War Measures Act. The story is dangerous. But I may have something else for you. A little more travel to take your mind off the great secret."

Berlin, October 19
Karin sat quietly holding a notepad and pen. Duff Stewart offered a day of work, someone to clarify words and meanings while he carried out a series of interviews. Local men were to be recruited for civil administration.

"Herr Altmann, you were a police officer?" Stewart put the question to a man in a threadbare three-piece suit.

"I was until last spring when I led volunteers in the defence of Berlin. Before that, in August of 1944, I was promoted to Detective. I worked primarily on property crimes, thefts and not political cases."

"And why was that?"

"The Third Reich had many levels of policing, the SD, the Gestapo and so on. On the local force, I worked on less sensitive cases."

"That's what we need." Stewart glanced at his notes. "Old-fashioned police skills. Local men should be on patrol. But there is an issue. Your party membership."

Altmann showed no concern. "Almost everyone was forced to join."

"Records of your wartime service were destroyed?"

"Yes, in the bombing. My papers are gone."

Stewart tapped the desk with his pen. "Another office must assess the Fragebogen questionnaire. And with all those questions, it does take time."

"Then, I thank you." Altmann stood but appeared to study the translator, as if memorizing her face. When he was gone, Stewart turned to Karin. "He seemed decent."

She shook her head. "I think he lied. He had to join the party to advance but must have had good connections. His promotion came after the July assassination plot against Hitler when only the most loyal were rewarded. As to leading 'volunteers' at the end…no. Men were forced to fight. And, his papers? Destroyed or conveniently lost?"

"That doesn't make my job any easier. I don't want to reject men that we badly need. Maybe he's reformed."

The sad smile returned to Karin's face. "I suppose he's only trying to survive. We all want more and better food."

"That's not going to happen anytime soon." Stewart lifted a document from the stack on his desk. "The latest order has come from the Allied Joint Chiefs, men at the very top. Germans will be given only enough food to prevent starvation, disease or civil unrest. And, there are other new rules, right down to seizing assets connected to the Reich, which with a broad interpretation could be anything. You would be wise not to discuss your inheritance."

Her heart sank as she thought not only of the deposit in Canada but of the payment promised for the diamonds.

"I've appreciated your help today." He began to clear his desk. "Can I buy you dinner? The Control Commission has a private dining room with a good spread and the 'frat' rules are relaxing."

"I'm definitely glad to hear the non-fraternization rules are changing and yes, a good meal is always welcome."

Their dinner extended late into the evening and their tentative friendship grew stronger. After initial small talk the conversation turned to harder questions.

"Is there any change in the immigration rules for Canada? There's nothing left for me in Germany." She spoke with a directness that Stewart found appealing.

"Immigration would be difficult," he explained. "Today the government might consider a few strong men, the manual labourers. Or, a woman could qualify but the work would be hard, in a clothing or textile factory. And some factories are nothing but sweat shops. I wouldn't recommend it." He saw she was hanging on every word. "Domestic service might be a route in the future. Rich Canadians will want well educated servants or nannies. If you were a scientist or someone with knowledge of the V1 or V2 rockets, the Americans are recruiting. Did you ever dream of flying to the moon? Rockets, designed by Germans, may carry us into space."

"No." She laughed. "My feet are firmly on the ground. And, when I was growing up, we had domestic help. I wouldn't care for that job."

"You could be a woman of leisure…" He regretted the words immediately. "I don't mean that the way it sounds…"

Her smile and gentle laugh put him at ease. "Let's talk of something safer. What about Canada? Is it like in America films, with cowboys and sagebrush?"

"Oh no. We've lots of lakes and trees. And European traditions still hold. My ancestors came from Scotland. One relative wanted to be King."

"Charles Stewart, the Bonnie Prince Charlie?" Her smile broadened. "I studied English history."

"Winners write history and the English won that dustup although there's still sympathy for 'Charlie.' But I don't pay much attention to family and pedigrees."

"I have no legendary relatives," she told him with a tone that showed she too didn't really care.

Stewart signalled to a waiter and pointed to empty glasses.

"Have you decided what to do when you go home?" she asked.

"Only that I want to be as far from the army as possible. One of my late father's friends controls the family business. We don't always agree but I can join the firm if I'm deemed responsible. I'm to meet one of the European partners in the next few days."

"I don't picture you as wild or irresponsible. From what I've seen, you accomplish what is expected." She was intrigued. He was unlike other men she had known, those driven to succeed at any cost. "Do you enjoy what are doing now?"

"Actually, I do. I'm not going to save the world but would like to see this country on the path to recovery."

"By watching the process, I see a danger." Her sad smile returned. "In western Germany former fascists may try for a comeback while in the east the Soviets promote Communists. The different ideologies could form a wall that divides the country."

"Is that why you want to leave?"

Karin considered the question before she responded. "That's part of it and I've been thinking, perhaps thinking too much. I've learned a lot in the last few weeks and no longer trust my own people. Those who knew the truth did little to stop what was happening during the Hitler years. So, I feel guilty and wonder if there's a way to make amends."

"Don't worry too much. The Allied governments are taking their pound of flesh. I hope something is left for the ordinary people."

CHAPTER 20

"**D**AYTON," THE TRAIN conductor called. "Dayton will be next. Exit to the rear." Todd Aiken stuffed a note pad into his small case. Over the years, the reporter learned to travel light; a change of clothes, soap, shaving kit, toothpaste, a brush and a bottle of liquor. A heavy duffel bag lay on the facing seat. His travel companion had yet to learn the lesson.

"A driver meets us at the train station and take us to the base." Cal Neil was an American liaison officer, officially an escort for a media tour but unofficially working to prevent any embarrassment for the military. "We can't waste time. This exhibition has been extended by a few days and the Wright Patterson base wasn't built for tourists. We'll meet other reporters, move fast and won't have time for a lot of questions. You should be pleased. Not everyone gets close to wartime booty."

"The Dayton paper says thousands of people are coming. That's hardly a restricted guest list."

"Just be glad the *Sentinel-Guardian* made the list. Think of what Canadian businessmen can learn from the German technology."

"Wow. A fighter aircraft in every driveway. Most families want new cars or refrigerators. But I'm prepared to be suitably impressed."

"The world is changing," Neil said and reached for a newspaper discarded by another passenger. The sports section headline announced the Brooklyn Dodgers baseball team had signed an African American. Jackie Robinson would join the Montreal Royals, a Dodger affiliate, in the spring. "Look at this," Neil passed the section to Aiken. "The black fella is sent to Canada where he's less likely to be lynched. A coloured player won't be welcome in the south or in some of the northern states."

Aiken scanned the page. "This fellow must have all-star potential. Maybe his arrival will change a few attitudes."

"Oh, I don't think so." Neil lifted his duffle bag. "That part of the old order isn't likely to change."

At the air base Nazi symbols decorated aircraft lining the tarmac. "Willy Messerschmidt and his engineers knew something about designing planes." Neil pointed to an aircraft as the tour group assembled. "This is a German ME 262. I won't bore you with specifications but it's called a jet and is faster than our fighters."

Aiken glanced at the plane and at the other spectators. Most were reporters but government and arms industry specialists from over twenty countries had been invited.

"Across the runway." Neil pointed. "Are the V1 and V2 rockets. No pilots, unmanned bombs or missiles. Americans rushed to imitate the Germans and were building rockets for use against the Japanese. Obviously, they weren't needed."

"I was in London," a uniformed American announced, "and those damn buzz bombs made a mess. Every bit as bad as the Blitz. We'd hear the V1 coming, the engine would cut out and down it came. V2's arrived with no warning. No chance for the poor souls on the ground when it exploded."

"Must have been quite a job to assemble all this material?" Aiken spoke quietly to Neil.

"Yah. Teams on the ground prowled through Germany and shipped tons of material home. Planes, rockets, blue prints, unusual chemicals, anything they could find."

"And what about the men behind all this?" Aiken asked. "What about German engineers and scientists?"

"We've a bunch of them too." Neil sounded smug. "They're happier with us than with the Russians. Probably not much of a choice, either a Gulag in Siberia or a safe, warm home in America."

"What is the average American citizen to think? I mean, learning from Nazi criminals?"

"I don't think they know and I'm not sure they'd care."

Berlin, October 24th

For Duff Stewart, it was another day of interviews with men who might rebuild Germany. At times, technical questions. "What will we need to fix the sewer systems?" Or, a query to assess the mindset of an applicant. "What do you think of the War Crime trials?"

"Obviously they are guilty," the latest job seeker answered. "The men on trial in Nuremburg gave the orders. Let them face punishment."

"Don't ordinary Germans share guilt?"

"Why? We didn't know what was happening."

"You supported the war."

"I fought Bolsheviks. If I hadn't, the Red Army would be on the English Channel. But, I'm only a working man. Give me the manpower, I'll fix the sewers and toilets will flush. Give me control of DPs. I'll make them work."

"Yes. I'll bet you would." Stewart shook his head. "Thanks for coming in. We'll be in touch when the de-Nazification process has been completed."

"Don't wait too long," the man said as he rose to leave. "The Fraulein," he nodded toward Karin, "appears to have passed her test. She should be rewarded with hot water for a bath."

As the door closed behind him, Karin stood to stretch. "The same story," she told Stewart. "None of us knew what was happening. Perhaps because we didn't want to know."

"My job would be easier with access to more records. From what you tell me, early party members were true believers. Those that joined later were often protecting themselves."

"Records existed but were stored in different locations and many were destroyed. The archive where I worked is buried under tons of rubble."

"Could you take me there?" Stewart suddenly asked. "At the very least, we'd get out of this office for a few hours."

Karin's description was on the mark. Giant blocks of concrete covered the underground complex. "The entrance was about... here." She moved carefully through the debris. "Herr Hauptmann set the charges. I suppose he learned about explosives on the Eastern Front. He was badly wounded but recovered to do his duty and..." She stopped suddenly, reached into the wreckage, lifted a mangled artificial arm and began to cry.

"Hauptmann?" Stewart guessed.

The answer came with a muffled sob. "We weren't close but he was kind. I had hoped he survived."

Stewart was covering the arm with debris, a token burial, when he discovered the hole, an opening big enough for a person to enter. Carefully, he poked his head inside and saw the outline of a corridor. "Karin," he called. "Bring a flashlight from the car."

Minutes later they cautiously made their way into what was left of a hallway. "It ran through the middle of the building," she told him. "Files were in rooms on either side."

"The engineers can determine if the structure is safe," Stewart said. "The records would speed de-Nazification."

Berlin, October 26

"I can supply small arms." Tim Murphy escorted a customer through what had become a black-market warehouse and where the inventory had grown beyond cigarettes and alcohol. "I have German revolvers, light weapons made in America or Czechoslovakia plus a few crates of Russian machine guns. Some have never been fired, still full of grease."

"Any heavier weapons? Mortars, Bren guns, antitank?"

The question shocked Murphy. "Good lord. Who are you fighting? My clients usually need firepower for small skirmishes, the odd hold up, a family vendetta, or simply protection."

"I pay for guns not to answer questions." The customer lifted a rifle and sighted along the barrel.

"From your accent I'll bet the weapons are for partisans in Yugoslavia. My suppliers can find pretty much anything."

"Suppliers?" The buyer laughed. "These guns are likely stolen from badly secured depots. But I'll buy. Small arms to start. Satisfied?"

"I guess. Maybe we can do more business in the future. Cigarettes, food, stockings for a little lady?" Murphy smiled. "And I'll keep my eyes open. I may stumble on something with a bigger bang."

Across the city, Evers Chance and Maria prepared for a night behind the walls of a British army compound. The house had undergone repairs but soot covered the beams and the odour of smoke lingered. Outside, sentries stood guard, another sign of the uncertain atmosphere in Berlin.

"The damage is much worse than I expected." Maria had just arrived from Paris. "And the Germans, once so proud, so proper and now utterly defeated. I'll never understand what happened. The country was full of intelligent people; scientists, writers, artists. How could they fall for what Hitler offered?"

"The times, the right conditions, intimidation …" Chance paused. "…I doubt we can fully understand. But there's a lesson for other countries and the future. It shows how an unsuspecting population can be led to ruin."

"Today it's a struggle for survival. Is there any chance of more relief before winter arrives?"

Chance shook his head. "All of Europe is in the same situation. Anything extra goes to Displaced Persons or former prisoners. Most food came from the east, what is now Russian territory. In our zone, the factories of western Germany could be back in production but where would they sell their products and what do the workers eat in the meantime?"

"I suppose memories of the war are still fresh. No one will rush to do business with a German Reich."

Chance bent to stir the logs in the fireplace. "Any thought of a Fourth Reich is too far fetched to be believable. The Allies prefer it that way. Without German competition the victors capture more of the international trade. Tomorrow, we'll get another view. I've arranged for a quick tour of the Soviet sector."

By morning, a cold wind and low clouds added to the gloom in East Berlin. A Soviet driver navigated streets lined with ruined buildings and carefully followed the directions of the officer beside him. Colonel Nicolai Bazarov spun to face Chance and Maria in the rear of the car. "Allied bombing caused most of this damage. Russian soldiers arrived to find a devastated city."

"The street fighting? Tanks and Russian rockets did no damage?" Chance asked and winked at Maria. Both were well aware of Soviet propaganda.

"The Red Army had to control Nazi criminals." The Russian turned his back but continued to speak. "We've since discovered the citizens were actually victims of Hitler and his cult. East Berliners now demonstrate an anti-fascist sentiment. And conditions are improving in the Soviet zone."

Chance decided not to argue. "East or West, it doesn't matter. Berlin faces years of rebuilding."

"The work has begun. New apartments are planned for the proletariat and with new collective farms, agricultural production will increase."

"We can't hurry nature. But hopefully rations increase. People can starve for only so long."

"There is no starvation with the Soviet system," Bazarov assured them. "Food is available."

"That's reassuring. Maria and I will make a comparison. We're going to a camp in the western sector this afternoon."

"Conditions there are very bad." The Russian swung to face them again. "Former soldiers, the so-called Displaced Persons, are crammed into overcrowded camps. Better to speed repatriation and return them where they belong."

"How we accomplish that? Many are afraid to return to Soviet territory."

"The fear is groundless. The issue must be settled."

Maria repeated the conversation for a United Nations relief officer a few hours later. "We tried force," he told her. "Fights broke out as our soldiers tried to put men on east bound transports and we've had a few suicides. You must understand, non-Germans made up entire divisions of Hitler's army. Russians see them as traitors or war criminals but many DPs saw Soviets as the greater evil. Memories of Stalin's secret police, the gulags and government-sanctioned famine are fresh in their minds."

"Can you simply delay repatriation?" she asked.

"Perhaps but for how long? UNRAA's mandate will expire in a few months. And men aren't the only problem." He pointed to a small bonfire and children warming beside it. "Orphans. The parents have disappeared, dead or perhaps in some other camp. These waifs are the lucky ones. Others live on the streets."

"Is there any chance of re-uniting them with their parents?"

"We try." He sighed. "But younger children often forget names of relatives or where their home was. And many are—damaged, traumatized by the last few years." A youngster stepped out of the dusk and threw more brush on the fire as if holding off the night for a few minutes longer.

Maria sighed. "Oh, what a mess."

"That's an apt description. Jews are the only ones who seem able to organize. Their orphans are being adopted. Well, adoption is an exaggeration but with the thin promise of a guardian, Britain allows a few children to emigrate to Palestine. Hopefully, someone there takes care of them. It's harsh but it's 1945."

CHAPTER 21

DUFF STEWART ANXIOUSLY tapped his foot as his new superior read the report on the German archive. Engineers were able to shore up the entrance and Karin was already sorting files. "Nice work, Lieutenant." The Colonel smiled, "And, I agree the woman deserves credit but don't go overboard. She was part of their system."

"She was a clerk." Stewart argued. "She didn't make decisions."

"Reward her with a larger food ration."

"She deserves more. And, she has a striking appearance. Men remember her. She could be in danger."

"Now that's nonsense." The Colonel rose and stuffed the file in a cabinet. "We're talking about low-level government workers."

"I've interviewed men for the police department. Some are tough characters with admitted experience in the Gestapo or the SS and don't like their countrymen or women getting too close to us."

"What would you suggest?"

"Let me work with her for a few weeks and then get her out of the country. She could emigrate to Canada."

"Oh, wouldn't Ottawa love that." The Colonel began to laugh. "No, I'm not about to recommend a Nazi for immigration. I'd be drummed out of the service. Give her extra rations or a clothing voucher. That should keep her quiet."

"But the danger?"

"I can't see a risk."

Berlin, November 4

Tim Murphy waited as the truck moved into position before closing the heavy door at his personal warehouse. He moved quickly through the merchandise, guided by the thin beam of a flashlight. The light fell on boxes marked as shovels and spades.

Johann Meisel stepped from the cab and pried open a crate. Under a layer of shovels were handguns and rifles.

"Keep the shovels on top," Murphy suggested. "Police are lazy and don't want to unpack heavy crates." He whistled and two men emerged from the gloom to begin loading.

"We didn't work together for long but it was profitable, for both of us," Murphy said and handed an envelope to Meisel. "That's the document you wanted; a form signed by a Dutch mayor showing you were born in Holland. Passports are hard to come by but proof of citizenship should get you through. Fill in the personal information. Make it look well used, creased, dirty and hard to read. But I'm curious where are you going?"

"Away," Meisel grunted. "To where I am welcome."

"I hear of SS officers using rat lines," Murphy said. "That's the name we give to Nazi escape routes. A man crosses southern Europe before a hop, skip and jump to the Middle East. The Mufti of Jerusalem might offer work."

"I wouldn't know."

"The Mufti has his hands full with the Jewish refugees who slip through the British blockade. What he may not know is that Zionists are also interested in weapons."

"Where would a Jew get the money to meet your prices?" Meisel watched as the last of the crates were loaded and covered with a heavy tarp.

"I didn't say they were buying from me. I just hear things. Like former German officers banding together, men who haven't given up on National Socialism."

"Again, I wouldn't know." Meisel began to count out American dollars. "But I might need more guns in the future."

Murphy checked the cash before stuffing the roll in his pocket. "Maybe I can arrange a little entertainment, an hour with Inga."

"Bah," Meisel dismissed the offer. "Too many women in Berlin are corrupted. Inga and the blonde woman are two examples."

"What's this? An interest in Karin?"

Meisel stepped into the truck cab and lowered the window. "Inga knows what she has become. The other one works with the enemy and makes it harder for our people."

"Let it go, Johan. Forget Karin. And Stewart won't hurt you. He's too busy finding men to restore city services."

Several miles away, Duff Stewart scratched out another note. The latest interview was not going well.

"Herr Fuchs, I don't understand these gaps in the record. A regular police officer when the war begins, a stint with the army in France, a vague reference to service in the east and back to Berlin." He glanced at a German-English dictionary, noted that Fuchs could translate to fox and decided the name was appropriate.

"I was sent east," Fuchs explained. "I got sick, a bug from a pestilent Russian village. I was too weak for strenuous work."

"But could work with the police?"

"Mostly paper work."

"And now? What do you see as issues for police in Berlin?"

"Oh, so many. Prostitution, the black market, street crime. Too many people live outside the law and…"

A polite knock on the door interrupted and the men watched as Karin entered the room, a set of folders under her arm. "That will be all," Stewart told Fuchs and motioned toward the door. The German nodded but continued to stare at Karin. Stewart pointedly cleared his throat, motioned to the door and waited. When the German was gone, he turned to Karin. "Did you find a file on Karl Fuchs?"

Her finger ran down a page. "An early convert, a party member since 1933." She flipped a leaf. "And oh, he served with the Einsatzgruppen. Those units massacred Jews. He could be investigated for war crimes."

"Fuchs...fox...whatever." Stewart crossed the name from his list. "We don't need men like him. But I'm often forced to make decisions based on who is least offensive."

Karin had heard his complaint before. "What I've learned in the last few weeks makes me sick but I can't condemn everyone."

Stewart crossed to her desk to retrieve a file. "We've another full day tomorrow."

He found himself closer than either expected. Their eyes met before she spoke. "No, please."

Embarrassed, he took a quick step back.

Ottawa, November 7

"I thought you'd been swept up in a revolution," Bert Thompson glanced at Todd Aiken. The latest editions of the Ottawa newspapers lay open in front of the managing editor and each detailed a growing wave of strikes at Canadian auto assembly plants. "Although, I couldn't picture you on the barricades. Good work though. I'm glad you telegraphed your story."

"I came back from the US to find Windsor on edge but not really on the verge of revolt." Todd Aiken dropped his travelling bag on a desk. "Strikers had blocked the entrance to a plant and there was no way to get substitute workers through the lines. The Provincial Police and RCMP that supposedly were ready to break the strike couldn't get close. Eight thousand Ford workers are on the picket line with sympathy strikes expected at Chrysler and other companies."

"The situation has caught the attention on our government," Thompson said. "A Federal Justice, Mr. Rand will be tasked to resolve the impasse."

"Good luck to him." Aiken shook his head. "Whatever formula Rand suggests won't satisfy everyone. The United Auto Workers says the dispute is over union membership but there's more at stake than labour theory. Ford laid off workers when wartime production slowed. The men fear more cuts are coming and fear demobilized soldiers will work for lower wages and take their jobs. There's a lot of high charged rhetoric from the left while arch conservatives see any strike as a threat to national stability. It's going to be tough to find common ground."

"I'd like to have left you in Windsor." Thompson raised his hands in a display of frustration. "But the boss says stories like this are why we pay for wire service reporters. I couldn't get him to spring for a night in a hotel, so we put you on the overnight train."

"And again, a lovely trip." Aiken grimaced. "The publisher should try travelling in coach. I'm tired of it."

"I'm sure you are but I'll make it up. Go home. Get a clean shirt. I'll take you to dinner."

That night Thompson and Aiken entered the Russian embassy. "Eat hearty," Thompson whispered. "A free meal courtesy of the Soviet Socialist Republic, in celebration of their 'glorious revolution'. But, hold your tongue. Don't say anything controversial."

Aiken could hardly believe his eyes. The room was packed. "The *Sentinel-Guardian* doesn't condone anything with a left leaning bent yet we sneak off to mark the Bolshevik coup of 1917. Does the publisher know?"

"What he doesn't know won't hurt him. This is the one night of the year I eat caviar and drink vodka. Look around the room.

Diplomat's, local politicians, a few members of Parliament and more civil servants than you can shake a stick at."

"Do I read anything into that? Is the government filled with leftists?"

"No. The biggest draw is a free meal."

"Maybe someone will enlighten me on Mr. Gouzenko?"

"Dammit," Thompson hissed. "Keep quiet or we'll be asked to leave before we sample the food. Besides, I have my own sources. The Mounties may be working with the Russians to locate your missing spy."

"That's crap." Aiken had the presence of mind to drop his voice. "The RCMP have him squirrelled away. If they claim to be helping the Reds, it's a ruse…"

"Mr. Aiken? What a surprise." A man in a Russian army uniform extended his hand. "I am Dimitri Carkov, special attaché. We spoke when my friend Igor disappeared? Have you any recent news?"

Aiken's mind flashed back to a terse conversation in September. The Russian first denied any knowledge of a defector then claimed Gouzenko had been led astray by western agents. Now he smiled. "Allies must work together as we did during our Great Patriotic War."

Aiken shook his head. "Friends don't spy on each other…"

"…Excuse us." Thompson seized the reporter's arm. "Mr. Aiken and I have to return to the office. Morning paper to produce and all that." The attaché appeared disappointed. "Perhaps some other time, a real discussion."

"You were about to say something embarrassing," Thompson said when they reached the street. "And there won't be another meeting. My diplomatic sources say Carkov has been ordered home and men have been known to disappear when they return to Moscow."

Aiken grimaced and drew his finger across his throat. "But wait. That may be another sign there's more to Gouzenko than anyone wants to admit."

Berlin, November 14

"We finally meet." Evers Chance smiled at Duff Stewart. "Vincent Russel wrote of your work. He's impressed by what he's heard of late. I understand you've been invited to join the firm."

Stewart nodded. "Russel didn't always appreciate my efforts. But I have to finish my stint with the army first and that can't come a day too soon. Although, dealing with the armed forces and government departments must be old hat to you."

"Something new every day." Chance smiled. "I'll do what I can to help you prepare. Things will be much different in Canada than here in Berlin. And, I must confess I'm killing two birds with one stone today. While we talk, I want to inspect this building."

Their voices and footsteps broke the silence of a deserted factory. "The Russian reparations teams were extremely efficient." Chance pointed around the empty plant. "Every piece of equipment is gone. Tools, wiring, plumbing, nothing left but bare walls."

Stewart scuffed at the outline left on the floor where a machine had been removed. "They clean up well."

"The Reds have lots of experience and the west gave them the green light." Chance took a deep breath. "At least we have the building. Give German people the tools and the plants will spring back to life. Their industrialists have a long and impressive record. It's a shame they got too close to Hitler's gang."

Stewart turned up the collar on his coat. An autumn chill had permeated the unheated factory. "I haven't been fully briefed on the political side but from what I hear Communists are working in governments all across Europe. One has to admit the message is enticing. If a man has watched the upper crust grow rich, a great levelling can be attractive. But then, communism appears to work only in theory or on paper."

"Good to see you noticed that." Chance too felt the chill and reached in his pocket for gloves. "But Russia is more Stalinist than Communist. That's the seed for failure in the longer term. Of course,

Capitalists have issues too. Our system all but collapsed in the 1930s and only the New Deal and war time spending brought it back. We may need another huge influx of spending to rebuild Europe."

"Europe's future is only an economic problem?"

"Yes and no. There's the military issue too. The Americans build more atomic bombs every month and their war gamers will have prepared a list of Soviet targets. US policies have shifted from extreme isolation to the dream of running the world. And they're refusing to share atomic secrets. That's likely to set off an arms race. The Russians, Brits, and maybe the French will try to duplicate the bomb-building process."

Chance began to pace off the dimensions of the factory floor. "But back to the immediate issue. All that's needed is cash and bright ideas. Hitler's car, the Volkswagen is one example. Only a few 'Beatles' were actually built. But today, with fuel shortages, a small, inexpensive car might be popular."

"A Mercedes is more to my likening." Stewart smiled. "Besides the American auto industry will dominate Canada."

"Ah yes," Chance agreed. "But in the longer term never underestimate the Germans. Watch what they accomplish in a peacetime economy."

"You don't see them rebuilding to threaten Europe?"

"That's unlikely. Years will pass before the basic infrastructure is fully restored. And the world is changing. Empires can't survive. The Dutch, French and yes, the British, will find it difficult to restore their colonies. You'll face a different issue in Canada, a flood of Yankee dollars. The British influence has waned. Canada has drifted into the American sphere."

"Americans can't buy the country." Stewart laughed.

"Don't be so sure. I think the Canadian business elite prefer to play monopoly rather than develop fresh ideas. Americans won't hesitate to take a run at Canadian markets. You'll have to pay as much attention to decisions made in Detroit or New York as those made Washington. And there's another major issue. The west must soon decide if the war was fought to preserve the status quo or if our leaders can truly lead us to some brave new world. In any case, our firm will continue to gather information, private intelligence if you like, and we'll do the odd special project for business or government."

"Any other advice?"

"Stay on top of the political and economic trends. Cultivate friends, contacts, informers, scour the newspapers, read between the lines. You never know what you'll learn. One other thing. I hate to be negative about a partner but I'm not sure Vincent Russell can be trusted completely. I tell him only what he needs to know."

"And what will you do?" Stewart asked. "I assume the firm will maintain an outpost in Europe."

"Hmm…oh yes, my work will continue." Chance glanced as his watch. "I must go but we'll talk again. Perhaps a dinner. You should meet my wife. Maybe bring someone for an informal evening?"

"Ha. A German girl at the office who would come just for the food."

"Bring her. Maria and I enjoy meeting new people."

Later that night Chance unwound a heavy scarf and hung his coat. His thoughts turned to what he saw while crossing the city. Groups of DPs from across Europe mingled with German refugees. Many met over small fires or huddled behind broken walls for protection from the cold.

Maria set a book aside and studied her husband. He had aged in the last few months and moved much slower. Now he appeared to be staring at a wall. "Hadn't noticed this before." he traced a faded outline. "Hitler's portrait probably hung here and was taken down before we could see it. Germans don't want to offend us."

He moved across the room to join her and she shivered as a cold hand touched her cheek. "Where are you?" she asked gently. "You often drift off."

"Hmm. Meeting Stewart has me thinking the world is again on the wrong track. We're warm and safe but those without shelter face a grim winter."

"Don't sound so dire," she chided him. "We've known this was coming. The Allies provide only a subsistence ration. That won't change overnight."

"A touch of urgency would be welcome." He slipped onto the couch beside her. "A hard winter and people will starve. The dispossessed are living on scraps and digging through garbage cans outside the barracks. Until now, they survived by what is called 'hamstering', digging in fields or forests for anything edible, but winter has come."

"Let the occupation administrators get control. They may have new ideas."

"Unfortunately, Americans don't understand the history, the culture. They think of a political system as it exists in the United States but Germans don't share a democratic tradition. The Nazis and the Prussians before them didn't hold power through the ballot box. They resorted to strong arm tactics. And, old habits die hard."

A few blocks away Karin pulled a blanket tighter. "It's so cold and not yet true winter."

Across the room Inga studied her finger nails before adding more polish. "Why not spend more time at the Control Commission offices? The Allies keep the heat on."

"I don't like coming home in the dark," Karin admitted. "In the last few days, I've felt someone was following me."

"Don't be so nervous." Inga blew on her fingers to dry the polish and began to brush her hair. "People are looking for shelter. Most are too weak to be any danger." She twisted her face in the mirror for a final check of her makeup before reaching for the light summer coat.

"That's not warm enough." Karin pulled the blanket tighter. "Take my fur for tonight."

Inga didn't need a second invitation. She slipped into the coat and spun in front of the mirror. "I'll look like a society lady."

Once on the street, Inga raised the collar and tightened a scarf so only her eyes were exposed to the cold.

Though muffled by light snow she thought she heard footsteps. She began to walk faster, threading through the piles of debris and glanced over her shoulder but saw no one. She'd be glad to be safely under Murphy's protection and their meeting place was only a few blocks away. Again, she heard footsteps and an echo from the ruins. A second later, a figure leaped from the wreckage and knocked her to the pavement.

"Traitorous Bitch!" The voice was oddly familiar.

As she tried to scream an arm tightened around her throat. "We'll teach you to work with the enemy!"

She recognized the voice of Johan Meisel before a heavy blow left her unconscious.

CHAPTER 22

DUFF STEWART HAD never seen Tim Murphy as angry. He stormed into the Control Commission office to tell Duff and Karin of the attack. Inga was barely alive when found by a passing army patrol. Police dismissed the assault as a street crime, the theft of a winter coat. "But Inga says Meisel was there. Something to do with the occupation and working with us."

Karin began to cry. "It must have been me they wanted. Inga borrowed my coat. Meisel and his gang know where I work and where I live. They mistook her for me."

"Well, they did a job." Murphy kicked at a chair. "My guess is brass knuckles. Her face is a mess. She's stabilized but doctors aren't sure about long-term damage. If the patrol hadn't come by, she'd be dead."

"We'll arrest Meisel." Stewart decided. "Charge him with assault."

"What does that accomplish?" Murphy spat out the question. "No judge would take Inga's word when there are no other witnesses. Besides local judges are German and could be secret Nazi sympathizers.

A conviction would mean only a few months in jail and he'd be a hero to his fascist friends. No, there are other ways."

"Be careful, Tim." Stewart warned. "If anything happens it could come back on you."

"So let the asshole get away with it?" Murphy swung his arm and accidentally knocked a pile of files to the floor. "We have to do something."

"First things first. Karin needs protection." Stewart tried to think of their options. "We'll move Karin to my place. In the meantime, track Meisel. Find out where he is but have someone else follow him. You stay out of sight."

"What about Inga?" Murphy demanded.

"I'll arrange additional medical help and post a guard at the hospital. Do this right. Meisel may have friends on the police force. Don't let him off the hook by doing something stupid."

"A bullet between the eyes wouldn't be stupid."

Stewart bent to retrieve the files scattered across the floor. "It's like with war criminals," he said, "a waste of a perfectly good bullet."

Murphy returned at dusk the following day. "Meisel is in the Russian zone. He was with a bunch of other Nazis last night, all of them drinking and singing that 'horse shit' song."

"Horse shit?" Stewart asked.

"Horse shit—Horst Wessel, the old Nazi anthem."

"At least we know what we're dealing with, men who refuse to believe the war is over. Is he living in East Berlin?"

"Yah. His gang took over a damaged tenement. Guards on the door, the whole shebang."

"Maybe catch him on the street." Stewart was thinking out loud. "But no, the Control Commission won't authorize a raid in the Russian zone. Are his men armed?"

"Yah." Murphy muttered. He pulled a flask from his jacket, "Drink?"

"No. Not yet. What kind of weapons?"

"Uh…handguns, rifles, Tommy guns."

"Wonder where he got them?" Stewart asked absently and studied a map of Berlin. "Are they deep in the Russian zone?"

"Too deep for a small force to get in and get out in hurry. And, we'd have to be heavily armed. That bunch might have hidden firepower."

"Like what?" Stewart asked.

"Bren guns? Maybe?"

"How do you know so much?"

Murphy took a deep breath. "Ok. I sold him weapons. I wasn't sure the damn things would fire. Cast offs, surplus stock, things armies don't want."

"Murphy! How could you be so stupid?"

"I made a few dollars and would have made more. He wants another shipment."

"What were you thinking? You'll be crucified."

"Not if my friends keep their mouths shut. I talked you out of a jamb on the dead prisoners. The least you can do is keep quiet now."

"Get out!" Stewart pointed to the door. "Get out of my sight. I need time to think."

Berlin, November 20

Duff Stewart waited as Evers Chance slowly made his way toward their meeting place, a small café with only a few tables. Chance walked with a cane but it was impossible to tell whether it was for support or a mere accessory. Still, he was breathing heavily as he lowered himself into a chair. "Cold takes my breath away. I thrive best in warmer climes."

Stewart waited while the older man caught his breath. "Might be difficult to find transport to the American South but what about the Mediterranean coast? Or Morocco?"

"Probably not this year," Chance replied and glanced around the room. The other customers were several tables away. "Maria and I enjoyed the dinner with you and Karin. She's a lovely woman. But that's not why we're here. You want advice?"

"Yes. I know you worked in the shadows, on matters that might not be considered entirely…legal." He too glanced around the room before explaining about Inga and the Nazi connection. "Meisel is guilty of the attack and there's more. He could be charged with war crimes." He told of what Karin had learned.

Chance was silent for a full minute but finally spoke. "The British and the Americans have their hands full with the trials at Nuremberg. At this point, they might prefer to concentrate on the leaders, the most serious cases, and let lesser offenders drift into obscurity. The drive for vengeance carries only so far."

"To add to the complications." Stewart continued. "Meisel's war crimes were in Russia."

"No evidence beyond a brief conversation with Karin?"

"That's right and I'm worried. If they were after her, they may try again."

"These men are living in East Berlin?"

"Yes, we have a watch on the building."

"What about the Russians?"

"The relationship with our former ally has soured. I wouldn't accomplish much through official channels."

Chance began to rub his hands together. "Try unofficial channels. A few discrete words to the right official." He began to button the coat. "It's almost time for you to leave Germany anyway. Ottawa doesn't feel the Canadian contribution to the occupation is truly appreciated and will soon begin to withdraw our troops. Once home, you'll be able to join the firm but Karin will be on her own. Think about that…too."

Berlin, November 23

Karin twisted the radio dial. The broadcasts concentrated on the opening of the War Crimes Trial in Nuremberg, coverage that she suspected would be a daily feature on German language stations. Through control of the media the victorious allies would force the grim reality into living rooms and kitchens around the nation. She had already decided the men were guilty.

Earlier she'd been to the hospital. Inga's condition had improved, thanks in part to Murphy. Somehow, he obtained supplies of penicillin, the new wonder drug. Doctors were confident of a psychical recovery but less certain of emotional damage and beneath layers of bandages was a badly scared face.

A tap on the door startled her but she quickly relaxed. Three sharp knocks, followed by two more was the signal Duff created. The code, she thought, might have been borrowed from a bad movie but the sound was somehow reassuring.

Stewart carried a box as he entered. "Food," he responded to her puzzled look. "Not much to choose from. Sausage, two potatoes and brussels sprouts. I can't guarantee what it's made from but the sausage is fresh. Sprouts appear to be only vegetable England will send to Germany and as to the potatoes, well, don't ask how old they are."

As the food cooked, she told of the hospital visit. "Inga can't talk much but a doctor says advances in plastic surgery could restore her face. The best surgeons however are in England and what's the chance of treatment for a German civilian?"

"I wonder. Chance has excellent connections, maybe he can help?"

And for the first time in days, Karin began to hope. "I have money," she told him. "But don't ask where it comes from. It could make your job more difficult. I'm sorry I can't say more."

"Then let me tell you what I've learned. Murphy is working in the black market. Not just cigarettes and booze, the damn fool has been selling guns and has more…inventory…than I expected."

"Yet you still protect him?"

"He helped me and I may be able to get him off the hook. It sounds nuts but all I have to do is dispose of a truckload of guns. Simple. Right?"

Karin's eyes widened. "You can't be serious?"

"Meisel wants another shipment. We'll take his money and ensure the weapons are never used but Murphy won't be in the clear until all of the guns are gone. I'm not about to start another war but there must be people who need protection. But, I'm not sure how to find them."

"That's lunacy." Karin scoffed and shook her head until a thought crossed her mind. "Maybe, I could help." She saw his shock. "Again, it's best you don't know…"

"Be careful. And, don't go the hospital for a few days." He warned. "Meisel or his friends are likely watching."

"I have to leave the apartment for a few hours tomorrow." A plan was already forming. "If I borrow your great coat and cap, I could disguise myself as a soldier."

"That body would be hard to disguise."

She smiled and sucked in her chest. "You might be surprised."

Saul Bornstein paid scant attention as a soldier entered his shop. "This will have to be quick. It's closing time," he called but then took a second glance. "Karin? Is that you?"

"Kenneth might be more appropriate." She laughed and raised the cap. "I'm trying out a disguise and I don't have much time. I need the money from the diamonds."

"That can be arranged."

She glanced about fearing someone else might hear. "I considered giving all of the cash to Jewish relief but I have to pay for a medical treatment for a friend. However, in addition to some money…well… would a truckload of guns be useful in Palestine?"

He was shocked into silence. The only sound was the ticking of a clock. "Yes." He finally answered. "But dealing in arms attracts unsavoury characters. Are you sure you want to be involved?"

"Yes, definitely. It might relieve my share of German guilt."

"But you're not really guilty. You didn't do anything."

"That was the problem."

CHAPTER 23

THE PLANNING TOOK longer than Stewart expected but he told himself nothing moves fast in occupied Berlin. December arrived before everything was arranged.

First, there was Murphy. Under the threat of exposure, he promised to end the arms trade but only after Stewart reluctantly agreed selling cigarettes and liquor might be acceptable. And Murphy made another confession. He had sold Dutch identification to Meisel, a document that could form the basis for a new identity.

Stewart told what he learned to a new Russian contact. Working through official channels was impossible but a one-on-one approach offered promise. Breaking a ring of neo-Nazis and seizing an impressive display of firepower would boost the prestige for the Soviet officer especially since Stewart wanted none of the credit. The background on Meisel's wartime crimes and his Dutch alias were soon in the hands of the Russian. And then there was nothing to do but wait.

Karin watched from the street as the truck was loaded and remained in the shadows as Meisel's shipment disappeared into the night. Moments later another truck appeared. The headlights flashed twice before entering Murphy's garage.

A guard stiffened at the approach of the Canadian soldier. A long great coat touched the ground and an army cap was pulled low over the forehead. "Stop!" The guard ordered. "What are you doing?"

"Making sure the job is done properly...Zev."

Several seconds of silence followed before he replied. "Gretchen?"

"Close enough." She laughed. "Have the men load. I've been watching. No one else is near by."

"Saul wouldn't say who arranged this." Zev moved closer. He wore a ragged jacket and could easily be mistaken for a refugee. "Who are you working with now?"

"It doesn't matter. I'm making up for past mistakes. How is Palestine?"

"Again, you know too much." He took a moment to carefully frame a reply. "It's warmer than Berlin and the Arabs threaten to make it hotter. With these guns we can protect our people."

"And without guns?"

"A massacre is possible," he told her, "But unlike what happened in the camps, Jews will fight. Eventually, if the British allow more emigration, Israel can become our true homeland."

From inside the garage the sound of loading rose in intensity.

"No regrets of leaving Russia?" Karin asked.

"None. And you? Regrets?"

"Only that I didn't act sooner." She glanced into the garage and saw the shipment was almost loaded. "Saul said you would destroy anything that was left."

"It will be done."

"Then I'll go." She offered a tentative smile. "I doubt we'll meet again."

Zev reached and clasped her hand. "We were told German women were stupid and weak. It was another of Stalin's lies. Good luck Gretchen."

Duff Stewart waited by the telephone, willing it to ring and end the uncertainty. Too much could go wrong. Dealing with Russians was never easy and Karin added the complication of the Jewish underground. Still, if it worked, his debt to Murphy would be settled and Meisel would face justice.

The phone rang and he seized the receiver. "Sergei?" He heard the voice of the Russian contact. "They tried to resist. We killed a couple but captured the one called Meisel and we have the weapons."

Stewart imagined the scene. A firefight in the ruins. "Were any of your people injured?" He thought of the repercussions that could flow from the raid.

"Nyet. But two Germans escaped."

"Damn! We'll have to keep our guard up. Did anyone else see what happened? Anyone who might talk to reporters?"

"I can assure you nothing will appear in the newspapers."

"Good then." Stewart heaved a sigh of relief. "Thank you, Sergei. Let me know if I can help in the future." The answer was an abrupt click as the connection was cut.

The receiver was hardly back in cradle when he realized someone was standing in the shadows by the door.

"The Russians have finished their work?" Karin asked.

"Done," he answered.

She undid the buttons on the great coat and tossed his cap on the desk. "And so am I. Murphy will need a new storehouse. His garage is on fire."

Stewart merely nodded. "He's already on the prowl for another location." He saw she looked haggard, as if weighed down by the recent events.

"I'm afraid, your coat is dirty." Karin apologized. "It was too long. The hem dragged on the street. And, your boots need a shine." She raised the coat to show the mud-covered footwear. "I didn't think you'd mind."

"I'm amazed. Our shoe size is identical?

"On no. I stuffed them with paper. I needed to look like a real soldier and now my feet hurt." Karin untied the laces and kicked the boots off. "A small price to pay."

"There's a complication," he told her. "Two of Meisel's men got away. You'll have to stay with me until it's safe."

"I don't mind." She began to rub her ankles. "I'll sleep better knowing someone is nearby."

"And I haven't given up on immigration. Ottawa is sending another official to work on refugee issues. I'll have a word with him. For now, let's get you home. We could both use some sleep."

At the apartment, she offered a feeble smile and as she said goodnight, felt the tension drain away. Money was available for Inga's treatment and the weapons on their way to Palestine were a personal act of atonement for Nazi crimes.

Stewart checked the locks on the outer door before he collected blankets for his bed on a couch and was soon asleep. It took a scream, a burst of pure terror, to wake him. He rushed into the bedroom to find Karin sobbing; knees drawn tight to her chest, her body shaking. "A nightmare," she gasped. "I've had it before. Bombs were falling. A man was in the street, his head exploded and there was blood and parts of bodies. I was back in those awful days of the war."

"You're safe." Stewart slipped an arm around her shoulders and thought of his own bad memories; the fighting in the Rhineland, the scenes as troops advanced into Germany and stacks of lifeless bodies. Mental images, he too, fought to suppress.

"I feel silly." Her speech had returned to almost normal. "But everything seemed so real." He gently touched her cheek and brushed away a tear.

"We've all seen things." He spoke softly. "I'm not sure when we'll be able to put it behind us. It's as if the war never ends."

She buried her face in his chest and for few moments neither moved, until she raised her head and the kiss seemed only natural. "Stay," she murmured and pressed tight against him.

Near Ottawa, December 6

"Try this road." Todd Aiken peered through the snowflakes collecting on the windshield. "The cottages are at the end of the lane." The cab driver tapped the metre as a gentle reminder. "Don't worry." The reporter assured him. "One last short detour and we'll return to Ottawa."

"Be a big bill." The driver warned. The short out of town run had become a long, boring afternoon. His passenger appeared intent on finding the most remote cottages along the Rideau waterway. He flipped off the windshield wipers as the snow shower eased and saw another isolated cabin. "Hey, I've been here before, took a fare to that cottage."

"When?" Aiken demanded and wondered if his luck had changed. He was running out options in the search for the Igor Gouzenko.

"Ah, I don't know, maybe October. We drove toward the cottage but then my passenger decided he'd walk the rest of the way. He was planning on staying. He brought a suitcase."

"Anything else?"

"Na. He was a glum bugger. Didn't say much. That was a lovely day, warm for fall. I got a glimpse of a family, youngish guy, a very pregnant woman and a kid. They scurried back inside when they saw my cab. I remember all this because I was paid with a travel chit and the government has been slow to settle up."

Aiken saw no sign of life. Rough wooden storm shutters protected the cottage windows. The path to the door was covered with a thin coating of snow and there were no footprints.

"I was to pick up a fare for the return trip." The cabbie remembered. "But the guy cancelled, said he'd rather be going home than playing nursemaid in Oshawa. My passenger shut him up and told me to skedaddle. And, when a police dick tells you to leave, you leave."

"Why do you think he was police?"

"I picked him up at Mountie headquarters. He wasn't in uniform but cops put a good shine on their shoes. His were spit and polish."

"Mid October?" Aitken pressed.

"Late October. I though it odd a family was on holiday so late in the season."

"Yah," Aiken agreed. "And, not high rollers if they were going to Oshawa."

"Takes all kinds," the cabbie told him. "Can we go back to the city now?"

At the newspaper office morgue, Aiken scoured back issues. A lonely librarian, one of the few survivors of the publisher's cost cutting, guided him along the shelves. "I doubt there's much from Oshawa. Not much happens there unless it's connected to General Motors and that would be filed with the auto industry." Aiken's only exposure to the city had come from a passing train and all he remembered were houses and the view of Lake Ontario. "What I want is not auto related."

"I do remember an odd story," the librarian opened a file drawer and ran her hand across the folders. "A reporter stumbled on a special facility, a secret training camp in maybe…'42. He headlined it 'Camp X' but the dispatch was killed by censors. I kept it in case the censors loosened up but it's not where it should be. It's probably lost but we can keep looking."

After another hour of a fruitless search Aiken faced the wrath of his managing editor. "You could have bought an old car with what the taxi cost?" Bert Thompson plucked the bill from his desk. "Was this more surveillance of the missing spy?"

Aiken closed the office door. "What if he wasn't a spy? As a cyber clerk he sent messages to Moscow. Maybe he's offered to surrender the codes and cut a deal for asylum."

"So, he's demoted from master spy to file clerk? Maybe he's taken the civil service exam and is working for the government."

"That's cute," Aiken answered. "But no. The RCMP have him and must be working to extract what he knows. After a few weeks of interrogation most prisoners tell their captors pretty near everything."

"Captors? Interrogation?"

"I don't know," Aiken confessed. "Gouzenko and family are hiding but I'm not sure where. I checked with a contact at Defence Headquarters. The British had a base near Oshawa early in the war, a school for spies and saboteurs. It was shut down before Germany surrendered but the buildings would be there and a few Mounties could maintain security."

"Have you thought of writing spy novels?" Thompson leaned back and knotted his fingers behind his head. "I liked the original premise but the plot has grown convoluted."

"Yah, I admit it's strange. But why keep everything under wraps? Maybe the Russian is singing and the police are looking for other spies."

Thompson tilted his chair forward and rested his elbows on the desk. "What if there is no story? All we know is a Russian walked out of the embassy with some papers. At first you thought atomic secrets were involved but now you think he was a mere clerk."

"A clerk who knows the system, knows what Moscow is looking for and who the Reds recruited?"

"I wouldn't run this story beside the comics much less on the front page. It's all conjecture."

Aiken braced for what he feared was coming.

"Time for a break from international intrigue." Thompson slapped his hands together. "I'm moving you to general assignment. A few weeks on the street might clear your head. Chase the rubby-dubs, the common criminals. Find a bit of old-fashioned larceny, the type of criminal activity a person can grasp in one quick read."

Berlin, December 14

The headline was large and black. *"Beast of Belsen-Executed."*

Tiny Barnett crumpled the newspaper and threw it into the fireplace. "I have no sympathy for a death camp commander but I can't get my head around hanging a female guard along with him. Irma Grese deserved the death sentence but I don't like what's happened with women. Our side is guilty too. We trained females in death and destruction before dropping them behind enemy lines. Take me back to a gentler time."

"It is the twentieth century." Maria nudged Chance and winked. "Next he'll tell us a woman's place is in the home, cooking, cleaning and making beds."

"A woman must know her place, Mrs. Chance."

"Oh Tiny, please call me Maria. Mrs. Chance implies I am under his thumb…"

"…Time to change the subject." Her husband interrupted. "I've had these arguments before and a man won't win. Besides we didn't get together to talk about war crimes. Have you made a decision on my job offer?"

"I have." Barnett appeared reluctant to share the news. "I'm sorry. I've decided to go home. I've an army pension and I'm going to enjoy the time I have left."

Chance felt a keen sense of disappointment but tried not to show it. Instead, he smiled. "That wife hasn't seen much of you these last few years." He glanced to Maria. She had hoped someone would lighten his workload and so he made another effort. "Tiny, what about part time? The odd bit of work every now and then?"

"It's nothing personal but no. Wife and I had a chat and she wants me at home. So, it wouldn't work. I'm sorry."

"I understand how your wife must feel." Maria's words were aimed at her husband. "The time comes to lighten the workload."

"Exactly what she said." Tiny chuckled. "Women must have a hidden book of truisms to quote from."

"It's part of our psyche." Maria too was hiding disappointment. "I think you are making the right decision."

"Well, honestly, I've grown frustrated these last few months." Tiny stepped closer to the fire. "Too many issues should be tackled and I can't do a damn thing. DPs for example. If we're not sending them back where they came from, we should look for new homes rather than those dismal camps. North American has empty space."

"Don't hold your breath," Chance warned. "I had the very devil of a job getting permission to move an injured German woman. A specialist on plastic surgery agreed to treat her but not without a bureaucratic struggle. That's one woman for a temporary stay in England. Imagine how Americans or Canadians would react to thousands of new arrivals looking for permanent homes. All the old fears return. Strangers, different languages, and different cultures." He stopped and appeared embarrassed. "Sorry. I didn't mean to run on. Maria says I too get worked up over things I can't control."

"And you too must slow down." Maria's voice had an urgent tone. "Tiny has the right idea. Relax. Enjoy life. Both of you have earned it."

CHAPTER 24

THE WAIL OF a siren brought Berlin traffic to a halt. An intersection was closed and a military policeman waved an ambulance through hastily improvised barricades.

"Nothing happens fast." Duff Stewart told his passenger and shifted the car into neutral. "There may have been an explosion, unexploded ordinance from the war. This city is a dangerous posting."

"Can't we go around?" George Belton was impatient. The Canadian Immigration officer had already weathered a series of delays and the traffic snarl meant night would fall before he reached the Control Commission offices. As an indication of his importance, Belton was to rank with senior members of the occupation army and was anxious to test his authority.

"Maybe get a good night's rest and come by the office tomorrow," Stewart suggested. "This sort of thing happens all the time. Berlin is a long way from normal."

As traffic inched forward, Stewart glanced to where debris blocked the side street. "Bomb disposal is risky. You never know what will trigger a blast. Explosive experts do the job today but last summer captured prisoners were sent in to defuse the ordinance. Some of them didn't come out."

Belton glanced to where a small group of soldiers had begun to dig. "I'm more concerned about living, breathing Germans, the kind who might be considered for immigration. I've a dozen to check out. Personally, I'd let them rot but their Canadian relatives claim the poor souls are misunderstood and opposed Hitler from the get go."

"We hear that a lot." Stewart shifted to a higher gear. "We stumbled across a cache of records that makes it easier to check some of the stories. My...uh...assistant...has been a big help. She knows the language and the file system but ...well...she's run afoul of her former countrymen. For her own protection, I'd like to get her out of the country. I have a request prepared with all the background."

"German?"

"Yah...no family left."

"Not much I can do." Belton quickly decided. "If she had Canadian relatives or someone to support her it might be different. Besides, she's likely a Nazi."

"Once, maybe, but not now...she's...."

"...I don't think there's a snowball's chance in hell but I'll take a look. Now get me to my quarters. It's been a long day."

Belton remained in a foul mood the next morning. He snapped a greeting to Stewart, ignored Karin and began to leaf through files. Several minutes of stony silence was finally broken when he announced his plans. "I won't be using translators from this office. I'm going to establish a relationship with local police. An officer has been assigned to help me."

"That's not a good idea," Stewart began to explain. "We haven't concluded the de-Nazification processes. A few police applications were approved simply to get patrols on the street. I can't vouch for those cops."

"Police Officers, not cops," Belton corrected him. "Don't worry. I'm can sniff out bad characters. Fraulein!" He snapped his fingers and pointed to Karin. "Cream and sugar in my coffee. Scamper off and see to it."

Karin glanced to Stewart who rolled his eyes. "Anything for you Lieutenant?"

"No thanks…"

"…Perhaps before you run off." Belton raised his hand. "Lieutenant Stewart left me a dossier on your case. A couple of questions? Born in Berlin in 1923, so twenty-two?"

"Yes."

"Hmm. So, fascism was in vogue during your formative years. Obviously white. Five feet…seven?"

"Five six actually."

"Uh-hum." He began to scratch notes on the margin of Stewart's report. "Full figure." He chuckled. "Very full figure. Middle name or initial?"

"Elisa."

"Any alias?"

The question surprised her. "No."

"You had Nazi friends?"

"Every German did."

"Do you keep in touch?"

"Not really."

"Any Jewish blood?"

Karin's eyes widened. "No. Why would you ask?"

"My job. How about ties to left-wing organizations?"

"No…I…"

"…That's all for now." Bolton dropped his pen. "Go and get the coffee like a good girl."

As the door closed, he looked to Stewart and raised his eyebrows. "She's very attractive. Submissive?" He saw Stewart was growing angry but continued to speak. "Just wondered. Your report is a glowing recommendation."

"She does excellent work but what was with those questions? Why ask of Jews or Communists?"

"We can't be too careful. Don't want the wrong sort getting into our country." Belton glanced at his watch. "Damn. Time is getting away. I have to go."

Karin returned with the steaming coffee to find Belton gone. "Isn't he a charming fellow? Are all Canadian officials like him?"

"I hope not," Stewart said with a grimace. "Maybe he'll come around?" He sniffed at the coffee. "Don't want your trip going to waste."

"Take it..." And before she could say more, an urgent knock sounded.

"Come in," Stewart called and saw an associate in the doorway. "Bad news, Duff. Your friend in the transport unit, Corporal Murphy. He's dead—killed in a building collapse."

It took two hours for Stewart to reach the site and talk his way past investigators. The shell of a building had collapsed sending bricks, girders, and other wreckage into what had been a large cellar. "Unexploded bomb?" he asked the military policeman in charge.

"Don't think so. No report of an explosion. More likely a vibration of some kind. A passing truck can bring down a fragile wall."

Stewart stared at the latest ruin.

"The body was recovered yesterday." The policeman pointed to the debris. "We found identification. This fellow, Murphy, was crushed when the walls came down. He must have had quite an operation; booze, tobacco, nylons, bottles of French perfume. Enough stock for a small department store. My men sort of helped themselves to what little could be salvaged." The policeman bent to retrieve the top of a whiskey bottle. "Since there's no government seal, I'm guessing the Scotch was doctored. Water mixed with tobacco juice or some other concoction to make it look authentic." He sniffed at the glass. "Smells real but we'll never know."

"Murphy was always on the make for a buck," Stewart kicked at more broken glass. "But he was always willing to help a friend."

"Did he have family?" The policeman asked. "Maybe you could send a personal note, something beyond the dreary official notification—*we regret to inform*—and so on. In cases like this the death is recorded as an accident. No one needs to know what he was up to."

"He never talked about family, pretty much a loner. He had an apartment. I'll clean it out."

"Body is in the ground but the War Graves Commission may move him. Big cemeteries are planned for the war dead."

Stewart turned aside and brushed at a tear. "Hmm...Murphy never expected to spend eternity in the ranks."

That afternoon Karin followed as Stewart unlocked the door to Murphy's apartment. The rooms were spotless with no sign of black-market booty.

"He must have moved everything in the last few days." Stewart opened a cupboard and found it bare. "A few weeks ago, a steady stream of men and a few women, came for...supplies."

"He brought 'gifts' for Inga at the hospital." Karin recalled. "And, he did make sure she got the best care. Between the money I collected and what he gave her she'll be ok. In a few weeks, she'll be released from the English hospital and can come home."

"I checked. Tim listed her as next of kin so she'll get whatever is coming from the army. I thought at first, he was using her but he must have developed real feelings. It's like so much from this war...so much we'll never know."

In the bedroom was a neatly made bed, a suit of civilian clothes, and an extra pair of boots. Karin opened the drawer of a bedside table and lifted an envelope. She passed it to Stewart. "I feel bad going through his things. He trusted you."

"Some kind of documents." Stewart glanced over the papers. "But not German. He served with the Canadian army in Holland so maybe Dutch? There's a signature but the rest of the form is blank."

"Let me help." Karin offered. "I don't speak Dutch but might be able to figure it out." And a moment later…"A certificate of birth or nationality, signed by a mayor or a city official."

"I wonder," he thumbed through the papers. "Two others, signed but blank. He sold identification to Meisel. Maybe this was part of a scheme to help establish a new identity?"

"Looks legitimate." Karin stepped to the window to study the document in better light. "The official stamp of a Dutch town." But before she could continue something in the street caught her attention. "That man leaning against the wall. He was there earlier today. He looks familiar."

Stewart stepped to her side. "Damn! That's Altmann. Remember, he got the police job. He may be a friend of Meisel or one of the guys that got away from the Russians."

"Why is he there? What is he watching?" Her voice began to quiver.

"Us," Stewart said and pulled her from the window."

The immigration officer was at his desk when Stewart arrived at the office the next morning.

"Set your own hours, I see." George Belton's voice was as harsh as the expression on his face. "The rest of the occupation force keep a regular schedule. Where's the little crumpet?"

"She wasn't feeling well."

"I expect you kept her busy through the night."

"Now wait…"

"No. You wait." Belton slapped a file closed and stood. "I'm using my authority to clean up this operation. Your demobilization papers are being processed as we speak. I'll give you an honourable discharge to save the army the cost and embarrassment of a deeper investigation."

Stewart didn't understand. "But we're making progress to restore water and the electrical grid."

"Someone else will take over, someone who is less forgiving."

"What are you talking about?"

"I had a successful day at the little archive," Belton answered. "The police officer assigned, Herr Altmann, knows his stuff. By chance, we stumbled on the file for Frau Werner. Based on what I've seen, she'll no longer be working with this office."

"But you were working on family reunification?"

"Yes. The dozen or so men on my list will be approved for eventual immigration. The whole lot worked in government jobs and so had nothing to do with the armed forces."

"But government jobs were held by Nazi party members. We haven't completed those investigations."

"Actually, on my orders, for the people on my list, we have. But that's of no account to you. Of more concern, the party affiliation of your 'assistant'."

Stewart fought growing frustration. "She was never a party member."

"Her last supervisor, a Herr Hauptmann, added a note to her file. He praised her dedication and wrote she displayed the very best of National Socialist values."

"She was a file clerk, a minor position."

"So, she says. We're looking for this supervisor."

"Dead. Killed at the end of the war."

"Too bad." Belton didn't appear to care. "Altmann says a bunch of young women got cozy with the Russians."

"We know all that." Stewart began to explain. "The Russians were out of control and acted like depraved beasts. She helped them to protect herself."

"She probably lied." Belton scowled. "She may have been a Nazi and a Commie. And you recommended her for work at the Control Commission."

"You have it all wrong."

"Do I? Altmann saw her at your apartment. That's a little too much fraternization."

"Now wait. Altmann may be connected with unrepentant Nazis. They're dangerous because…." He paused. Telling the full story would reveal Murphy's black market operation, the weapons transfer and the secret arrangement to turn Meisel over to the Russians.

"Because…?" Belton prompted.

"It doesn't matter, does it?" Stewart gave up. "You've made up your mind."

"Oh, she really fooled you but I've done my homework. Little things are important clues. The women of Berlin have taken to wearing bring red lipstick. Hitler didn't like the garish appearance and most females use bright red to show they reject the legacy of the Fuhrer. Except, for the hard core. Frau Werner, I noted, prefers a lighter colour. The Fuhrer would be pleased."

"This is nonsense." Stewart clenched his fists. "What you say means nothing."

Belton shook his head. "I think it does. She'll never meet immigration standards. But you…you'll have a clean discharge, a flight home and no one will know of the indiscretion. And when you're gone, Herr Altmann will begin a full investigation."

"Forget about me. Karin could be in danger. Altmann and his kind have scores to settle."

"Let the Germans sort it out. It was their mess to begin with."

"When will you leave?" Karin asked that night. The news left her cold. Again, she would lose the protection so vital in postwar Berlin but Stewart was also a friend and in the last few days had become a lover.

"A couple of weeks," he answered. "New orders for a de-mobbed lieutenant won't be a high priority."

"I'll look for another room." She turned to hide her face. "Maybe another girl at the Control Commission will take a roommate."

"There's more." He gently took her hands. "Belton has ordered your dismissal. You see…" And Stewart explained what Belton thought.

What she heard left her in tears. "Everything comes back to haunt me. I had forgotten that Herr Hauptmann had written a commendation. And now, lipstick is dangerous. We didn't use much makeup during the war. It was too hard to find."

"Don't give up." Stewart looked deep into her eyes. "Trust me. Give me a couple of days."

Again, she fought for control and pressed her face against his chest to conceal the tears.

CHAPTER 25

EVERS CHANCE COULD only nod in sympathy as Stewart told of the latest crisis. Maria swore softly. "Give a bureaucrat a bit of power and look what happens."

"We won't change his mind." Chance predicted. "Belton is reflecting what he considers government policy. But it simplifies matters for you. You'll be joining our firm, just much sooner than expected."

"But Karin is in limbo and in danger," Stewart said. "She doesn't have the 'proper' papers to leave the country."

"Proper?" Chance asked.

"She has German documentation but that won't help. I have an idea to get her away on false papers but there's a risk."

"There's always risk. What are you thinking?"

Stewart told of Murphy's Dutch certificates and how Karin's name could be inserted on a form. Black market documents, ration cards, and travel permits would back up the deception.

"I remember false papers." Maria laughed. "In fact, we've used them often over the years. Create a story, keep it simple but act brazen."

"How would you get her away?" Chance asked Stewart.

"I thought of sending her with a boatload of war brides."

"No." Chance quickly dismissed the idea. "The authorities will vet those passengers. And, she'd have to get to England to board which would trigger more questions. Better if she took a ship from a European port. Let me see what I can arrange. Obviously, she'll have to change her name."

"Which is another complication." And Stewart told of the inheritance Karin had waiting in Toronto. "She has to be Karin Werner to collect."

"We'll work it out." Maria laughed. "Chance and I have done this sort of thing before. This will be like old times. I'll have a chat with Karin. She's a bright young woman. Someone like her deserves to be salvaged from Berlin."

"Yes. I agree completely and..." Chance suddenly froze. His face twisted from a flash of pain.

Maria rose and came to his side. "What is it?"

It was a few seconds before he was able to answer. "Indigestion... must have been something I ate. Never mind. I'm already starting to feel better."

Returning to the apartment, Stewart waited and watched the street but saw no sign of surveillance. Inside, he tapped the coded signal but Karin didn't answer. He pressed an ear to the door, heard voices, and used his key to quietly enter.

"Karin?" He called softly but there was no reply. He moved slowly down the hall and only relaxed on recognizing a radio broadcast. The washroom door was open. He felt guilty but watched as she stepped from the tub and began to towel dry. Only when she reached for a robe did he slip back down the hall. "Karin?" This time he called loudly and slammed the apartment door.

"A minute," she answered. "The hot water came on and for the first time in months I was able to soak. It felt so good. I'll be right out."

She tightened the robe on entering the room and Duff took another deep breath. The house coat was short, reaching barely to mid thigh. "This was Inga's," she said. "I'm sure she wouldn't mind."

He tried not to stare. "You do it justice."

The answer was a shy giggle. "Am I distracting you?" She sat on the sofa, tugged on the robe, gave up and instead pulled her legs beneath her.

This time he chuckled. "Yes, but a lovely distraction." He forced his eyes to her face. "But we have to talk. I may have a way to get you to Canada."

Any levity vanished.

"Karin Werner must disappear," he began. "With Murphy's Dutch documents, we'll create a new identity. Canadian authorities will pay less attention to someone from the Netherlands. Ration cards are relatively easy to obtain and we'll create a portfolio of other identification."

"Is it that simple?"

"No. There are complications, lots of them. Canadian borders are essentially closed to immigrants unless there is a family connection."

"I have no family, no Canadian relatives."

He took a deep breath. "How about a husband?" Her eyes widened. "A marriage of convenience. I'm betting other war brides have complicated relationships."

"War brides?"

"Thousands of them, married to Canadian soldiers and on their way to a new home. The government won't stand in the way of love. Once aboard the ship you should be home free."

"Ship? What ship?"

"Chance knows the skipper of a freighter than leaves Antwerp later this month. It's not first class but there's a private cabin. I'm flying home and will meet you in Halifax. From there, we go to Toronto and a meeting with the lawyer for the inheritance."

"You've thought this through."

"You'll claim to have been born in Holland, near the German border and during the war you were recruited...no...better yet... forced to work as a maid in Berlin. After the war, you spent time in a DP camp and met the husband."

"Tell me about him?"

Stewart smiled. "He's very handsome and extremely intelligent."

"You?"

"We fell madly in love. You may be—with child. Make up whatever sounds plausible. I'll carry the documents in Karin's name so there's no danger of a customs inspector finding a second set of papers."

"I'm not pregnant." She assured him. "Does that affect the marriage plan?"

"No." He laughed. "But we need a marriage certificate signed by a Canadian Army Padre. He won't be in on the story so we'll have to be convincing. You'll need a new name. I checked. Vanderhoeven sounds Dutch. Pick a first name. Who would you be if not Karin?"

It was all too much.

"Tomorrow," she said. "I need time to absorb this."

"Don't think too long. The Padre is booked for Christmas Eve."

Berlin, December 24

Stille Nacht, Heilige Nacht. A German version of *Silent Night* echoed through the room as a youth choir rehearsed for a midnight tradition. Karin's eyes misted. "So many memories come back. Did you know the carol was written by an Austrian Priest after Napoleon's war?"

"You can reminisce with me," Duff told her. "But when we get to Canada don't mention it. Too many Canadians remember a more recent Austrian...a Corporal Hitler."

She nodded but the music kept her mind in the past. "At Christmas, the church near my grandfather's estate would be lit by candles and the whole family would be there." She choked. "I'm the only one left." For a few seconds she struggled for control. "I never expected *Silent Night* at my wedding. A girl doesn't get many chances for marriage even if this is...what do you call it? A marriage of convenience?"

"For the record, you are a beautiful bride." He took her hand. "Any man would be proud. And remember the war has changed social standards. Divorce is no longer tabu."

"Yes. We must keep our options open," she said and he thought he sensed a hint of regret. The choir reclaimed her attention but a few moments later she spoke again. "Perhaps the music is a message from the other side. I don't speak of family but think of them often. So much has changed. Germans call 1945, Year Zero. It's time to start over."

The music director brought the rehearsal to a close and as the choir dispersed, the couple made their way to the adjoining church.

The sanctuary had suffered from bombing. Stained-glass windows were replaced by thin plywood while soot and blacked timbers showed the extent of fire damage. Yet, a few pews had been cleaned near the pulpit. The witnesses, Chance and Maria sat quietly while Stewart, in his army uniform led Karin forward. She wore a light summer dress, the only white in her meagre wardrobe.

The Military Chaplain raised his hands. "Dearly Beloved..." He paused and frowned as Stewart glanced at his wrist watch and whispered. "Make it fast. I have a plane to catch."

"I could skip part of it..." He had been warned of time constraints.

"Yes, please," Stewart answered and Karin nodded.

"Do you Duffield Stewart take this woman. Er...sorry miss, someone left the name blank on this certificate."

"Gretchen..." Karin answered, "...Gretchen Vanderhoeven."

"Not for long." The Chaplain scratched at the documents. "Soon to be Gretchen Stewart. We'll carry on."

He turned back to the Lieutenant. "Do you take his woman as

your lawfully wedded wife…in sickness…" He stopped as Duff again glanced at his watch.

"I guess you do." And turned to the bride, "Do you Gretchen…"

The answer was a brusque, "I do."

"I understand the rush but this should be a special occasion." His eyes rose to the damaged roof as if in search of divine inspiration. "But the marriage is legal."

Stewart laughed. "I wish we had time for a honeymoon."

"From what I hear you've experimented." The Chaplain scolded but signed the certificate. "The consummation of a marriage is supposed to follow the vows. This should be a solemn occasion, one filled with religious significance."

"Yes, thank you, Father." Gretchen shook his hand.

"Father?" He blanched. "Father is for Catholic's. I'm a Presbyterian."

"Ah yes." She attempted to cover her mistake. "Duff said a protestant denomination would be more acceptable for moving to Toronto. If we were to live in Quebec, immigration authorities prefer Catholics. I'm trying to learn Canadian ways, really, I am. And, thank you for what you've done."

"No thanks are necessary. Or, thank Mr. Chance. He's been most generous toward my adopted flock."

Chance stepped forward and slipped his arms around the newly weds. "I'm afraid there's more disconcerting news. The Canadian Immigration department has ordered a special watch on new arrivals. Use extra care."

Stewart nodded. "I feel better knowing you and Maria will get Karin to the ship. I'll protect her on the other side."

"It's our pleasure," Chance spoke. "And, we'll have a few days to work out the rest of this scheme. Nothing too elaborate, only enough to be convincing. And, let me handle Vincent Russel. I'll provide enough background to keep him satisfied. The fewer people who know of this charade the better."

CHAPTER 26

Halifax, January 1946

"LIAM, GET A move on." A Halifax customs inspector called to a member of his team. "I don't want to spend a minute longer on this ship than I have too and it's not only because of January cold."

Liam clapped his hands to keep the blood circulating. "Yah. This ship should be sent to the wreckers. I'm amazed she's considered sea worthy. The cargo hold is a mess after the rough crossing. Broken crates and boxes are spread all over hell. Apparently, shipments of war time artifacts destined for Canadian museums."

"Let the dock workers sort that out as they unload," the inspector grumbled. "The only passenger left is a Dutch woman who lost her voice. Nice looking girl, a war bride. The husband was to meet her but is a no show. He probably had second thoughts and abandoned her. We'll see more of that as more brides arrive. Apparently, thousands are coming."

"This one speaks English?" Liam asked.

"Pay attention. I told you she can't talk…"

"…Ahoy swabbie!" a soldier called from the dock and sprinted up the gangway.

"Ahoy? Swabbie?" Liam repeated in a loud whisper. "That one watched too many pirate movies."

The inspector moved to block the passageway. "Stop right there. I'm Gallagher, Immigration Department."

"Lieutenant Duff Stewart. I'm to collect my wife." He was out of breath, the result of a late train, the hunt for a taxi and a long run from the dockyard gate. "My wife," he panted. "Her name is Gretchen."

"Good thing you arrived. I was about to send her to the brig." Gallagher frowned. "Captain says she lost her voice."

"I hope she's not sick again." Stewart stepped closer to the officials. "She picked up something earlier in a camp for Displaced Persons. Those places are cesspools of disease."

"Yah well, that's your problem now." Liam began to sort through custom forms. "Her name is Stewart?"

"We're just married. She might be under her family name, Vanderhoeven, Gretchen."

Liam moved to a cabin door and banged loudly.

The door opened to reveal a blonde woman in heavy, dark makeup.

"I'm a little late, lambchop." Duff threw his arms around her. "Welcome to Canada." The reply was a grating squeak as she pointed to the cloth around her throat. "Don't worry, cupcake." Stewart grinned. "Get the suitcase and we'll go. With what I've planned, you won't need to talk."

"Hold on!" Gallagher interrupted the reunion. "We've notices of people who might try to enter the country…illegally." His voice had an officious and threatening tone. "Papers!"

She stepped back, cowering in fear.

"Try to be pleasant," Stewart snapped. "She's dealt with Nazis and belligerent guards in the camps. Life hasn't been easy." With that, he softly said, "Paper's, my dear, they want to see the documents."

She nodded, slowly opened several buttons at the top of her dress and retrieved an envelope.

Gallagher's eyes locked on the exposed cleavage before finally shifting to the worn papers. "We had an alert for a woman who matches her description. Blonde, full figured, about her height and age."

Stewart sighed. "From my experience in Germany and Holland, thousands of women fit that description. Blonde, blue eyes. Nordic countries are full of them."

"He's right," Liam agreed. "North West Europe, probably a lot of in-breeding. Finish and we can get supper."

Gallagher glanced again at the papers then studied the woman. The heavy makeup made her appear darker than she probably was. He studied her intently before he spoke again. "Ah hell. Ok. Go. If there's a problem, the police can track her down."

Stewart grinned. "Come on, buttercup. Tonight, will be our second honeymoon."

Two hours later, she stood by a sink and washed away the makeup. They were finally alone, in the compartment of the train that would carry them west.

"We forgot something," she said and tossed a wash cloth aside. "The ship captain and crew spoke Dutch. I don't. And since I'm supposed to be from the Netherlands anything I said might have given me away. But I remembered what you told me of the secret mission to Berlin and how you used a dirty bandage to fake a throat injury. All I had to do was croak, wheeze and cough."

"Good thinking." Duff fought the swaying motion of the train, gave up and stretched on the bunk. "The makeup was a nice touch."

"Maria gave me advice. I learned a lot from her. She also suggested the immigration inspectors might be distracted by a flash of skin. That worked too. He didn't spend much time on my papers. By the way, the Atlantic crossing was dreadful. Another war bride was on board, a woman with a baby. The child was a mess, oozing from both ends. Sea sick? Diarrhea? The smell was awful."

He tried to suppress a chuckle. "Sounds like a delightful crossing."

"Memorable. But I'm here."

"Everything is in place," he told her. "The lawyer has been told to liquidate the investments. The funds will be available in cash in Toronto."

She crossed the compartment to where he lay. "One other thing. Don't use pet names like lambchop or cupcake. Simply call me Gretchen. We both have to get used to it."

She began to remove her clothes. "And, this will be tight but we'll have to share this bed."

Washington, January 16

"Moving?" Vincent Russel asked the obvious question as he saw the boxes piled haphazardly in the Pentagon office.

"Demobilized," Ben Wiley answered. "I'll be glad to be a civilian again." He reached to shake Russel's hand but abruptly stepped back. "You look awful."

"Florida sun and Canadian skin. Bad sunburn. I'm on my way home from a southern vacation." Ever so slowly he settled into a chair. "Everything hurts."

Wiley began to laugh. "I'll remember this. I'm going south next month, a quick vacation before I look for work. Any chance your firm might need an American associate?"

Russel hesitated before replying. "We might. I'm going to keep the old firm running, at least for a while. Thought it best to let the dust settle and see what the end of the war brings."

"The dust isn't settling." Wiley continued to pack. "All those war time agreements, those no strike deals with labour are expiring. Coal miners, men in the oil sector, railway workers, autoworkers… everyone wants to catch up on lost wages. You can't blame them. The cost of living is soaring."

"And what of the future for Intelligence?"

"That's going to be a dog's breakfast! The various agencies added men during the war. Naval and Army Intelligence, Hoover's FBI, and a host of others. Truman shut down the Office of Strategic Services but may establish a new super department, a Central Intelligence Agency."

"You might find work there."

"Who'd want it. In Washington, politics, no matter how petty, is all that matters. With the strikes, the hunt is on for left-wing agitators or communist infiltrators."

"I do hear continual rumblings about Reds." Russel nodded. "Mackenzie King is anxious."

"Still over this spy?" Wiley closed a box and sealed it. "The case set off alarm bells in Washington. We've wondered about subversives in our government. Hoover loves it. He'll ask for more agents to root them out."

"You don't think it's a major issue?"

"I don't. A whisper campaign perhaps, clear away a few people with questionable backgrounds. That's what I'd expect. On the other hand, Americans can be easily aroused. A few stories in the papers or a politician beating the drum of an anti-communist agenda and everything could change. Siding with the Communists or leaning too far left might be considered—Un-American."

Ottawa, January 22

Todd Aiken brushed snow from his coat and stamped his feet in a vain effort to clear the icy residue from his boots.

"A little nippy out there." His managing editor smiled. "Don't bother removing the boots. I have something for you to chase."

"I need to file on the courts." Aiken sounded dejected. A day at the courthouse produced only the tale of a third-rate burglary. "A simple ass made off with an old bicycle," he explained. "Cycling in a snow storm attracted the interest of the constabulary."

"Our publisher would consider that an attack on law and order and a violation of the property rights of an esteemed citizen of the capital." Bert Thompson slid the glasses down his nose and peered over the frame. "Why not simply add a couple of lines in the news digest column."

"We finally agree." Aiken smiled. "I did have a conversation with the legal clerks. They're posturing for new jobs. The rumour mill says a Royal Commission will be established to investigate a matter of national security."

"Oh, not again." Thompson slumped in his chair, "Not the spy business. You've controlled that overcharged imagination in the last few weeks but appear to be falling off the wagon."

"Gouzenko is out there…somewhere." Aiken nodded. "When a Supreme Court Justice is asked to investigate it must be important."

"Only when there's confirmation." Thompson pushed the glasses back into place. "And you don't have it. Besides, I've a special request from the publisher."

"What now?"

"War Brides. The story of the Canadian boys who fell madly in love with the maidens of Europe."

"Aw no, not that. Give it to a female reporter."

"We have no female reporters. He fired the last one a week ago. Didn't like the way she dressed. Slacks, trousers were too modern for his tastes."

"I wouldn't know where to start."

"Find a heart wrenching story of love, a story so sweet that it won't need sugar. A brave Canadian lad falls head over heels for a charming Fraulein…wait no…" Thompson rose and began to pace the office. "…No…she can't be German, a French girl maybe…no… better yet…English. Yah. He'd like that. Women from the continent won't fit his image of the ideal immigrant."

"Are you serious?"

"Perfectly. He won't approve extra spending so you'll have to see what the boys of the Ottawa Valley brought home."

"Eventually the story will break. We could be the paper that does it."

"No, at least not yet but we never know in this business. Oh, the boss wants pictures. Make sure the war bride is pretty."

Toronto, January 23

The deep throated steam whistle sounded as another train rolled into Union Station. "I'd forgotten how much I missed that sound." Duff Stewart smiled and set their suitcases on the platform. "I never got used to the shriek of a European engine. Give me the blast of a heavy locomotive."

"Strange what we notice." Her voice was almost lost in the background noise of the railway depot. "I find it odd to see undamaged buildings and streets that aren't clogged with rubble. It's like something from the past."

"Let's hope it's a model for the future. A cab to the apartment or we can walk? It's not far."

"Let's walk," she suggested. "We've been cooped up on the train. A little exercise will feel good. I'll carry the new suitcase."

"It's a shame you spent so much time looking for used clothing while in Montreal. That city has a reputation for high fashion. Toronto shops sell more conservative attire."

"The clothing store was strange. Another customer complained about the selection. I, on the other hand, was impressed, even if the dresses were second hand. The racks in Germany are empty. And, food. Diners complain about the portions but I haven't eaten so well in years. I feel guilty. The papers say the food ration in Berlin has been cut again."

"I suppose Canadians at home had it easy during the war, at least compared to Europeans." Stewart stopped to survey a grocery stand. "And, with access to army stores during my time on the continent, I never went hungry. I know you did."

"Yes. It's another thing I'd rather forget. Food and shelter were always a worry. From the train I saw so much empty land. And I thought of the people living in the camps. So many would welcome a new life here."

"The government is in no hurry to welcome new immigrants." Stewart hefted an apple but returned it to the stand. "The Prime Minister wants to be sure newcomers fit with existing society. That's English or French speaking and decidedly Caucasian."

They stopped on a corner and waited for a streetcar to pass. As the sound faded, she asked, "This lawyer. How much does he know?"

"Only that you're coming and want the inheritance in cash. It's your show."

The next morning, a bedraggled refugee appeared at the law office. As a lawyer with international connections, Walter Nesbitt cultivated business from abroad but with a single glance decided Frau Werner would not be a continuing client.

Her faded yellow dress had seen much better days. Her eyes darted nervously around the room and she rubbed dirty hands together before running them through uncombed hair. Vibrant red lipstick was smudged around her mouth. A ragged black stripe on the back of her legs provided a bad imitation of nylon seams.

"The paperwork is in order." Nesbitt flipped through the documents. "Who ever set this up wanted a simple process. Your grandfather, was it?"

The woman nodded.

"Came at a welcome time, I imagine." Nesbitt began to verify the forms with his signature. "No doubt you had a difficult time during the hostilities. And, it hasn't been easy here in Canada with the rationing and shortages. And the rise in income taxes, a terrible burden."

"But women weren't raped by occupation armies."

He glanced up, surprised by the anger in her voice. "Well...no."

"You'll never understand. Those of us who lived through it find it hard to go on. Terror bombings night after night...and...now...

nothing but wreckage and constant nightmares. Canadians are so lucky. My people could rebuild their lives here."

"No need to uproot the European population. DPs should stay where they are. Canada has enough problems without waves of refugees."

"Yes, save yourself." The anger rose in her voice. "And, you'd like us to forget the innocents who died in the Allied fire bombings." Her hands tightened into fists. "So many are gone."

"No sense refighting the war." Nesbitt urged. "Try to stay calm."

"I can't forget." She leaned forward on the chair. "And those stories of crimes committed by German soldiers. Lies. Allied lies. Germans are not all beasts."

"I'm sure it's been difficult." The lawyer signed a final form. "And truth be told we probably don't know enough of what went on in Europe." He pushed the papers across the desk. "A signature here." He tapped the paper. "And here."

"How much money?" Her mood began to change.

"A small fortune. $50,000 Canadian dollars."

"How much in Reichsmarks?" She sounded like a child at Christmas.

"Uh...I'm sure we could work it out," Nesbitt stammered. "But it's more than many working men will earn in a decade."

Suddenly she dropped her face into her hands and began to moan. "Not enough. Nothing makes up for the suffering."

Nesbitt opened a brief case to show neat rows of hundred-dollar bills and again her mood changed. She gently caressed the currency before closing the case and pulled it tight to her chest. "That's all there is?"

"Yes, a large sum of money." Nesbitt rose, eager to see her on her way. "I suspect Miss Werner you can now afford special help. Doctors may have suggestions to help with postwar trauma."

"No doctors!" Her temper flared. "I'm going to see the Niagara Falls and then...then...I don't know."

Niagara Falls, Ontario, January 24

The police officer thumped a gloved hand on the bell at the hotel reception desk. "I'm here to collect evidence on this missing person."

"There's not much." The night clerk placed a small paper bag on the counter. "I went through her room. German ration cards, that sort of thing, and oh, a business card for a Toronto lawyer. She checked in alone. Seemed a bit…off…kept muttering foreign gibberish."

"I don't have much," the investigator admitted. "A young lieutenant saw someone climb the railing, a woman clutching a case. She must have dropped her papers and the room key. That's how I knew to come here."

"At least you have a witness."

"The soldier? He's no help. He'd been drinking, heavily. I was going to take his name but, in his condition, he'd have made a poor witness. Not sure what he'd remember when he sobered up."

"So, what do you do, constable?"

"I'll file a missing person report and I'll contact the lawyer but it looks like suicide." He glanced at the identification. "If this…Karin Werner…went over the Falls, we may never recover a body."

The next morning the Toronto lawyer answered the phone call from the police. "Constable, I don't know much about her but the legal papers were in order. She left here with fifty thousand dollars in cash." Walter Nesbitt then listened impatiently as the policeman spoke. A full minute passed before he was able to break in. "The cash was in a briefcase and yes, she certainly appeared the type who might do herself in. It underlines the problem with all the refugees. Allowing them into this country would be an added strain on our resources."

The police officer began to speak again and Nesbitt shook his fist in silent fury. Finally, he interrupted. "Constable, there's nothing suspicious. She was mentally unstable. As to the money, she demanded cash. No one else has a claim and there's no way to trace it. And, please don't mention me if you release the story to the press. I'm just a lawyer who did the job to the best of his ability."

Berlin, February 1

"This is sad." Evers Chance stood at the desk in a police office in Berlin. "I've an article from a Canadian newspaper. A young lady was swept over the Niagara Falls. The report suggests she was German."

A bored desk sergeant sent for a senior officer. "Herr Altmann deals with refugee issues."

Chance hadn't met Altmann but the man in the uniform of the Berlin police and with the swagger of a Prussian army officer met all his expectations. The entrance lacked only the Nazi salute. "This might interest you." Chance unfolded the newspaper clipping and waited. It was several minutes before Altmann spoke. "A surprise. I am aware of her. We opened an investigation last year. I wonder how she got to Canada?"

"Doesn't take much imagination," Chance answered. "Other fugitives slipped away. Men like Martin Borman, vanished. German SS officers are showing up all over, as close as the Middle East, and as far away as Argentina. It's almost as if there was a planned escape route…"

"…Fabrications." Altmann interrupted. "Don't believe those stories. As to men like Borman, bodies are found in the ruins every day."

"Well, at least we know about this woman," Chance said and waited as Altman reread the clipping.

"Almost certainly a suicide," Altmann decided. "Murder would attract more attention from the gutter press of the west. This is a very short story. Even the money, a small fortune, didn't excite the reporter." He folded the clipping. "If I may keep this, I'll add it to her file and close it."

"Yes." Chance nodded. "Obviously further investigation would be a waste of time."

"And will you be leaving soon?" Altmann asked. "Many Canadian soldiers are going home. The British and the Americans appear ready to consider at least a partial withdrawal. Only the French and Russians are intent on continuing this cruel occupation."

"I'm a businessman," Chance explained. "My objectives are different from those of the army. I'll stay to watch the New Germany emerge."

"First, we must restore law and order and German pride and..." Altmann's voice trailed off as he studied the visitor. "Are you feeling well? You've become quite pale."

"Maybe, I'll sit..." Chance almost fell into a chair. "These weak spells hit at random. My wife thinks I should see a doctor but I believe a change in the weather will help. We all feel better with spring."

CHAPTER 27

"**D**UFF? DUFF STEWART?" Todd Aiken shouted as he recognized his old friend among the pedestrians on an Ottawa street. "Last I heard you were rebuilding Germany."

Stewart laughed and wrung the reporter's outstretched hand. "Imagine running into you. Of course, it's Ground Hog Day, you'd leave the burrow."

"And I'm thirsty after a long winter nap. The beverage room up the street is open. Buy me a drink."

The pair soon caught up with Stewart bringing news of Murphy's death and the attack on Inga. He decided not to speak of Karin. "Sad about Murphy." Aiken sipped on a glass of beer. "He'd have had a field day in the postwar world. And Inga is recovering. That's good to hear." He smiled at her memory. "Now what about you. Civilian clothes? Off duty?"

"Demobbed," Stewart said. "I've joined my father's old firm. I had a series of meetings and will catch the overnight train to Toronto. Any hot news that I should know?"

"Oh, things are happening." Aiken leaned across the table. "A Russian defector shocked Mr. King with a story of a spy network but the Prime Minister doesn't believe Joe Stalin would condone such skulduggery. It will come out eventually and the shit will hit the fan."

Stewart faked surprise. Russel had told him of the defection and how the fear of undercover agents had sparked investigations inside western governments. So far, the same governments had kept the story secret.

"It's the bomb." Aiken's voice dropped to a whisper. "The Brits and Canadians were involved in the research. The Reds can't let the Americans get too far ahead on a major weapon."

"And, the blue prints were in the Canadian capital?" Stewart laughed, "That's a stretch."

"A big stretch. The so-called spies didn't get much. But the fact they were here shows the wartime alliance is shattered."

"I'm not surprised. The Russians in Berlin were hard to deal with."

"A year ago, the Nazis, the fascists were the enemy. Now, our angst grows over Communists." Aiken signalled for another glass. "One war ends and another threatens. Hard liners compare the situation to 1938. Appeasers, people willing to negotiate with the Russians, are losing ground to those who demand a tougher approach. I hear rumours that any refugees from Europe will come from very conservative, from right-wing backgrounds. Those on the left, even a simple union member, might bring revolutionary ideas. Why even a man with a record of opposing Hitler might be under suspicion. A lot of Reds played major roles in the resistance."

Stewart's mind flashed to the men and women in the refugee camps spread across Europe. "But this country could use new blood and new ideas."

"Ah, but it might upset the immigration applecart. We may accept blitzed-out Brits but our leaders are reticent about other refugees." Aiken drained the glass and signalled for another. "And, I suspect they'll keep a closer watch on our own people. Civil servants, for example, may find promotion difficult if there's a strong left-wing connection or for that matter, questionable moral standards, like a child out of wedlock, a drinking problem or an affair with the same sex. I expect we'll soon demand very rigorous righteousness."

"Have you reported on this?" Stewart asked. "Sounds like a great story."

"No. My publisher doesn't like to rock boats. He's more interested in war brides."

Stewart tensed. Did Aiken know about Karin and the deception that brought her to Canada? But he relaxed as Aiken told of his latest feature story. "I stumbled on a city girl from a very fashionable part of Brussels. The newly weds are sharing space with the soldier's family on an isolated farm. No phone, spotty electricity and outdoor privy."

"There's likely to be a big adjustment for all the war brides," Stewart said.

"Yah, but those ladies will soon have a fresh Canadian passport. The government is updating the citizenship act. To this point, all of us are legally British. The fellows on the Hill want to show the world we have a distinct identity and will create a separate Canadian status. They considered a new flag but decided the old guard would object. Citizenship is less controversial."

Stewart was intrigued. "So, after a certain period, these war brides could be legally Canadian? And, conceivably they could go off on their own way and leave the husband?"

"That's what I hear. Why the interest?"

"Just curious." Duff glanced at his watch. "Look, give me an address or a phone number and we'll meet the next time I'm in town."

Toronto, February 3

Stewart quietly opened the door and glanced around the apartment. All seemed as he left it. Except, dishes were washed, floors were swept and the rooms had the tidy appearance few single men could create.

"Duff?" Her voice came from the bedroom and a moment later

she appeared in the doorway. The blonde hair was neatly combed and fell to her shoulders. She wore a thick, high-necked sweater and a plaid skirt. He drew her into his arms and felt an eager response.

A few moments later she stepped back and took his hands. "I did as we planned and opened a number of small bank accounts. In fact, creating a new identity has been quite simple. I wonder how many other refugees will quietly establish themselves in Canada." Her hands swept down across the skirt. "And, I spent a bit of my inheritance. The sales clerk told me the tartan was Royal Stewart so I couldn't resist. The rest of the money is under the mattress and you're the only one who gets near my bed."

Stewart laughed. "I was remembering how much you enjoyed the beach in Zurich. You could buy a lake house, what we call a summer cottage."

A broad smile crossed her face. "By a lake, with a garden, and flowers…lilacs. They thrive anywhere."

"I hadn't thought of the landscaping but why not. The money would be safer if invested in property, a long-term investment because you're going to be here for a while. You see, I've heard from Chance. Karin's demise has been accepted in Berlin."

"It all worked?"

"Yes. The police believe that Karin and the cash went over the Falls. That part of the story is ended and there's other news that may be important. The Canadian government is making changes to citizenship regulations. In a few years, you can make a life on your own and have the papers to go with it. The war made it more acceptable for women to chart their own course."

"Why? Why would I want that?" She took a step back. "I'd rather be with you."

He felt an instant wave of relief. "I hoped you would say that. I feel the same way." Again, he took her in his arms and gently nibbled on her ear. "Did you know, it was those ears that first caught my attention?"

"Ears?"

"At Potsdam. The girl in the Russian army uniform, the huge brim on the hat and only those ears kept it from falling over your face. I had no idea how important you would become."

The reply was a throaty laugh and a wide smile. "That is amazing. And, I was already becoming Gretchen."

Ottawa, February 4

"Where the Hell is Aiken?" The managing editor shouted across the newsroom. "He's been begging to write this story."

Bert Thompson leaned over the desk of another reporter. "Maybe he doesn't know? Drew Pearson broke the spy story wide open on his American radio program last night. Spies in Ottawa. Spies in Washington..." and then he noticed the envelope on his desk. Inside were several pages of freshly typed copy and a handwritten note. "Following a new lead. Hold space in the final edition."

Thompson studied the pages and found a concise, well-written summary of events since Igor Gouzenko defected, the role of the RCMP in the investigation, and government reluctance to make the details public. He grasped his red pen but made only a few minor changes.

"I thought you'd like it." Aiken appeared in his office door. "And, I do have a fresh lead. The police are about to make arrests."

"They won't want to tip off the guilty," Thompson guessed. "If I was under suspicion, I'd book passage to Moscow."

"I'm still not sure who is guilty or of what?" Aiken leaned against the door. "A few of these *spies* gave the Russians information that was public knowledge, stuff already published in newspapers or in academic journals. Is that a crime?"

"I'm not sure it matters," Thompson rocked in his chair. "The fact the Russians recruited our people shows the Reds can't be trusted."

"Trust is in short supply." Aiken nodded. "We're on the verge of a witch hunt. I wouldn't be surprised if anyone with a hint of leftist sympathies became a target for investigation."

Berlin, February 5

The morning newspaper told of sensational spy revelations based on the American radio broadcast but Evers Chance was not surprised. "Communist agents have been in place for years. A good intelligence service would have found them."

"Don't get too excited," Maria poured the breakfast coffee. "It's no longer our concern."

"Oh, I know." Chance sighed. "I'm out of the official loop but a spy story gets the blood flowing." He read the article a second time. "Drew Pearson is well known commentator and someone leaked the details. Why?"

"Eat your breakfast before it gets cold. The cook will be slighted if there are too many scraps."

"Breakfast be damned. Someone in Washington wants money for counter spies. Before the war, only a few of us kept tabs on the other side."

"Try the eggs." She opened another section of the newspaper. "I'm hoping for a trip to Paris soon. New fashions will be on the runway."

"Bugger fashion. I'd like to root out the bad guys." He ran a finger down the column. "The Brits will be up to their necks in this. Although, I've always believed the Reds infiltrated British intelligence. Moscow often knew too much and too soon. But, with this revelation the gloves come off. No one has to toady to the Russians...and...I...I... think...there..."

Maria raised her eyes in time to see his face contort with pain.

He fought for breath, an agonizing struggle before he slumped head first to the table.

"Chance?" She was on her feet beside him. "Chance? What is it?"

His head rose but the eyes refused to focus and again he slumped forward.

"Chance!" Her voice rose in panic. "Speak to me?"

"What is it ma'am?" The cook appeared in the door.

"Call a doctor!" she screamed. "Chance! Damn it! Breathe!"

Toronto, March 6

"A pleasure to meet you, Mrs. Stewart." Vincent Russel presented a bouquet of flowers. "I've known Duff for many years." She smiled and sniffed at the arrangement. "Thank you. I'll put them in water. He's in the living room."

As Russel entered, Stewart tossed a newspaper on a growing pile. Russel smiled before he spoke. "She's a fetching woman."

"I've asked her to give us a few minutes," Stewart said. "At one point, I thought she'd go off on her own but that's changed. We've grown close and she could help the firm. That's why I sent the letter."

"Which was a surprise." Russel lit a cigarette. "I found the idea silly at first." He saw Stewart grimace. "She's not the first woman to catch your eye. But I reread the proposal. Her experience, intelligence and the language skills are impressive. I was reticent until the word came of Chance and his illness. We'll likely need extra help."

"I'm not suggesting she become a full partner. But I don't want to leave her in the dark."

"Women have a way of knowing what a husband is doing in any event. But both of you must be cautious. We couldn't have leaks on business ventures or contacts with governments."

"I trust her discretion."

"So, this isn't really a discussion." Russel guessed. "It's more ultimatum?"

"I suppose it is."

Russel settled into a chair. "If doesn't work out, both of you would have to leave the company."

"We're prepared for that."

Russel ran his hands across his face knowing he faced a key decision. "Any other…demands?"

"Actually, yes. I want to put an Ottawa reporter on contract with a small stipend. He's frustrated and can't make use of all he learns."

"Well connected?"

"Todd Aiken would not be considered an insider but he hears things."

"I'll want to check him out."

Stewart nodded. "I expected that. And you'll want to do background on Gretchen."

"Already done. Ask her to join us."

Moments later she entered the room. No longer a Displaced Person or an uncertain refugee but a woman with a new lease on life. Russel passed her a newspaper, the front-page photo showing Winston Churchill and President Harry Truman together at an appearance in Missouri. "Have you read of Churchill's tough talk, a call for a stronger stand against the Soviets?"

"Duff and I listened on the radio. We stay on top of current events."

"And what did you think?"

"Oh, a fine speech. Mr. Churchill has a gift with words. He wants to rebuild the wartime alliance. America and the British Commonwealth could form an English-speaking coalition and stand up to Russia."

"And will it work?"

"Only parts of it. Duff says America doesn't care about the Empire and would prefer to see independence for British colonies. He also believes Americans will want to run the show. The British won't like that." She paused but he motioned for her to continue. "As to the Russians, those I knew were tired of war but used bluster to get their way. Europe must rebuild and while that's happening, Canada could snap up new immigrants...including people from the camps. I met some of them. Bright, industrious and need only an opportunity."

"It will be years before we see large-scale immigration." Russel predicted. "It will come eventually but we'll want to know the full background on every person who arrives on our shores."

"Yes. We can't be too careful," Duff said and she saw him hide a smile.

"And this..." Russel pointed again to the newspaper. "What about this...*Iron Curtain*? What did Churchill say...*From Stettin in the Baltic to Trieste in the Adriatic, an iron curtain has descended across the continent.*"

"Obviously a fact," she answered. "Russia will dominate Eastern Europe but the thought is not original. Dr. Goebbels used almost identical words when he warned about the Russians during the war."

Stewart began to laugh. "So, that quote may be Churchill's private reparation." He reached and took her hand. "Gretchen has an excellent grasp of what is happening in Europe. She'll need time to study North America."

"She may have to study the world." Russel cautioned. "Tension in Europe could spread to the Middle East. Jews and Arabs are at each other's throats and the winner will control the vital oil shipping routes. I'd like a word with the damn fools supplying arms to the factions in Palestine."

This time, Gretchen hid a smile. "Good luck finding them."

Russel nodded and gave her his full attention. "I had you investigated by the best. Chance did the legwork before his illness. He said his report contained all I need to know. I'm sorry your family was wiped out in Holland. The war must have been an awful experience."

She was silent and thought of the story conceived with Chance and Maria. "I try not to dwell on it." She hoped to sound convincing and with relief saw Russel accepted her account. A silence fell over the room before she asked. "How is Chance?"

"In bad shape." Russel shook his head. "He's getting great care, the best doctors and nurses but I'm worried. The prognosis is...grim."

"And how is Maria?"

"About what you would expect from a strong woman. She has hope but is a realist. I've assured her whatever happens, the firm will stand by her. It's the best I could offer. That and our prayers."

Ottawa, March 14

Todd Aiken swore as he entered the newsroom. "I didn't get there on time. The police were searching the apartment but wouldn't talk. I had the feeling if I pressed, they'd arrest me too."

"Our national constabulary doesn't often arrest a member of Parliament." Thompson snickered. "A real coup for the RCMP. Unfortunately, you were beaten. Another reporter was on the phone with Fred Rose when the police arrived. A Labour Progressive MP would be a natural target during a Red Scare, just as you predicted. What else do you have?"

"A dozen or so arrests. The police were breaking down doors at dawn. Beyond Rose, there's a fellow that may, I stress may, have had access to material on explosives. There's an information officer from the Air Force, a female secretary and an assortment of others who may have had access to important files. They're all being held—incommunicado. No access to lawyers. No access to family. No calls. Lights on in their rooms twenty-four hours a day. Almost sounds a bit like Gestapo tactics?"

"Careful." Thompson warned. "Certain words might inflame those we eventually will have to rely on for information."

"I'm waiting for confirmation but I think one of those 'detained' was connected to atomic research."

"Will this confirmation come soon?"

"Probably not." Aiken had grown used to dealing with frustration. "The government is setting up a Royal Commission to investigate and our judges are not renowned for moving fast or for sharing secrets. But we'll finally see Igor Gouzenko. He'll be a star witness."

"Eventually everything will come out," Thompson said. "Although the Prime Minister would like everyone to forget the spy scandal that began on his watch."

"It won't be forgotten if it brings on World War Three."

"Oh, don't go down that path." Thompson smiled. "A war of sorts, a *phoney* war or maybe a *cold war*, one where the combatants make threatening gestures and spy on each other. No one wants shooting. We've had enough of that. But who would have imagined the first act of this new struggle would play out in Ottawa?"

Berlin, March 18

The nurse rose as Maria entered the room.

"A quiet night, Ma'am." The accent was English, a matron recruited from a British hospital. "He's not due for any medication until noon and the next shift will see to that." She checked his pulse before collecting a coat.

Maria sighed. "I keep hoping for an improvement. A few times he appeared to be getting better."

"Don't get the hopes too high." The nurse warned. "I've seen similar cases and very few miracles."

"I understand." Maria looked to the bed where Chance lay, silent, motionless.

"At least we have sunshine." The nurse pointed toward the window as she left the room. "I'll see you tonight."

"Yes, thank you." Maria moved to the window but the bright sun couldn't lift her spirit. Outside, the songs of chirping birds swelled to a chorus. She pushed the window open and spoke aloud, hoping somehow, he might hear. "Chance. The birds are singing, a beautiful early spring day, the kind of day you wouldn't want to miss."

Suddenly it was all too much and she surrendered to wracking sobs. Until something, a movement drew her attention to the bed. His eyes had opened and a feeble hand motioned her closer.

"Stop the damn blubbering." His voice was barely a whisper. "I want to hear the birds too."

"You're awake."

"I'm not dead yet despite those storm troopers who masquerade as nurses."

She laughed and caressed his cheek. "Chance. Are you truly back?"

"Ah, Maria. I couldn't leave you. We'll try for a few more years."

A FINAL WORD

Salvaged from the Ruins is the third instalment of a series that began with the events of the Great War.

1917, An Angry Sky, and *Salvaged from the Ruins* were written as stand alone novels but several characters reappear and offer their impression of the first half of the twentieth century.

I've tried to remain true to the historical record. Hundreds of books deal with the World Wars, from academic studies to personal accounts and collectively produce a host of different views. The fictional characters offer yet more exposure to those uncertain times.

For more background, brief bibliographies and a list of real and fictional characters see www.almcgregor.com

My thanks to Deborah Phibbs for the cover design and to Catherine Boyd for the edit and to both for their encouragement and patience.

Al McGregor

2022

ABOUT THE AUTHOR

Salvaged from the Ruins is Al McGregor's fifth novel of historical fiction. *A Porous Border, To Build a Northern Nation, 1917,* and *An Angry Sky* are available through Amazon, Kindle, and Kobo. The former television news anchor and reporter remains a self-confessed history buff and speaks frequently about history and the writing process.

Made in the USA
Middletown, DE
05 May 2022

65188404R00172